HAILED BY FIENDS

EVA CHASE

The Heart of a Monster

Book 4

Hailed by Fiends

Book 4 in the Heart of a Monster series

First Digital Edition, 2022

Cover design: Claire Holt with Luminescence Covers

Ebook ISBN: 978-1-990338-85-4

Paperback ISBN: 978-1-990338-86-1

Hardcover ISBN: 978-1-990338-95-3

CHAPTER ONE

Quinn

The reporter on the TV screen looked like a fish dragged out of the water, her eyes bulging and her mouth opening and closing breathlessly as she tried to explain what had happened on the outskirts of L.A. just a couple of hours ago. Shaky footage that looked like it was from a cellphone showed a distant view of a massive dark shape moving over a large building I recognized far too well.

"Reports are coming in of a huge form that smashed into an old factory building, causing most of the roof to collapse. Some witnesses to the event saw smoke billowing into the air, though no signs of fire have been observed. The form itself appears to have been long and cylindrical, leading some to describe it as a 'giant snake.' Presumably it was a large machine, but it has since been removed with no traces remaining other than the ruined building."

There mustn't have been much video captured, because the footage quickly switched to the wreckage around the factory. Next to me on the sofa, Lance snorted. "A machine," the dragon shifter said with rough amusement, shaking his head so his dark brown curls jostled wildly. "Mortals don't have very good eyes."

I made a face. "It's hard for us to accept that something we assume couldn't possibly exist is actually real. I had trouble to begin with, but having the three of you right in front of me made it pretty much impossible to deny the facts."

It was still difficult to believe that this was the life I was living right now. I had a man who sprouted tentacles from his sides and could turn into a massive octopus-like creature sitting at my other side. A gargoyle still in his hulking, rocky form with wings flexing over his shoulders leaned against the back of the sofa behind me. The demon who owned this apartment stood near the sofa's arm, at the moment looking more like a movie star who'd walked straight off a theater screen than any kind of monster.

And the incident the reporter was attempting to describe had been caused by a being even more immense and monstrous than any of the men around me: an ancient sea serpent the shadowkind called a leviathan.

He and his partner in crime, an earth-shaking behemoth, had been terrorizing this city and sorcerers around the world for months. I'd thought we'd struck a victory against them with the trap we'd put together, which had killed the behemoth. But his co-conspirator had been lurking in wait, springing out at the first opportunity to feast on the behemoth's essence.

Which meant instead of two very powerful, ancient, murderous monsters, we were quite possibly dealing with one very *very* powerful fiend. I sucked my lower lip under my teeth to worry at it.

I didn't know if I could tackle the leviathan if it'd taken in the behemoth's powers as well as what it'd already possessed. I'd only been able to draw the behemoth into our trap using my sorcery—sorcery enhanced further by drawing in the essence of one of its fallen minions—and I'd barely been strong enough. I wasn't sure I could make myself twice as powerful to match the leviathan's new strength, if its macabre meal had worked the way it must have hoped.

I glanced at Rollick, the former leader of this group of shadowkind, who still had more authority and resources than the rest of us. "He appeared so blatantly," I said. "It was only evening—lots of mortals saw him, even if they don't totally believe what they saw. That's against the most basic shadowkind rules, isn't it? Will the Highest shadowkind send more of their warriors to try to deal with him?"

Would it matter even if they did? The last time the oldest and most feared of all the shadowkind had sent their underlings to the mortal realm from the shadowy world where they lived, the villainous duo had managed to capture two of the warriors' minds and slaughter the rest.

I suspected Rollick was remembering that incident too. The demon rubbed his sculpted jaw, his dark blue eyes pensive. "They may hear about this situation. It depends on how much fear and magical control the leviathan has been able to exert over the other shadowkind in the area. But even if they hear about it, I'm not entirely sure what they'd *do*."

Crag straightened up behind me, his muscles flexing across his brawny gargoyle body. "They have to do *something*. Showing his shadowkind form like this—openly destroying mortal buildings—it's even worse than having his lackeys attacking humans from the shadows. Even harder for them to explain away."

Beside me, Torrent's forehead had furrowed under the fall of his scruffy dark red hair. "Did he need to make that much of a spectacle of it? He could have slipped inside through the shadows and kept out of view while he devoured his 'friend.' It's almost as if he *wanted* to be seen."

I shivered, liking that idea even less than what I'd already been thinking. "Maybe with all the silver and iron, he needed to smash his way in to get good access."

"No point in overthinking the problem," Rollick said in a typically languid voice, but when footage of the battered factory building appeared on the TV screen, his body stiffened in a way that brought my gaze jerking to him.

He seemed to recover within seconds, lifting the remote to switch off the TV, but a chilly flicker of uneasiness had passed from him into me in that moment. Ever since he'd force-fed me a bunch of his essence, I'd been able to pick up on his stronger emotions. Something had unnerved him deeply.

The demon caught my eye with a warning look that seemed to say, *Don't bring it up in front of the others*. I shut my mouth against the question I'd wanted to ask, my teeth gritting. But I guessed I couldn't blame him for not wanting to advertise his unexpected vulnerability to the entire crew. He'd only just found out about it himself earlier today.

How could so much have happened in just one day? I pressed my hand to my forehead, where a faint ache pulsed. My limbs still felt heavy, the crackling sorcerer energy that'd become familiar now simmered down to a soft sizzle in my chest.

I'd expended a lot of power getting the behemoth under my control. I'd have insisted on racing back to the scene and trying to harness the leviathan too, but I'd been able to tell in the moment that there was no way I could command even a lesser shadowkind beast, let alone one of the most intimidating monsters out there.

I'd recovered a little in the past couple of hours, but I didn't think I'd be back at full potency for a day or two. And probably only with some sleep, not that I felt much in the mood to rest my head while my nerves were still jangling with a sense of impending disaster.

Lance stirred restlessly on the sofa cushions, his bright green eyes flashing. "He's a problem for sure. Giving dragons a bad name. I'd carve him into little pieces if I could get my hands on him." He made a jabbing gesture in the air with the three-inch-long, viciously sharp talons that protruded from his fingertips even in human-like form.

I found myself checking him for any signs of deeper anguish. I'd used my sorcery on him, Torrent, and Crag before we'd gone to launch our trap, to try to block any chance that our enemies would manipulate their minds.

Casting magic on any of them had made me nervous, but I'd been particularly concerned about Lance. He'd gone through a lot of trauma at the hands of crueler sorcerers in the past. I hated reminding him of those times, even when my power might help him.

I touched his arm, giving his bicep a light squeeze. "Are you okay after the sorcery I worked on you? It didn't rattle you at all?"

Lance shot me a smile that was somehow sharp and sweet at the same time and slung his arm around my shoulders, careful as always to angle his claws away from my skin. He nuzzled my hair with the open affection he offered up so easily. "You were my shield while I was yours. There's nothing to be rattled by."

A warm glow lit in my chest at his phrasing. If it could always be like that, I wouldn't have minded using my magic. But it was hard not to cringe away from it when I knew how the sorcerers before me had awakened that power in themselves—the horrible rites where they tore apart shadowkind and human lives alike.

I'd shied away from doing everything I could with my supernatural talent, and we'd almost paid the price. I hadn't given Rollick any commands, and when the behemoth had come up on us faster than we'd been prepared for, the ancient being had cast enough power at the demon to leave him reeling in a struggle for control. He'd nearly attacked me in the last few seconds before the monster had met his end.

I couldn't balk again. I had to do whatever it took to protect the men around me and all the other beings, mortal and shadowkind, the leviathan threatened.

Even if we still weren't totally sure what the beast's endgame was.

"We can't just wait around and see what the leviathan's next moves are," I said, sitting up straighter with a rush of determination. "We know he wants to hurt people—we know he's got worse things up his sleeve, and now he'll have an easier time carrying his plans out with the extra power he's consumed. Where would we be able to find out more about what he's up to?"

My men looked grim, but none of them argued with me. "He's been sacrificing shadowkind at that rift down the coast," Torrent said. "He might be back to that as soon as tonight. It seemed like the two bosses wanted to handle that process themselves."

"He might have other beings seeking out those fish he likes," Crag added. "If we can find them without it becoming a trap." His last few words turned into a growl, and he gripped my shoulder protectively with his firm hand.

"That's a couple of starting places," I said, trying to lift my spirits and hopefully theirs at the same time. "And Rollick has his people keeping an eye on things. We could—"

A sudden jolt of pain shot through my body, so abrupt and unexpected that I doubled over in response. A gasp tumbled from my lips.

My men gathered around me in an instant, Crag's grip on my shoulder tightening, Lance and Torrent scooting closer, Rollick striding over from across the room.

"Is it your wound from the attack?" Lance asked, worry

and anger twining together in his voice. "If I didn't heal it well enough—"

"I—I don't think it's that," I mumbled, breathing raggedly. The pain ebbed but also seemed to spread, radiating down my back and unfurling into stiff fingers that squeezed at my chest. I couldn't seem to pull enough air into my lungs.

I pushed my hands back through my hair, riding out the sensations. A tendril of nausea wound through my stomach as the pressure higher up finally started to ease off. I inhaled and exhaled as steadily as I could, waiting as the pain continued to dwindle.

Even when I straightened up again, an impression of tightness lingered, wound through my ribs. I felt as if I'd just run a mile, even though I hadn't left the sofa.

Rollick peered at me intently. Concern wafted off of him. "What's the matter? What are you feeling?"

"I don't know. Just cramping up or something." I dragged in another breath, and the realization smacked into me like someone had thrown a bucket of water over my head.

I knew the warning signs. I'd been watching for them carefully my entire life. Lately I'd just gotten so distracted by the external threats to my life that'd become so vivid in the past few weeks that I hadn't focused that much on the other risks.

The chill that tickled through my limbs had nothing to do with any physical ailment. I swallowed hard and wet my now-dry lips.

"I think—I think my heart might be starting to fail."

CHAPTER TWO

Quinn

At my statement, Lance spun all the way toward me with a snarl as if he thought he could intimidate my transplanted organ into behaving itself. He stared at my chest and then at my face, his eyes wild. "What can we do? We need to fix it!"

Crag had come right around the sofa, his wings unfurling. "She would need a hospital, wouldn't she? I can get her to one quickly."

One of Torrent's tentacles curled around my wrist protectively as he glanced around the room. "Where's your medicine? Did you miss a dose?"

"She didn't," Rollick said before I could answer, with a firm certainty that sent a more welcome twinge through my chest. I knew immediately from the way he said it that he'd been keeping track, monitoring to make sure I was as safe as possible.

As much as the demon liked to pretend he didn't care all that much about anything, he hid an awful lot of compassion.

He crouched down next to the looming gargoyle so his face was level with mine and held my gaze, all serious intensity. "You know your specific condition better than any of us could, Quinn. What do you need?"

The flurry of concern and affection around me had me choking up. It took a second before I could speak.

"I don't think we can really do anything right now. My medical team is back in Jacksonville."

"Then we go back to Florida," Lance broke in before I could go on, leaping to his feet.

I shook my head. "I need to be here, dealing with the leviathan. We might *all* be dead if he goes through with whatever he's planning, no matter what happens with my heart."

I tested my body, shifting my arms, and found the pain had almost completely dissipated other than a faint pressure in my chest that I only noticed when I focused on it. Maybe it was all nerves now.

"It was just a brief spell," I said. "Usually these things don't happen in an instant. That's just an initial warning sign. I probably have months before my heart is weak enough to give out completely." As long as nothing sped along the process.

Torrent was frowning, his whole body tensed. "I thought you should have at least a few more years before that happened."

I offered a tight smile. "So did I. I don't know—maybe using the sorcerer magic that came with this heart is putting a strain on it that's worn it out faster. Maybe it wasn't the strongest heart to begin with. The estimate they give you is just an average. Some people get more... and some people get less. And I could be wrong. Maybe it was just the stress getting to me and my heart's fine."

My men didn't look convinced, and to be fair, I wasn't really either. Rollick stood again, folding his arms over his chest. "There are medications to help sustain the transplant in a situation like this, aren't there? I can bring in a doctor. We'll do what we can without drawing attention to you. If you went back to your team in Jacksonville, there's a possibility the leviathan has minions keeping an eye on the hospitals there."

I hadn't even thought about that. I nodded, hating how weak I felt, worn out by the brief but intense burst of symptoms.

I had the impression that Rollick meant to summon up a doctor from someplace or other right away, but before he could so much as reach for his phone, Crag stiffened. The gargoyle jerked around, his gaze skimming the room as his muscles flexed.

The other men braced themselves too, knowing Crag was the most sensitive to the presence of other shadowkind out of all of them. I pushed myself to my feet, relieved to find that my legs only wobbled a little, and grabbed my trusty crossbow off the coffee table. I kept it loaded with the three silver-and-iron bolts it could hold at all times, just in case.

"Please don't hurt me," a squeaky little voice said from the vicinity of the window. A small form moved in the shadows beneath the ledge. "I wanted—I wanted to say thank you."

My men formed a barricade in front of me, even though the creature that'd arrived hardly seemed like much of a threat. One of them could probably have stomped on it without breaking a sweat.

"Show yourself," Rollick said in a voice that was both smooth and ominous.

A miniature human form eased into the glow of the overhead lights, only tall enough to reach my knee, with spiky blue hair poking up over her pinched face and iridescent bug-like wings fluttering at her back. She cringed looking up at the much larger shadowkind, but she held her ground.

"Pixie," Crag muttered. "What are you doing here?"

She quivered before she spoke. "The behemoth had my mind. I saw you all leaving after the sorcerer killed him and freed us. So I followed you. I—I'm so grateful that you stopped him from using us any more, but I'm so scared— the being he was working with—the leviathan..." Her words seemed to dry up as her whole body shook.

"So you came here looking for protection?" Torrent said dryly.

"Not just that," the pixie insisted with a sharper squeak to the words. She sought out my gaze where I was peeking from between the men. "I'll help any way I can. Whatever you're going to do next. Whatever you need. I know you're not like the usual sorcerers." Her gaze flicked over my companions. "You obviously know that too. And there are others—lots of the beings who broke free from the behemoth's sorcery would help too. They're waiting nearby. I said I'd talk to you first."

They'd realized that a whole horde of them invading the apartment at once probably wouldn't have gotten them the result they were looking for, no doubt. I took a step forward, but Lance caught my arm.

"We don't know if she's being honest or tricksy," he said. "That little friend of Torrent's turned on us before."

Goldie the leprechaun. Torrent grimaced at the memory, but Lance did have a point. Rollick cocked his head, with another tic of his muscles that I only noticed because I was standing so close. What was up with him?

"You could be under the leviathan's compulsion right now," he said to the pixie.

She held up her hands. "No, I swear, everything I said was true. Please—if you don't want my help, I'll leave. It's enough just to say thank you. But I don't like what they've been doing. It feels wrong. And I don't know what it'll take to stop the leviathan now."

"Do you know anything about their plans?" I asked. "What they were trying to do?"

She shook her head with a miserable expression. "They didn't tell us very much. But they were killing other shadowkind by a rift near here. They were making some attack the mortals when they didn't want to. And now, bursting into that building in front of the whole city... I have a very bad feeling."

As did we. I hesitated, and then the most obvious solution came to me. "I can use my sorcery on her—to confirm that she isn't under anyone else's sway and make sure she's answering us honestly."

Lance spun to face me. "You can't work more magic. It could make your heart worse."

I squared my shoulders. "It's the one way I can contribute. It's the whole reason I'm in this mess to begin with. We probably won't get *out* of this mess if I back down. Anyway, it shouldn't take much just to ask a few questions." I yanked my attention back to the pixie. "If you're okay with it."

I didn't want to use my powers on an ally without their permission—that was one line I hoped I'd never feel the need to cross again.

The pixie raised her chin without hesitation. "I have nothing to hide."

I couldn't help admiring her spirit despite her small stature and the four deadly, not particularly friendly beings she was facing off against. My men watched me warily as I stepped to the front of the group.

"If you feel at all out of sorts," Rollick started.

I glanced back at him. "I know. I like defying death, not running headlong into it."

The demon gave me a crooked smile. "From what I've seen, you're not always clear on the difference. But go ahead."

I glowered at him half-heartedly and then focused on the pixie. The energy inside me had faded with my earlier efforts, but enough of a tingling remained in my chest that I should be able to pull off a little sorcery.

I willed the magic up into the back of my mouth. The words in the odd language sorcery almost always seemed to come out in spilled over my tongue. *You will answer my questions truthfully.*

The energy leapt out of me and sank into the pixie without any sign of other sorcery blocking my command. "She isn't under anyone else's control," I announced quickly, keeping my gaze on her. That fact didn't guarantee that she was trustworthy. "Why are you here? Tell me the truth, like I instructed you."

The pixie's voice came out fierce. "I want to stop the leviathan from enslaving me and other beings like me the way the behemoth did. You brought down the behemoth, so you seem like the best person to turn to. And I at least wanted to say thank you for breaking me from that spell."

"Do you intend any harm at all toward me or these beings?" I asked, gesturing to the men around me.

She shook her head. "I only want to help. I don't want to see anyone else get hurt."

I couldn't sense any reason to doubt her in her words or her body language. I glanced around at my men. "Is that enough to convince you?"

"Well, she isn't some kind of traitor, anyway," Torrent said, still looking skeptical. I guessed it was kind of hard to figure just how much help the pixie would actually be.

She didn't appear to be affected by his tone. She jerked straighter as if standing at attention and beamed at me. "Thank you for giving me a chance! Can I bring the others who'd like to offer their gratitude and support too?"

Rollick hummed to himself, the sound casual but the ripple of emotion I caught from him unsettled. "We should probably test all of them to be sure of their intentions. I'm not sure our lovely sorcerer is quite up to that at the moment. How many beings are we talking about?"

The pixie bobbed eagerly on her feet. "Oh, at least a

hundred when I left them to come to you. More might have gathered since then. A lot of them are lesser creatures who probably don't totally understand what's going on, but they want to put an end to all this trouble too. I think there were a couple dozen higher beings like me or, well, bigger." She let out a little giggle.

I blinked, having trouble wrapping my head around what she'd just said. Rollick had been working on building his connections up into some kind of shadowkind army, but he hadn't made a whole lot of progress from what I'd gathered. Shadowkind didn't tend to band together for larger causes—they liked to look out for themselves.

Now we had a couple dozen higher beings and over a hundred shadowkind altogether ready to push back against the leviathan's attacks? A shiver of exhilaration ran through me that lifted me above the melancholy of my uncertain health.

Maybe we really could do this. Defeating the leviathan, enhanced powers or not, no longer felt like quite such a huge hurdle to conquer.

Rollick's expression had turned unusually grim, though. He narrowed his eyes at the pixie. "And how close is this swarm that's waiting for you? They followed you most of the way to the apartment?"

She nodded. "I told them to stay a little ways off—they don't know exactly where you are. I understand you're being cautious."

"Not cautious enough." Rollick snapped his fingers at the rest of us. "Grab your things. We're going to regroup elsewhere. A flood of shadowkind in the neighborhood will almost definitely have caught the attention of other beings we *don't* want finding us. The leviathan's minions have been spread out all over this city."

My pulse stuttered. I whirled to grab my shoulder bag and backpack, keeping my crossbow close by as I stuffed the smaller bag into the larger and swung the pack over my shoulders.

Rollick had turned to the pixie. "Tell the bunch waiting for you to head to the grotto near the southeast rift and wait there for further instructions. You can come with us for now, but not the rest of them—not until we've had a chance—"

The rest of the orders he would have given were cut off by the crash of heavy bodies through the two windows, the glass panes shattering. Several more forms sprang from the shadows beneath the door. I yelped and snatched up my crossbow as the first of the new arrivals lunged at me.

It was too late. Our enemies had already found us.

CHAPTER THREE

Crag

It was obvious from the first instant that the beings who'd charged into the room had just one goal in mind: tearing Quinn apart. My body immediately sprang into action with the only acceptable response: tear *them* apart first.

Already in my gargoyle form, I didn't even need to shift. With a roar, I sprang at the nearest beings. I smashed one's skull with my rocky fist, its brains exploding into a smoky pulp, and pummeled another's head right off its neck. Hazy essence gushed through the air from their crumpling bodies.

More shadowkind were flooding into the apartment from what seemed like every direction, many of them animalistic lesser beings interspersed with a few higher beings who made their lunges at Quinn more strategically. Hisses and snarls rang through the air.

Lance whipped around the sofa in his dragon body, incinerating a beast with a gush of scorching breath here, ripping another into fleshy shreds there. Expanded into his demon shape, Rollick gouged out a vampire's throat with his bare, clawed hand and drove his other fist straight through another attacker's chest.

Torrent had brought out every tentacle he could while staying upright. The sinewy appendages lashed around us, knocking creatures off their feet, crushing their bones with vicious slaps. He swiped his limbs through the air more frantically as the barrage of shadowkind kept growing in their onward charge, his jaw clenching beneath the hollow of his scarred cheek.

And in the middle of it all, Quinn's breath rasped as she fired off shot after shot with her crossbow, fumbling for the bolts she'd stashed in her bag in between. I whipped my head around to take a glimpse at her, and my chest wrenched at the paleness of her face, the sweat that'd beaded on her forehead.

How much was this fight taking out of her when she'd already started to feel ill? These brutes were putting even more strain on her heart while it was struggling. What if it failed completely because of this onslaught of fiends?

Anguish and rage seared through my body in tandem. Every being that was threatening the woman I loved should pay in the most painful way possible.

A deeper roar reverberated up my throat. I flung my fists even faster, leaping from place to place, carving a gap with battered flesh and plumes of essence in the incoming flood.

Part of me wanted to hurtle right out into the street and track down the shadowkind who'd led our enemies to us. Smash and pummel the leviathan until even that gigantic menace lay bashed and bleeding. But I couldn't leave Quinn behind. There were too many vicious maws and sharp talons snatching at her right here.

And more and more kept coming. I had no idea how many the leviathan might have already had under his sway and how many were new recruits, but it seemed as if every shadowkind in Los Angeles must be racing into the apartment with murder on its mind. The air was thick with smoke that pricked at my eyes and blurred my vision. My companions were little more than blurs of motion rippling through the clouds.

A reptilian beast wriggled close enough to Quinn to snap at her arm, and I slammed my heel down on its spine with a fleshy crunch. My teeth set on edge. There were even more swarming us every moment.

Rollick hadn't given any instruction, but I didn't need his commands to know what I needed to do. I flung my arms around Quinn, yanking her off her feet into my embrace, and bellowed out to the others, "I'm getting her out of here!"

Quinn froze in my arms, tensed from the battle but obviously not wanting to make it harder for me to carry her. She was always so starkly aware of how her protections against our foes might hurt me, but the silver and iron threads woven into the undershirt Rollick had gotten made for her only sent a faint pinching of discomfort through my skin, not even as bothersome as the beaded vest she'd used before.

It hadn't stopped these monsters from finding her, though. We had to get her so much farther away from here and the ancient being that wanted her dead.

As I barreled toward the nearest window, Quinn clutched her crossbow to her stomach and hunched her head under my chin. I threw myself through the already broken pane and whipped out my wings to propel us up into the sky. The warm night air rushed over us, sweeping the acrid essence from my lungs.

Unfortunately, the leviathan's minions had gotten wise to our usual tactics. Several winged beings leapt into the air to soar after us. They must have been waiting outside in case we attempted an escape.

I wasn't going to let those beasts bring me low this time. Before, that thicker metal vest had weakened me in ways the new undershirt didn't, and I'd gotten more used to fighting while carrying her. I bared my teeth. These creatures were going to regret ever tangling with a gargoyle.

With vast flaps of my wings, I careened straight upward into the darkening sky. There was no point in heading toward our precautionary meeting spot outside the city until I'd dealt with these fiends, or one of them might follow us and then tell the others to bring another attack down on us.

My thoughts narrowed down to the movements of my body, the feel of Quinn nestled safely against me, and the strikes I'd have to make to end each of the lives closing in on us.

Somehow, my fierce mortal had managed to maneuver

her crossbow around to take aim. The moment I swung toward our pursuers, she shot three of them in quick succession. The first bolt slammed into a harpy's shoulder, making her spasm but not falter more than that. The other two projectiles caught beasts in the forehead and the neck. As they plummeted with blood steaming from their wounds, I tightened my grip around my woman.

The fact that she was so capable, so determined to fight for herself, only made me more furious at the creatures that wanted to wrench her from this world. I bellowed a battle cry that resonated up from my chest and heaved toward them.

While I held Quinn with one arm, I could do damage with my other fist, but my best weapons in the air were my legs. I kicked and clawed, whirling this way and that with rakes of my broad feet. I grabbed the harpy's hair and rammed her head into my knee hard enough to split her skull open. The talons on my toes tore open a hawk shifter's gut. My body twisted, jerked, and jabbed with all rage-driven might behind it, lending me strength and speed.

By the time the last body fell, my shoulder was aching where I'd taken a swift but shallow slash and my breath was coming hard, but we were alone. I pushed off a forceful current of air and soared toward the spot Rollick had picked out where we should meet if anything went wrong in the city.

Quinn shivered against me. I glanced down at her with a pang of concern. "Are you all right? Did any of them manage to hurt you?"

Had *I* inadvertently hurt her while I fended off our attackers?

Before guilt could dig in too deeply, she shook her head. "I'm just... I'm tired of all this fighting. Of always having to be on the run. And seeing so many creatures dying."

She nestled her head under my chin, and a different sort of guilt rose up through my chest, more an ache than a jab.

I'd dealt out a lot of the death she'd witnessed today. I'd pummeled dozens of creatures without any thought but of her safety, as savagely as I could manage. I didn't think she'd have told me I'd done anything wrong, but I didn't like that I'd contributed to the violence that had disturbed her.

"We'll do whatever we can to make sure they don't follow us again," I said gruffly, even though I had no idea how we'd accomplish that. Our enemies kept tracking us down nearly everywhere we went, and the leviathan would be even more desperate to get rid of Quinn now that she'd managed to destroy his partner. Now that she'd shown that she *could* tackle a being that powerful.

She was in more danger now than ever before. Both from the weakening organ inside her and our most unshakable enemy in the outer world.

That knowledge had me sweeping my wings faster. We careened over the suburbs and onward until the lights of buildings and roads below came few and far between. The chemical tang that laced the city air gave way to fresher natural scents.

"How can you tell where the right spot is from up here when it's so dark?" Quinn asked, craning her neck to peer at the ground, which was drenched in black.

"I feel it rather than see it," I said. "The patterns of earth and stone all have their own resonance. I made note of the sensations when Rollick showed us the place."

My stomach itched with the urge to gulp down some quartz to bolster my gargoyle strength and awareness. I hadn't had the chance to munch on many minerals since I'd started down this chaotic path with the woman in my arms weeks ago.

I could manage without it. But maybe Rollick would be able to obtain some for me quickly without much hassle if I asked.

I picked up on the vibe I'd been watching for and swerved to the left. A few minutes later, we descended through the air with a rush of wind to land on a rocky hill where several boulders would have hidden us from view even if the sun had been out.

Quinn shifted so she could stand, and I released her carefully, studying her in the thin moonlight for any sign that her heart was affecting her badly again. Her legs held her firmly enough, and her face might have been a bit pale, but her eyes scanned our surroundings with total alertness. Remembering how she'd hunched over earlier this evening, the pain that had marked her lovely face, made my gut twist up.

"I guess it could take a while for the others to get here," she said. "They'd have left as soon as we did, right?"

"That would make sense," I said. "There'd be no point in them lingering once you're not there to protect. If they can catch a ride on a vehicle, it will carry them close pretty quickly."

She nodded and rubbed her mouth. "I hope the pixie was okay. After she tried so hard to offer us her help... She looked terrified when the other beings burst in. I think she hid under the TV, but I didn't see what happened to her."

With a jolt of chagrin, I realized I hadn't even remembered the pixie had been in the room. I couldn't recall seeing her after the moment when the attackers had swarmed us, I'd been so focused on destroying them.

Nothing had mattered to me except Quinn. Quinn, and pulverizing anything and anyone that might threaten her.

"I—I'm not sure," I admitted. "I don't imagine the beasts would have bothered her. And she was swift enough finding us—she should have been able to slip away."

Quinn frowned. "I hope so."

I didn't know how to answer this soft side of her. It'd always been her softness that'd both called to me and left me uncertain, so different from my own nature.

I would batter, maim, and kill to keep her safe. But even if I managed to avoid ever hurting her by accident again, how could she *not* see me as the same sort of being as the creatures who'd meant to do the same to her?

And how long would her love last, the more she saw of my brutality?

That question dug into me as sharply as Lance's claws could have, but it came with a resigned sort of resolve. This was what I could contribute. Defending her with all my strength was what I did best. And with everything that'd happened, the next few days might call on me to become even more brutal than ever before.

If Quinn ended up seeing me as nothing more than a monster after all, that was how it had to be. I wasn't letting any of those fiends touch one hair on her head if I could help it.

CHAPTER FOUR

Quinn

I skimmed my fingers over the smooth plaster walls as we descended the concrete steps into what I could only describe as an underground bunker. Cool air closed in around us despite the summer heat above. Ahead of me, Rollick flicked a light switch at the bottom of the stairs, and a room that looked like an immaculately Ikea-furnished studio apartment flashed into sight.

"Wow," I said, taking it in. "You put a lot of work into this setup. You were expecting the apocalypse to come sometime soon?"

The demon shot me an amused glower. "It's brand new. I commissioned it and a few others around the country after it became clear what level of threat we were facing. But it's not for *my* protection. With the amount of silver and iron embedded in the earth around this room, I'd rather be outside it in the safety of the shadows if worse came to worst. This is all for you."

I blinked, studying the elegantly functional space again with a lump rising in my throat. I'd thought a lot of harsh things about Rollick over the past month, and early on he'd deserved some of them. But he'd been more devoted to my well-being than I'd had any idea about for longer than I'd imagined.

"Oh," I said, groping for the right words. "You managed to get this built that quickly."

He shrugged. "I pulled together your massive sorcerer-inspired trap in just a few days, didn't I? It's amazing how speedily things can come together when you simply ignore red tape and pay your workers enough."

I could believe that. I ventured a little farther into the space, my sneakers whispering over the thin but soft rug. There was a kitchenette at one end, a small birch dining table and a linen sofa, a TV mounted on the wall, and a big boxy shape that I guessed was a Murphy bed, ready to drop down when it was time to sleep but kept upright for the time being to maximize the floor space.

The only thing the room was missing was windows. I could feel that I was underground in the lack of natural light, and a faint sense of claustrophobia itched at me as if I could feel the earth all around us pressing in.

"The leviathan and his minions won't stand a chance of finding Quinn here!" Lance declared happily, but I noticed he gave a tiny shiver as he bounded around the room, peering at all its contents. The metals toxic to shadowkind would affect him and my other men even more than they irritated Rollick, who was the oldest and strongest of the four.

I glanced at the demon. "Just how much silver and iron *are* there around this spot? You had plenty at your house in Texas, and it didn't seem to bother the rest of you there."

"I pulled out all the stops," Rollick said. "And those layers are concentrated much closer to the living space here. But we should all be able to tolerate it for as long as necessary, and we can take turns ducking out for a break before it wears on any of us too much. You can remove your threaded shirt while you're down here without any worry at all that your presence will be detected. I figured a safe house should be as comfortable for its primary occupant as possible."

A safe house. As he said the words, it sank in that this wasn't just a temporary resting place. "You're expecting me to stay here for a while."

"The leviathan does seem very eager to get you out of the way," Torrent put in from where he'd appeared at my other side. "If you stay down here, we can be sure you're safe."

Rollick nodded. "If your heart is acting up, we don't know how that might affect the energy it's giving off. The threads in that shirt might end up not being enough to ward off notice if you're walking around in the open."

A surge of defiance cut through my exhaustion. "No. I can't just hide away for who knows how long while that monster does whatever it's planning to do to the rest of the world. I might be the only person who has any hope of stopping it before things get so much worse."

Crag frowned. "Quinn—no one could ask you to take all that on by yourself."

"I'm not by myself," I insisted. "I have all of you, and whatever other beings we can rally. We defeated the behemoth, and we'll figure out what to do about the leviathan." I rubbed my temple, the momentary spurt of energy fading under my exhaustion. It had to be well past midnight by now, and it'd been a very long day.

Lance veered back around to catch me in his arms. He nuzzled my jaw. "You need to rest now, baby girl. You'll make yourself sicker if you push yourself too hard, right?"

Torrent nodded. "You've been through a lot in the past twenty-four hours. Once you've gotten caught up on sleep, you'll be in a better position to make decisions."

I made a face at him. "I don't think any amount of sleep is going to make me think it's a good idea for me to bury my head in the sand while the world goes to hell."

He gazed back at me, his sea-green eyes as steady as ever. "Then you'll be in a better position to make plans about how we'll stop it from going to hell. You're wiped right now."

"As owner of this humble abode, I whole-heartedly agree with what my mutinous former employees have said." Rollick strode over to the bed and hit the control to bring it swinging down from the wall. "I'll only entertain further arguments about your next exploits *after* you've recovered."

Lance eased off his embrace, but only so he could tug me toward the bed, which was already made up with ivory sheets and a thin blanket. "I'll keep you company. And not in the distracting way. So you know for sure there's no way anything could hurt you here."

I swallowed thickly and let him guide me over to the bed. They weren't *wrong*. I wasn't going to do anyone any good if I collapsed before I got around to figuring out my next brilliant plan.

"Fine," I muttered, and crawled onto the bed. Lance tucked the covers over me and snuggled in next to me, perfectly chaste as he'd promised. Rollick flicked the light off again. As I leaned my head against the dragon shifter's warm shoulder, breathing in his smoky scent, his warmth did ease my jangling nerves.

I closed my eyes, and despite the chaos of the day, it wasn't long at all before I drifted off.

When I woke up, finding my head muggy but my body somewhat refreshed, I was alone. As I squinted in the darkness around me, the lights flickered on and Lance appeared at the other end of the room by the stairs that led to the main door. I had the impression he'd just returned from a jaunt outside.

"You're awake," he said eagerly. "How do you feel?"

"Not too bad." I sat up. "Where did you go? Where's everyone else?"

He tipped his head toward the door at the top of the stairs. "That little pixie woman who came to the apartment managed to follow us here. We were all having a chat with her."

I pushed off the covers and shoved myself off the bed. "I want to talk to her too. Has she brought along any of the other shadowkind she said wanted to pitch in?"

Lance shook his head. "She's very sorry about causing any trouble in the city, so she was careful. But she says she can find them again." He paused. "I don't think Rollick will like you coming out of here until we agree on a plan, but I can tell the others that you're up and they can come down."

I glanced down at myself, abruptly aware of the clothes clinging to me with a day's accumulated sweat and other grime. I'd been so wiped last night that I hadn't even taken off my threaded undershirt despite Rollick's assurance that I could. "Give me five minutes to wash up a bit."

The bunker had a tiny bathroom with a sink, toilet, and shower stall all crammed next to each other. My phone alarm went off in the middle of the world's hastiest shower, and I hopped out to take my morning pills. My schedule had changed so much with the different time zones I'd traveled between that I had no idea how I'd have managed without the automated reminder.

Within five minutes, I managed to pull on a reasonably fresh change of clothes from my backpack. I'd just grabbed a granola bar from the box I found in one of the kitchenette's cupboards when four shadowkind figures appeared in the living room area.

Crag wasn't with them—I assumed he'd stayed aboveground to patrol the way he liked to. The other three of my men surrounded the little pixie, who looked even tinier with their tall, well-muscled bodies looming over her.

"She's very persistent," Rollick remarked.

"I think that's a good thing." I swiped my damp hair back from my face and sat down on the floor so I was almost eye to eye with the little winged woman. "I have a feeling we're going to need all the help we can get. I'm glad you made it through the fight all right."

She ducked her head. "I went to warn the others and made it back in time to see the gargoyle and you flying off. I was able to follow—but I made sure no one noticed me. It was my mistake, letting the others gather so close by before. I'm sorry."

"Anyone could have made that mistake. You don't know what we've already been through with the leviathan's people."

I sighed and leaned back on my hands, glancing up at my men as well. Torrent and Lance had sunk onto the sofa while Rollick propped himself on its arm. The demon took one look at my expression and chuckled softly. "You're still determined to throw yourself right back into the fray, aren't you, stubborn sorcerer?"

I let out a huff. "I don't think that should be a big surprise. The question is how."

I inhaled and exhaled slowly, gathering my thoughts, and the men waited to see what I would say. My thoughts gradually came together. "We still need to find out what the leviathan is up to. And the more of his supporters we can peel away from his ranks, the better. I think targeting his minions, especially the ones he's forced into serving him, is our best bet. If we can figure out where to find them without getting swarmed again, anyway. Do we know for sure that he's still active at the rift?"

Rollick inclined his head. "I took a little trip to check while you were sleeping. He's sacrificing away, tossing up lesser beings like they're nothing more than shark chum. If that doesn't make the ones watching eager to find a new master, I don't know what would." He shot me a narrow grin, but I caught one of those odd twitches of his jaw and a flicker of emotion that sent a jolt through me that was too swift for me to focus on it.

"You wouldn't want to go at him there," Torrent said before I could worry too much about the demon. "There are too many minions milling around, and he'll be reinforcing his sway over them regularly. We need to pick off stragglers."

I turned to the pixie. "He and the behemoth were working pretty closely together before. You might have some idea where the leviathan would have sent beings like you in smaller groups where it'd be easier for us to deal with them."

Her eyes brightened. "Yes! I can think of a couple of places near Los Angeles that might work. The rift could be a good start, actually. There would be a lot gathered right around it, but they always sent out a few here and there to make sure no mortals came near, even during the day, between the nighttime sacrifices."

I smiled. "Perfect. Then we can start there."

Lance let out a faint hissing sound. "We're going right back to the place where they attacked you so many times? I don't like it."

"I'm not exactly excited about it either," I told him. "But holding off on tackling the problem isn't going to make anything better. The leviathan is out there already, probably terrorizing the city and who knows how much else of the world even more than before."

Rollick pushed to his feet. "You're going to need to put your protective gear back on, then. And we're giving the areas he's claimed a *very* wide berth this time." He checked his phone. "And I have a medical professional I'm going to insist you speak to before we go anywhere else."

I glared at him, but he simply gazed back at me without any sign of budging. I could tell from the expressions on Torrent's and Lance's faces that they'd side with the demon on this particular subject no matter what I said.

Grumbling wordlessly, I stood up. "All right. If that'll make you feel better."

The visit with the doctor Rollick had picked out went both more smoothly and more awkwardly than I'd anticipated. She checked me over quickly and efficiently, listening to my heart and my breathing and running a handful of tests. But there were hesitations between her questions and moments where she knit her brow that reminded me that she had no idea of my patient history beyond what we could fill her in on. This wasn't an ideal scenario for giving a diagnosis or treatment.

In the end, she wrote out a prescription that Rollick grabbed and then told me to take it easy for a little while. I managed not to laugh out loud at those instructions. We also hadn't been able to explain to her how the supernatural powers I'd been wielding might have been speeding along my borrowed heart's demise. She did look concerned, though, which left me with a knot in my stomach.

The transplanted organ was definitely starting to falter. And I had no idea how the trials ahead of us might rush me toward my end even faster.

Our next stop was the beach quite a stretch up the coast from L.A. My men had wanted to scope out the area near the leviathan's chosen rift from a distance first. As I stepped onto the rocky shoreline where we'd come down to the ocean, my gaze was immediately drawn to the swath of dark clouds that smothered the sky from just a little south of us to as far as the eye could see across the water. Even where we stood under hazy afternoon sunlight, the waves were frothing wildly as they smacked the shore.

"It looks like a storm's settling in," I said.

Torrent dipped a tentacle into the water, and his expression turned grim. "The water's being churned up. I did hear that the leviathan has summoned tidal waves in other parts of the world in the past several years. He might be attempting the same thing here."

My heart sank. When I looked at Rollick, he was eyeing his phone again, scrolling through something on the screen. The tensing of his mouth unnerved me even more.

"There's been quite a barrage of weather hitting L.A. and the nearby coastal regions since early this morning," he said. "I was hoping from the early reports that it was a natural stormfront, but from what I'm seeing now, the way they're intensifying... I'm sure that menace is behind it. There's already been flooding along the beaches."

A shiver ran through me. "We might not even be able to get close enough to look for his minions. And what about all those people—the mortal ones?"

"The city is starting to evacuate everyone in the neighborhoods closest to the sea," Rollick told me.

Crag scowled at the roaring waves as if he could frighten

them into chilling out. "We should get Quinn away from here."

I set my hands on my hips. "Forget about that. We only just got here."

Torrent turned to face the rest of us. "I'll take a closer look, see exactly what's going on. The ocean is my domain. I'll have the best chance of determining how he's working his powers on it and whether there's a way to interrupt the effect. It shouldn't take very long."

I hadn't thought I could get any more worried than I already was, but it turned out I was wrong. My lungs constricted. But I couldn't tell Torrent not to go when I was insisting on taking my own risks, could I?

"Be careful," I said instead.

He held my gaze for a moment with a small smile. "I told you I'll always come back to you, and I plan on keeping that promise."

Then he leapt into the waves.

CHAPTER FIVE

Quinn

The pixie—whose name, I'd finally learned, was Paisley—stamped her foot as she looked around the shallow grassy dip a few minutes' walk from the coast where she'd hoped to find some of her former fellow lackeys.

"They must have moved on from here," she said in her squeaky voice. "I don't know where else they'd have gone."

"The leviathan might have moved all his operations since the behemoth's death," Crag rumbled. "He knows we've been looking into his activities and trying to interfere."

"Wonderful." I hugged myself, my tee and the protective undershirt beneath it clinging to my skin with a growing dampness. It wasn't exactly cool, considering we were in the midst of a southern California summer, but the storm clouds condensed around L.A. had been creeping ever closer. The gray haze overhead had been spitting on us for at least a half hour now.

Lance shook himself as if he didn't appreciate the moisture either. "His minions have to be around somewhere."

I glanced back toward the sea—and toward the gloom hanging over the distant city. "We could go closer to their main base of operations. We'd probably run into someone eventually."

Crag frowned. "We don't know how many we might run into all at once or who else might see us. I don't like it."

"You don't like me being here at all," I reminded him. "You think we're going to get pummeled by a tidal wave at any moment."

He glowered at me, but he couldn't manage to put much annoyance behind it. "We might. Rollick said the flooding was getting worse all around the city."

The demon had gone off to meet with some contacts and sort out business he hadn't gone into a lot of detail about, but that I gathered had something to do with arranging the army we were supposed to be building. Paisley had also told him where to find the freed beings who'd wanted to pitch in. I expected to be spending a lot of time tonight casting minor sorcery on one after another to confirm their loyalty the way I had with the pixie.

"Well, we're not getting anything done here," I said, holding in a huff of my own frustration. I was a powerful enough sorcerer to have compelled a behemoth to his death, and here I was wandering around mostly trying to avoid running into our enemies. How was that helping anything?

But I knew that getting caught—and maybe killed— wouldn't be particularly helpful either.

We trudged back to the shoreline not far from where Torrent had left us a couple of hours ago. I wasn't sure how long his investigations would take. He'd been gone for a few days the last time he'd slipped into the ocean to find out more about the leviathan, but then he'd traveled all around the world. I'd gotten the impression he was planning to stay local this time.

What if *he* was caught? I couldn't imagine the leviathan would go easy on him if the monster realized he'd gotten his hands on one of my closest companions.

I clambered along the rocky shoreline restlessly. The waves splashed higher than before, drenching my sneakers, and I grimaced with a prickle of apprehension. The giant serpent was definitely stirring up the salty waters in ways that could be awfully destructive.

Lance let out a little shout of triumph and vanished from view. I hustled over to find him in a small dip where a stretch of sand had gathered within a circle of taller rocks that framed it from three sides, a few trees looming even higher around the edges. Their branches rattled with the rising wind, but between them and the arched boulders, they held off most of the rain.

Lance was stalking around on the sheltered sand. He gave a disgruntled sound. "I thought this looked like a good place for beasties to want to hide. No one down here, though."

Crag was studying the spot with a pensive expression. He rubbed his rocky jaw. "Maybe it would be a good place for Quinn to hide—as long as you keep an eye on the water and make sure it's not surging too high. I could fly farther down the coast and see if I can find a minion to pick off from the rest. It'd be better for me to bring one back here to question than for Quinn to get closer to the leviathan's territory."

It said something about how concerned he was about what the ancient shadowkind might do to me that he'd rather leave me with just Lance for protection than bring me with him on his quest. I sighed and hopped down into the natural alcove. "Fine. But search quickly, and if you don't find anything, come back. Otherwise I'm going to do more searching on my own."

Paisley fluttered her wings. "I can fly with you," she offered to Crag. "Cover more ground. I mean, I'll need to come to you to do the rest if I spot any of them, since I can't carry much of anyone off myself, but it could mean we find them faster."

Crag paused, eyeing the tiny woman, and seemed to decide that she'd be more use scanning the terrain than protecting me from whatever threats might arise. "Fine," he said gruffly. "Let's go."

As they vanished into the shadows, I walked across the sand, testing the grains under my feet, until I reached the driest section where the overhead rocks formed what was almost a cave. I sank onto the ground, finding that the pale grains were at least pleasantly soft, and Lance dropped down next to me. He tucked his hand around mine. The gesture came so easily now that I barely noticed the claws that could have sliced open my skin in an instant if he hadn't maneuvered them so deftly.

"It's good for you to have a little time to relax," he told

me in his breezy way. "You've been on your feet for a long time now. Did you bring some food? Maybe you should eat something. I could try to hunt if you don't."

A crooked smile crossed my face at the barrage of concerned suggestions. I reached into my trusty messenger bag and pulled out the apple I'd packed. "Not a bad idea, but no hunting necessary. And I'm fine. I had that bad spell with my heart yesterday, but I don't feel so different from usual today. It was probably just the strain of tackling the behemoth and—"

Before I could finish my sentence, my hand tremored. As if my body was determined to prove my words wrong, my pulse started to race, a chill washing over me that had nothing to do with the damp air. The clenching sensation that'd gripped me before tightened around my chest, making my breath hitch as I struggled to catch it.

Lance leapt to kneel in front of me, his eyes blazing with urgency. "You're sick again. What do you need? Did you take the medicine Rollick got with that paper from the doctor?"

I managed to nod, my fingers digging into the sand as I fought for control over my body. My voice came out ragged. "Yeah. But it'll—probably take a while for that—stuff to kick in." If it did at all. If the reasons my heart was acting up had anything to do with normal transplant issues and not the supernatural energies that'd been passing through it.

Lance stroked my arm from shoulder to elbow, obviously uncertain about what else to do. But I didn't think there was anything he *could* do for me right now. I breathed as deeply and evenly as I could, focusing completely on the rhythm of the air moving in and out of me, and I wasn't sure how much time passed before I felt like myself again. I inhaled shakily and raised my head, barely aware of having lowered it.

The dragon shifter peered at me with concern shimmering in his violet eyes. I'd rarely seen him look so serious. "It was bad again. Two times in two days, when it never happened before since I've been around you. Should we go look for Crag and tell him we need to go? Or I could find a way back to Rollick's safe house on my own, I think."

I wasn't sure how likely that was. We'd driven here, and Lance didn't know how to handle a car. I could drive, but I doubted Rollick would appreciate us taking off with his ride anyway. If he'd even left it where we'd parked instead of using it himself on his business, which I didn't know.

And besides...

"It's okay," I said, grasping Lance's forearm. "It's over now. I'm probably going to have to deal with moments like that every now and then for the time being, and that's okay. They're not really doing any damage."

They just meant that my heart was starting to wear out to the point that it was giving off warning signals.

Lance's brow knit. "Maybe you *should* stay in the bunker. Away from everything. Then you can get better. We'll fight the leviathan, the four of us and the other beings who want to. Shadowkind to shadowkind is more fair anyway."

I wished fairness was a factor that mattered. A lump rose in my throat. I scooted closer to the dragon shifter, my forehead coming to rest against his.

"I won't get better," I told him, more steadily than I'd expected—but then, these facts weren't news to me. I'd just never before had to explain them to someone I cared about who didn't already know. "No matter how much I rest or what medications I take, a transplanted heart was never going to last me my entire life. If I'd been really lucky, I might have gotten twice as long as I have so far. But it was a strange heart, and obviously I'm not so lucky." I paused. "Well, I wouldn't even say that. I don't regret that the strangeness of the situation let me meet you."

Lance growled low in his throat, a pained sound. "You made us go away, and you promised you wouldn't do that again. *You* aren't allowed to leave us either. I want you to stay right here with me. That's where you belong."

I leaned into him more, an ache spreading through my gut. "It is. And I don't want to go. But I've known since I first had the operation that this was going to happen someday. To some extent I'm lucky I even made it past the first year. I've been prepared for this moment my whole life since I had the transplant. That's why I tried to make every day count. To experience as much as I could while I could. So holing up underground and doing nothing really isn't my thing."

"I don't want to see you hurting," Lance said, and looked down at his claws, curling them away from me as if suddenly scared that *he* might hurt me, the way Crag had once feared.

A spark of inspiration lit in my head. The idea wouldn't fix everything, but maybe it would help him accept the way things were and make the most of them like I hoped to. It was exploring excitement that'd brought us together in the first place, after all.

I slid my hand down to his palm and unfurled his

fingers. Then I raised his hand to my face to trace the tips of his claws over my cheek. Even now, with the dreary weather around us and my body still a little shaken from the brief glitch of my heart, their delicate touch woke up a quiver of delight that ran straight to my core.

"I *still* want to enjoy every moment as much as I can," I said. "In all the ways that you can help me enjoy it. The thrills you give me won't hurt me at all—I promise. They'll just make the time I have sweeter. Will you remind me of how good we can feel together?"

Lance made a rough sound. Then he was sliding his fingers from my cheek into my hair, his other hand rising to trace across my neck. His mouth collided with mine.

As his tongue flicked between my parted lips, its dragon ridges forming across it the way he knew I liked, I couldn't think of any place I'd rather be, no matter how much longer this heart kept beating.

CHAPTER SIX

Torrent

I caught the siren just outside the underwater rift that lay out in the depths of the Pacific. She'd been traveling through the shadows that swirled around the ocean currents, but that suited me just fine. I could only talk to her in our shadow forms, since my physical shadowkind form couldn't produce speech and my human form would have drowned down here.

I shot out my shadowy tentacles and snagged them around her essence, holding her tight when she tried to squirm away.

"I'm not going to hurt you," I said in the strange voiceless way we spoke through the shadows. "I just want to talk for a minute."

The siren shuddered, still trying to work her presence

free. But I had twice as many limbs as she did, even if a few of them were no longer whole.

"I have nothing to say to you," she spat at me.

I picked up more panic than anger in her ephemeral voice. Had she been compelled toward her destination? I'd sensed her leaving a small group of water-dwelling beings that'd clustered around the much vaster impression that I knew belonged to the leviathan.

"I want to know where you're planning on going after you pass through that rift," I said. "Are you simply going back to our home, or were you supposed to continue on to some other part of the mortal realm through another portal?"

"Why should I tell you?"

"Because I don't think you really want to be doing whatever that menace sent you to do. And maybe if you tell me, I can make sure you won't have to."

She snorted, but there was desperation to the sound. That convinced me even more that she was under the leviathan's magical compulsion. I'd have to tread carefully with her—past minions we'd interrogated had ended their existences rather than allowing us to continue to question them.

But I had no means to really force her to answer. Quinn was leagues distant, and I wasn't sure I could drag this being all the way to her unnoticed. We'd be in even deeper shit if I led more of our enemies back to the woman who was determined to save us all.

Possibly that lack of direct threat stopped the siren from attempting to harm herself. She thrashed in my grasp again to no avail. Then she went still for a moment. I felt more than saw her attention on me, studying me.

I didn't know what she saw, but she seemed to decide it was worthwhile to offer up a small tidbit—probably the most she could without violating the commands on her. Whether it was an attempt to bargain for her freedom or in the genuine hopes that I could help, I couldn't tell.

"There are many oceans in this world," she said. "And mortals live alongside all of them. Pressure is more effective from more than one side."

Uneasiness rippled through my amorphous body. She was heading to the Atlantic ocean then, I guessed—to carry out some destruction on the opposite coastline of this country? Many sirens could conjure sea squalls, a talent the more vicious among them used to put their sailor prey in a vulnerable position or punish those who eluded them.

She was the only being who'd headed toward this rift, but others had moved off from the apparent meeting in different directions. How many spots was the leviathan directing his minions to? How much destruction did he intend to carry out?

And what was the point of all this anyway?

I doubted the siren I held prisoner could have told me any of that even if she'd wanted to. I paused and said, in recognition of the covert way she'd replied to my first question, "It's a shame when a disaster causes many of those mortals to die all at once."

"Yes," she said grimly, "it is. But sometimes it can't be helped."

"I wonder what possible reasons an ancient being might have for wanting that to happen. Hypothetically speaking."

She sighed. "So do I."

She didn't know his plans any more than the other minions we'd captured did. Did *any* of the lackeys he'd drawn into his scheme have a clue, or were we kidding ourselves that we had a chance of undermining him this way?

Well, I knew more than I had before. And at least I could take a little comfort in the awareness that one siren could cause a lot less watery turmoil than the leviathan already was on this coast.

But it would be better if she didn't go at all. I relaxed my grip slightly. "Can you delay? If you can manage a detour, I know someone who could—"

Apparently not, or at least she didn't trust me to have her well-being in mind. She twisted sharply and slapped hard against the newly damaged tip of one tentacle that still ached now and then even when it wasn't being attacked. Agony speared through my limb, and the siren's shadowy presence managed to wriggle free.

I lunged after her, but she'd already caught a current that sent her careening right through the rift.

I hesitated outside the portal to the shadow realm for a moment, debating giving further chase. But what was I going to do if I caught her? Kill her to prevent her from carrying out orders she didn't want to follow anyway? Or rather, if I found her in the shadow realm, try to batter her essence into such a state that she couldn't follow through with her mission, since shadowkind couldn't die in our natural environment?

No. I didn't want to torment a being who'd had no choice in the matter, and it hadn't seemed as if she was a critical piece of the plan. The leviathan had hundreds of lackeys now. It was a waste to spend much time focusing on just one.

I turned away from the rift and moved on through the sea, letting myself solidify into physical form to make full use of my body and enjoy the caress of the water over my skin. I tasted every movement and flavor in the currents with my suckers, watchful for any other minions who'd headed this way. But I wasn't sure there was much else to learn.

Before the siren, I'd caught a kelpie who'd known even less than she had and followed a school of shark-like lesser beings who'd disappeared into that same portal. They'd been too animalistic to offer any answers, so I hadn't bothered trying to question them. The leviathan was definitely rallying his watery minions to a much greater extent than I'd encountered when I'd first gone searching for information on his activities several days ago.

Maybe there *wasn't* anything else to learn. It'd been hours now. I should check in with the others, let them know what I'd discovered and see if any of them had big ideas about what to do about it or how it might fit into the leviathan's larger intentions. Or if they'd encountered something more informative in their own search.

The span of ocean near the L.A. coast, where the water closer to the surface was churning and heaving, had nearly emptied of mortal creatures. The disturbance and maybe the leviathan's presence in general had driven most of them off. They might not have been able to tell what kind of threat he posed, but they had their own instincts. They knew danger when they saw it.

As I swam onward, a twang of discomfort reverberated through my gut. I'd roamed all over the mortal world, partying and indulging in every possible vice, when my physical body had been undamaged, but I'd spent a lot of time enjoying the seas in my monstrous form as well. Even after my beating, after I'd started working for Rollick, I'd come out to these waters regularly to claim this one small bit of enjoyment I still could.

But I'd never sensed anything was amiss in the expanse I'd soaked in so often. The leviathan had been traveling all around the globe, stirring up catastrophes, and I hadn't caught wind of the wrongness that was growing in the part of this world where I most naturally fit in.

Before, I'd been too caught up in my selfish pleasures to care. And after, I'd still mostly dwelled on what mattered to *me*—avoiding any more blows to my ego, impressing the boss I'd dedicated myself to so I had some sense of achievement and purpose. That had been selfish in its own ways too.

Would the leviathan and the behemoth have managed to get so far in their plans if I'd cared more about the world I'd derived so much enjoyment from? If I'd been inclined to do something about any strangeness I noticed rather than dismissing it as irrelevant?

Would I even be sticking my neck out now, doing everything I could to stop whatever new catastrophe the fiend was planning, if Quinn's life and safety weren't at stake? That was a kind of selfishness too. I wanted her to survive because I wanted her in my life, with all the joy she'd woken up in me.

The uncomfortable thoughts followed me all the way

up the coast. Finally, I tasted the shifting traces of minerals and organic matter that told me I was nearing the spot where I'd left the rest of the group behind. Hopefully they hadn't needed to depart in a hurry because of some new threat, but I could make it to our agreed-upon backup meeting spot if they had. It'd just make for a longer journey.

As I came closer to the shore, I noticed another creature that wasn't quite mortal slinking through the shallows. Was it a shifter of some kind in its mortal-like animal form or a lesser being? The vibe it gave off made me think it was more purposeful than a thoughtless creature would be.

I eased closer, following its movements, and lashed out in an attempt to snatch at it. But the fishy body dipped and dodged before darting through my grasp with its slippery scales. I whirled to chase after it only to find it lunging at me, transformed into something now human shaped and sized but with fins jutting from its forearms.

Fear flashed through me. I had to stop this thing before it stopped *me*. It might have already spotted the others—it might mean to report their location to its master. No normal being would have gone on the attack with me like that when I still had a huge advantage of size.

I snatched at his limbs, and he sank spindly teeth into one of my tentacles. With a grunt, I shook him off. Seeming to decide he'd made a miscalculation, he leapt away from me, back into fish form.

But I couldn't let him leave either.

If I could capture him—if I could bring him to Quinn —I might have brought back real answers after all.

I hurtled after him with swishes of my tentacles. I could move faster than his small body, no matter how he veered one way and another in an attempt to lose me. I closed in on him, my tentacles braced to lash out—

Some instinct or a thread of sorcery in the fish shifter's brain must have told him there was no escape. Instead of racing onward, he jerked downward without warning—and speared his skull on a sharp spire of bone protruding from a half-crumbled skeleton on the sea floor.

I stared at his sagging body for a minute as his smoky essence flowed into the water, my chest tight. Then I returned to the shore empty-handed.

At least, if he had been a spy, he wouldn't be reporting to anyone now. Small comforts.

I passed from the water into the thin shadows that draped the shoreline beneath the clouded sky, knowing I'd move faster that way once I was on dry land. All the same, my heart felt heavier than usual as I flitted across the terrain, feeling for impressions of any of my companions nearby.

I heard Quinn first—a gasp that echoed through me with a jolt of desire. I knew that sound so well. As I veered toward the spot it'd come from, the dragon shifter's eager growl reached my ears next. I glided around a stretch of larger rocks toward a hollow shadowed by looming boulders and a few trees, and spotted the two of them entwined on a sheltered patch of sand.

I'd thought I was beyond jealousy when it came to Quinn and the beings I trusted my life with. But seeing Lance swipe his tongue along her jaw as he traced his claws over the bared skin around her waist woke up an emotion that wrenched at me.

In the back of my mind, I could hear him announcing his love for her in that brashly confident way he had.

Completely certain of the depth of his emotions and what label he could put on them.

She'd said it back to him before… and she'd said it to me too. But I hadn't been able to answer her with a similar declaration of my own. What did love mean to a shadowkind? How could I say that what I felt matched the devotion she'd shown me, as much as I adored her?

So maybe I didn't really deserve her the way the others did. After all, what had I done to prove my worth as a partner beyond offering the same indulgences I'd once treasured?

But how could I change who I'd been for centuries in a way that would transform me into someone who'd truly earned my spot by her side?

CHAPTER SEVEN

Quinn

Lance paused in his death-defying caress of my torso with a cock of his head. "Torrent's come back."

Now that we'd started on this course, every nerve in my body was quivering with the need for him to continue toward its blissful end. But that didn't mean I *only* wanted him. I teased my fingers into his chaotic curls. "Is that a problem?"

The dragon shifter flashed a grin at me, baring the fangs he'd already grazed along my neck with glee. "Not at all. The more thrills for you, the better, right?"

I beamed back at him. "Definitely." But even as the generosity of his love lit a warm glow inside me, a sharper pang hit me underneath.

This interlude wasn't just about thrills, as much as I enjoyed those. Depending on what I had to do to stop the leviathan, I didn't know for sure whether we'd ever have another moment like this again. This might be the last time I'd get to soak in my men's carnal affections and offer my own devotion so intensely and concretely in return.

I didn't know how much of an impact losing me might really make on their vast lives, but if I was going to have to leave them, I wanted it to be with them knowing how fully I embraced and appreciated every part of them.

As he resumed his stroking of my stomach, Lance glanced over his shoulder. "Don't just stand around watching from the shadows. Bring those tentacles over here."

Torrent wavered into view just a few steps away at the base of one of the looming boulders. I couldn't read his tense expression, but his eyes looked stormy with the emotion behind them.

For a second, I forgot the moment I'd wanted to create here, the little bubble of happiness I'd known would only be temporary anyway. I rested my hand against Lance's knuckles to stop his caress. "Did you find out anything in your search?"

Torrent shook his head. "Nothing clear enough that we could do anything about it immediately. You can carry on." He paused. "I wasn't sure that you'd want me to join in."

Lance snorted. "I can give our woman my claws and fangs and tongue, but you can make her feel even better on top of that. We might as well put all we have to good use." His mouth stretched into an even broader grin.

In case the other man had any doubts about whether I agreed with that sentiment, I held out my hand to Torrent to beckon him over. "I wasn't accomplishing much wandering around here," I said, as if I needed to explain why I wasn't saving the world this instant. "It seemed like... a worthwhile way to pass the time. While we can."

I'd only meant to refer to the fact that we'd been pretty busy with tackling and then fleeing from our enemies in the past couple of days, but I suspected from the tightening of Torrent's jaw that he understood the other implications as well.

I didn't want him thinking about the limited time *I* might have in general. "Come here," I added softly, and something about my tone convinced him.

He sank down onto the sand next to me, leaving me encompassed in heat between him and Lance. As the dragon shifter nuzzled my jaw and pressed another kiss to my neck, I turned my head toward Torrent. His gaze held mine as my breath hitched and my eyelids fluttered with the sliding of Lance's claws farther down my body to the apex of my thighs.

Torrent raised his hand to trace his fingers over my cheek, but he didn't lean in for the kiss I was anticipating. "Always trying to find a way to make everything better, Ms. Fix It," he said lightly, though his expression was still pensive.

My lips twitched with a smile. "I'm not trying to fix anything right now. Just to make the most of what I have. Which I think is an awful lot."

His throat worked. Then he finally kissed me, his mouth capturing mine at the same moment as he trailed one of his tentacles across my chest. Even through the fabric of my tee and undershirt, my nipples stiffened at the brush of the suckers over them. The tingles of pleasure brought an eager murmur up my throat.

I gripped his shoulder and kept my other hand tangled in Lance's hair. The tips of the dragon shifter's claws grazed my cunt through my shorts, and I only partly swallowed the moan that followed.

He swiped his tongue over my throat as Torrent kissed me harder. When the exploring tentacle slipped right under my clothes, trailing bliss up my torso, Lance tugged my face around to claim my mouth for himself again.

Torrent swept my hair back from my shoulder and pressed kisses to the crook of my neck as his lithe limb worked over both of my breasts in tandem. He didn't give any sign that the contact with the threaded undershirt bothered him, and I didn't want to offend him by implying any physical weakness.

He knew what he could give, what he was comfortable with. I wanted my men to trust that I knew what I could handle, and I should respect them just as much.

I reached for Torrent's shirt and unbuttoned it blindly so my hand could roam over his leanly sculpted chest. Every ripple and dip of a scar was a testament to how far he'd come to be here with me now. He hesitated at first and then pushed even closer to me, welcoming my touch. When I stroked my fingertips over the dappling of suckers on the back of his upper arms, a hungry noise resonated through his breath over my skin.

Lance let out a grunt that sounded like a mix of amusement and impatience and vanished from my grasp for a split-second. I wasn't at all surprised to see him reappear fully naked, his well-muscled, golden-brown body on full display with his erection jutting impressively from between his thighs, ready for action.

He'd thrilled me in so many ways with that dragon tongue of his that I wanted to return the favor. I leaned in, bringing my mouth to his golden-brown skin. His warm, smoky scent filled my lungs as I kissed my way down the planes of his chest and abdomen, all the way to his groin.

When I reached his cock, I didn't hesitate to swirl my tongue around its thick head. As it twitched under my attentions, Lance groaned.

"So good, baby girl," he murmured, teasing his claws around my thigh and across my lower back. He stroked back and forth as I took him deeper into my mouth, pressing just hard enough to send the prickling of pain that came laced with delight through my flesh. Then he tugged at the waist of my shorts as well as he could without severing the fabric. "A little help getting these off?"

The second comment was directed at Torrent. A moment later, another tentacle flicked across my belly to undo the fly and yank the shorts down. As I helped squirm out of them, sucking Lance hard enough to provoke a growl as I did, Torrent kept squeezing my nipples with his suckers. His second tentacle delved right between my thighs to glide over my pussy.

A tingle raced through my clit. I moaned around Lance's shaft, and the dragon shifter grazed his claws across my scalp. His hips pumped instinctively, seeking even more stimulation.

When I tucked my hand lower to fondle his balls, his breath turned ragged. But with my next slick of my tongue around his cock, lapping up his musky flavor, he gripped my hair and tugged my head up.

"I don't want to finish there," he said in a rough voice. "Too many other parts of you I'd like to be inside."

At the raise of my eyebrows, he didn't elaborate, only pulled me into a kiss. I clung on to him, my body undulating as pleasure radiated through it from Torrent's attentions, pouring all the emotion I could into the meeting of our mouths.

But it didn't feel like enough. When I drew back, I caught Lance's violet gaze. My pulse stuttered for no reason other than the joy of having had this man in my life. "I love you."

Lance gave another growl and slammed his mouth back into mine, kissing me so hard my head spun. "I love you too, Quinn," he murmured against my lips. "So much. You are *mine*."

Not only his, though. I kissed him back just as passionately, but when he released me, I shifted onto my side to let Torrent wrap me even more fully in the embrace of his tentacles. The pluck of a sucker against my clit had me gasping, but it couldn't distract me from my sense of purpose.

I brought my mouth to his and kissed him as eagerly as I had Lance, reveling in the wild, salty flavor that laced his lips. Then I cupped his jaw with my head bowed close. "I love you."

Torrent let out a rough sound, the storminess coming back into his eyes. "I will always come back. You're the brightest thing in my life. But I don't know if—"

"I know," I said quickly, without any disappointment.

Torrent had made it clear before that love wasn't a concept he knew what to do with. I wasn't looking for him to pretend a feeling that didn't come naturally to him. The affection he did offer me was more than enough in return. "I just want you to remember. Always. I'd be right here with you forever if I had the choice."

His mouth twisted, but then it crashed into mine again. His tentacles picked up their rhythm, strumming at every sensitive spot on my body faster. Pleasure swept through me, but I didn't want to reach my release like this either.

I groped at Torrent's pants, and he flickered away and back again like Lance had, leaving behind everything but the boots that covered the damaged ends of his legs. I pushed him over onto his back. As I straddled him, he adjusted his tentacles around me, still stroking my breasts but easing up to uncover my cunt.

Lance knelt at my flank and licked his tongue along my shoulder blade. "I like this position. I'd like to feel you the way only Torrent has gotten to before." He grazed a knuckle over my back entrance.

Ah, so that's what he'd meant about other places, plural. I couldn't help pushing back into his touch at the quiver of bliss it sent through my nerves. "Yes, please," I mumbled.

Torrent let out a dry chuckle that was cut off by a groan when I rubbed my pussy against his rigid cock. "Make sure you get her good and ready first," he instructed his friend.

I sensed Lance's grin in his intake of breath. As I sank down, taking Torrent inside me, the dragon shifter peppered kisses down my spine—and kept going.

At the first swipe of his tongue over my other entrance,

I both whimpered at the shockingly heady sensation and started to tense. It felt even more intimate than anything we'd done before. But Lance showed no sign of hesitation or reluctance, lapping at me there and coating me with his slick dragon saliva until my uncertainty unwound.

Torrent stroked my clit with his tentacle and gave my nipples a tighter squeeze. A jolt of giddiness shot through me. I took that as my cue to start moving over him, rocking up and down, taking his cock deeper with every iteration.

The tentacled man lifted his hips to meet me, and the dragon shifter matched our pace unwaveringly. As Torrent thrust forcefully enough to hit the perfect spot inside me, a whole chorus of sounds tumbled from my mouth. Lance worked me over with his tongue for a few seconds longer and then lined himself up behind me. The head of his cock —the slimmer humanesque version—nudged against my opening.

"All good, baby girl?"

"The best," I said in a ragged voice.

As wild as Lance could be, he was nothing but careful when he knew one wrong move could hurt me. He slid in slowly, letting each pump of my hips against Torrent's guide him another inch. And with every one of those blissful inches, the pressure inside radiated farther through me, making me tingle all the way to my toes.

Lance wrapped an arm around my waist and hummed happily against the back of my neck. "Different and yet just as wonderful."

I started to giggle and lost the sound to a moan as he and Torrent both thrust deeper at the same time. After that, I wasn't aware of much at all other than the ecstatic sensations unfurling through my body and the grunts and groans of my lovers' pleasure alongside mine. We moved together as if we'd always been meant for this, even though a few months ago I'd had no idea beings like these two men even existed.

"Fuck, Quinn," Torrent muttered raggedly. "You are amazing."

I could only whimper in response. I bucked harder, faster, chasing the release we were all hurtling toward. Torrent pushed himself upright with his good hand to close his mouth around the tip of my breast. Lance dragged the tips of his claws down my sides, Torrent nipped my nipple in time with a flick of my clit, and I tipped over the edge, feeling as if I were both soaring upward and careening from a great height at the same time.

My body shuddered, and Lance growled. He slammed into me with the most force he'd yet dared and let out a choked sound as he came with me. Torrent thrust up into me with his tentacles gripping me tight, and I cried out again with one last wave of bliss as he flooded me with his heat.

Lance didn't pull back as he softened inside me. He nuzzled my back and hugged me close. "Still strong, our baby girl. We won't let anything take her."

I glanced down and met Torrent's gaze. I had the feeling he understood better than the dragon shifter did how little say they'd have when it came to certain problems threatening my life, but he didn't correct the other man. Instead, he pushed his torso even farther up so he could form the other side of our joint embrace more fully.

I nestled between their bodies for several minutes until

the thump of heavy feet sounded just beyond the trees, as if a large form had landed on the ground.

"Crag!" Lance said cheerfully, leaping up and flickering into his clothes as easily as breathing.

My cheeks flared with the awareness that I couldn't make myself presentable quite that quickly. Thankfully fixing my shirt was a simple matter of tugging the hem farther down. Torrent snatched up my shorts with a tentacle and passed them to me. I'd managed to squirm into them and was just buttoning them up when the gargoyle appeared at the seaward end of the sheltered hollow.

Paisley fluttered after him, but she wasn't Crag's only companion. He had a rotund figure about half his substantial height in his grasp, his massive hands clutched around the being's stout neck. It squirmed in his fingers, its eyes bulging, but obviously couldn't flee.

If Crag had taken notice of what we'd recently been up to and had any feelings about it, he didn't show them. He nodded to me with a grim smile. "I caught one."

"So you did." I let out a halting laugh, jarred by the sudden switch in mood. I had to gather my powers quickly and focus on the important tasks at hand.

But reconnecting with Lance and Torrent had been important in its own way. As I sucked in a breath, I found the passionate interlude had refreshed my spirits. It wasn't that hard to concentrate.

I focused on the plump human-like being the gargoyle held and willed a surge of sorcerer energy up from my chest. The words spilled off my tongue with a crackle, compelling him to answer our questions.

My energy smacked against a barrier inside him like it

had with other beings in the past. No surprise—he was under the leviathan's sway. I squared my shoulders and braced for a much bigger punch of power. I had to shatter the magic that already bound him... and then, if he was still unwilling to cooperate, use more sorcery to force him to.

"Quinn?" Crag said with obvious concern, but I shook my head. It wasn't any good preserving my strength if the world fell apart around me in the meantime.

I repeated the order in the sorcerer language, flinging the words at the being and my sense of the magic inside his head with all my might. My pulse hiccupped—but the barrier cracked. With a flash of triumph, I hurled the command at him once more.

The leviathan's sorcery disintegrated completely. The stout little man blinked and gulped a breath through his constricted throat.

"Put him down," I told Crag. "But don't let him leave yet." I drew myself even straighter, this minor victory steadying me on my feet.

We were finally getting somewhere. Maybe I'd end up getting a chance to fix this mess after all.

After Crag lowered him to the ground, the being rasped a few more breaths. He shook himself and peered up at me. "You broke me out. I can do what I want again."

"You can," I said. "But I'd appreciate it if you tell us what you know about your former master's plans first."

The round face fell. "I—I'm not sure of much. He just ordered me here and there, back and forth." He made a wiggling gesture with his thick fingers. "But..." His equally round eyes brightened. "I did hear just this morning—he was sending a bunch of watery shadowkind off into the ocean. He wanted them to gather in a few different places in the sea around this country."

A chill tickled down my back. "And what were they supposed to do then?"

"I only got the gist of it. But I think... they're supposed to summon the big waves."

"Big waves?" Lance repeated. "How big?"

The little man grimaced. "Big enough to wash away all the mortals near the shores, all around this country. 'Drown them all,' he said."

CHAPTER EIGHT

Quinn

Drown them all. The portly shadowkind man's words were still ringing in my ears when Rollick returned to our shoreline location not long afterward. He took in our combined gloom and cocked his head with his usual authoritative air. "All right, what's gone wrong now?"

"We managed to catch one of the leviathan's minions that knew a little about his plans," I said. "And Torrent talked to a siren near a rift in the ocean whose story lined up with it. The leviathan is sending a bunch of water-based beings through the oceans all around the country to hurl tidal waves at as many places as they can."

I rubbed my arms against the growing chill, which wasn't all internal. The clouds overhead had thickened even more, their spitting turning into a full if light rain.

Rollick frowned at the sky and motioned us toward his car to get out of the weather. "I'm not sure how much he could accomplish by attempting that. *He* can create a real tsunami, but a siren isn't going to have much impact. It takes at least a few of them just to upend a boat."

"A big boat," Torrent put in, walking stiffly in his physical form with his tentacles for balance so that he could continue the conversation where I could hear. "And we don't know how many beings the leviathan has under his sway at this point—or helping him willingly. How are things in L.A.?"

"The flooding is getting worse," Rollick admitted. "But that's more due to a bunch of small waves rather than one particularly big one. I'd imagine he's in the process of building one at least for that spot. But he can only tackle one place at a time himself."

My heart skipped a beat. "They'll need to evacuate even more people. A tidal wave can cover a lot of ground. If it comes on too quickly..."

Rollick nodded as he opened the passenger-side door for me. "They're already moving a lot of the residents to temporary shelters farther inland. I'm not sure about this approach our foe is taking. He could have stealthily built up a wave with less obvious preamble. It's as if he wants us to be aware of the threat."

"Maybe he likes knowing we can't do much about it," Crag rumbled somberly.

Rollick's forehead furrowed. "I can't help thinking there's more to it than that. But I haven't been able to put my finger on it yet. I took a look at his pet rift that he's been expanding, and while it's noticeably bigger and giving off more energy than I usually see, I can't tell why he and the behemoth were so obsessed with it either."

"I don't trust anything that big snake is doing," Lance muttered. He leaned past the open car door to steal a kiss from me before hopping into the back seat. Paisley fluttered after him, and Torrent and Crag disappeared into the shadows. There wasn't much more for them to report anyway.

As Rollick started the engine, I hugged my messenger bag to my chest. "If the leviathan is sending shadowkind to the Atlantic side too, and we know he has it in for me... He'll probably have them targeting Jacksonville before anywhere else, won't he?"

My parents didn't live super close to the ocean, but I didn't know how far any of the waves the leviathan's minions summoned might reach. Or whether Mom and Dad would be at home if one hit and not taking a stroll on the beach. Or what other problems our enemies might cause out there.

The villainous duo hadn't figured out who my family was, as far as we knew. But they'd been aware I'd been staying in Jacksonville. It wouldn't be hard for the leviathan to guess that there'd be people I cared about in the city. If he targeted the entire area, no one was safe.

My stomach knotted. I didn't want *anyone* dying because of the monster's campaign against me. But my parents had already been through so much both because of my childhood illness and now my long, unexplained absence. How could I leave them unprepared when the threat might be coming right to their doorstep and it wouldn't take more than a quick call to warn them?

The demon could obviously guess at my concerns. As heavier droplets started to drum on the windshield, he shot me a tight smile. "I whisked your parents away to safety once before. I'm sure I can manage to do it again if it seems necessary. We'll keep a close eye on the reports from all North American coastal areas."

"Why is he specifically after *this* country?" Lance asked from behind us, clicking his claws restlessly. "The worst sorcerers are over on the other side of the ocean."

He had to mean the enclave where experienced sorcerers led novices through the vicious rites that granted them the power to "harness" shadowkind. I couldn't disagree with his assessment of them, having witnessed those rites and the sorcerers' attitudes about the shadowkind they enslaved firsthand. Oh, and also after having those sorcerers almost murder me. That gesture hadn't made me feel all that friendly toward the bunch of them either.

"I don't know," I said, glancing at Rollick. "It sounded like the leviathan and the behemoth were going around in Europe and Asia plenty before, although maybe that was before they joined forces. You said there doesn't seem to be anything special about that rift other than the way they've expanded it. They could have done that to any rift anywhere, right?"

"As far as I know." Rollick rubbed his jaw. "It could simply be that they joined up and decided to go on their sorcerer-murdering rampage, and they found it easier to track down the families here in the 'new world.' Many of the sorcerer lines on the other side of the globe are more established and practiced at hiding themselves."

"And the storms?"

He shrugged. "I'm already unconvinced that he'll be able to wreak all that much havoc with his lackeys even on one country. If he tried to take on the entire world all at once, he'd be spreading his forces even thinner. He probably wants a certain amount of concentrated impact. The real question is, toward what end?"

I thought back to the minions we'd managed to capture before. There'd been one who'd been helping the duo of its own free will. "That one creature did say something about taking the mortal world for themselves. But a few tidal waves and some storms... I mean, they'd cause a lot of destruction along the coasts, and that's horrible, but it wouldn't really turn the tide for an all-out invasion. You didn't think they had any hope of managing that no matter what they did."

To my relief, Rollick responded with the exact same confidence as before. "An attempted takeover would be bloody and catastrophic on both sides, but there's a reason it's never been attempted before. There are far too many mortals, and you have an abundance of the substances that can easily weaken or even kill us. I truly hope he's not so delusional that he's going to attempt that kind of invasion anyway."

"It'd be a strange way of launching it," I said, knitting my brow as I gazed out the window into the falling rain. "Where are we going now?"

"I thought we'd take a little detour over to—"

Rollick's remark was cut off by a strangely fleshy thump from behind me. A thump that sounded like it'd come from *inside* the car.

I spun around just as Lance lunged at Paisley. The pixie was flinging herself at the window next to her headfirst, her skull smacking against it for a second time. She pounded at it with a few swings of her fists as well before the dragon shifter caught her in his grasp and clamped her arms to her sides, holding her well away from him to dodge her now-flailing legs.

"What are you doing?" he demanded, looking bewildered.

"Have to go," Paisley muttered through clenched teeth. "Have to get to him. He needs us."

My eyes widened. "I broke the behemoth's hold on her. The leviathan shouldn't have any control—unless the sorcery can hide and activate later—"

Before I could finish that thought, Lance twitched. He snarled and whipped his head around as if trying to shake something out of it. Next to me, Rollick shuddered. The wheel jerked in his hands with a screech of the tires.

I jolted against my seatbelt, my breath knocked from my lungs. Swearing, the demon swerved all the way onto the shoulder and slammed on the brakes. His hand fumbled as he reached to shut the engine off. A cold smack of terror passed from him into me, like nothing I'd ever felt from Rollick before.

"Quinn," he grated out, sounding as strained as Paisley had. "You need to drive. East. As fast as you can. There's a" —he cut himself off with another shudder, smacking one hand to his temple—"a turn off onto another highway up ahead. Take that and keep going."

I shoved open my door and stumbled out into the rain, my heart thudding. "What's happening?"

Lance was twisting and squirming in the back seat, groaning with frustration. "He's trying to take us. The slippery magic is tickling around in my head. I can't get it out."

The pixie had darted from his grasp. I yelped as she shot past me, her wings fluttering so fast they were a blur. In an instant, she'd vanished into the shadows along the darkened road.

Rollick heaved himself out of the car and around the hood to the passenger side, unsteady on his feet. The sight of him so off-balance sent a flare of panic through me. I dashed around to take the steering wheel like he'd said.

"Our serpentine 'friend' is sending out a general call," the demon managed to growl as he threw himself into the seat I'd just vacated. "I wouldn't have thought—for him to reach this far with this much power—but he did absorb so much from his partner." He let out a hiss through his teeth.

I started the engine, but my mind was spinning. "If it's his sorcery, I could try to cast my own to block it."

"No. We don't have time for that. We don't know if you're strong enough, and if you don't manage all of us—I can feel Torrent and Crag grappling with it too—it isn't hitting us as forcefully as it would have up close. Even Lance is holding off the leviathan's influence for now. You just need to get us farther away before the bastard ramps it up even more."

I didn't need to be told twice. I hit the gas and tore down the road as fast as I felt I could control the car on the increasingly slick road. My pulse pounded louder than the raindrops drumming on the roof. Lance was still thrashing in the back seat, the leather tearing as he dug in his claws. Rollick had bowed his head over with his hands clutched around it, breathing in halting gasps I could tell he was fighting to even out. More fear wafted from him into me.

How far were we from the leviathan right now? L.A. was at least fifty miles away. And the leviathan had managed to extend its influence all the way out here.

How many other shadowkind, not quite as powerful as my own or closer by, had already fallen completely under his sway like Paisley had?

I couldn't answer any of those questions. All I could do was take the exit Rollick had mentioned and speed farther away from the coast and the city that was the leviathan's current haunt. Thankfully with the stormy weather, there was even less traffic than when we'd driven out here. The gas tank was still three quarters full.

We'll be okay, I told myself over and over. *We'll be okay.*

As we roared along the highway to the east, the rain dwindled. The drumming became a patter and then faded away completely. Afternoon sunlight streaked out across the landscape up ahead where the clouds thinned.

Rollick gradually straightened up. His stance was tense, but even so, he couldn't hold in the tremor that ran through his body. He glowered through the windshield for a few minutes before he let himself speak again.

"Just when I thought that fiend couldn't become any more of a menace."

He glanced toward the back and sighed, I assumed at whatever wreck Lance had made of his seats. The dragon shifter had quieted down, but I still heard the occasional grunt and rustle as he fought off the lingering effects. It was several more minutes before his bright voice, unusually mournful, carried to us. "I'm sorry."

"It's all right," Rollick said in a resigned tone. "Blame the beast that caused it. You did a good job fending off his commands."

"I think... I think there was still a little of Quinn's sorcery in me from taking on the behemoth. I reminded myself of her orders, even though they didn't totally make sense anymore. That helped."

At least my magic had done a little good. I swallowed thickly. "Can I assume Torrent and Crag are all right?"

Rollick nodded. "Still with us in the shadows, taking a much-needed rest after dealing with that crap." He shifted his gaze back to the horizon ahead. "It seems we won't be doing much more investigating around L.A. for the foreseeable future. But I don't think that's where we'd want to be heading right now anyway."

I glanced at him. "What do you mean?"

His mouth twisted. "If the leviathan is powerful enough to send out his sorcery that far, he'll have enslaved hundreds more beings than he had under his sway before. Maybe enough of an army that he *will* be able to send tidal waves all along both coasts. We'd better get your parents out before he has time to see that plan through to its brutal conclusion."

CHAPTER NINE

Quinn

I couldn't sit still in the back of the limo parked on the tarmac. Rollick had insisted on going to collect my parents on his own, since he could travel through the rifts to reach Jacksonville in a matter of minutes, faster than even the private jet he'd be taking Mom and Dad on to return to the area near his bunker. But I could only imagine how confused and terrified they'd be once some stranger had forced them to leave their home, no matter what he said to them.

Crag had commandeered the seat next to me, peering out the car windows watchfully and rubbing my shoulders with his solid hand when I shifted in my seat for the hundredth time. Lance had gotten restless himself and gone out to prowl along the edges of the airfield, even though we were well away from L.A. and anywhere the leviathan was likely to send his minions searching for us now.

Torrent's voice carried from the front passenger seat, speaking into a cellphone in his usual low, even tone but getting a bit louder here and there as he added emphasis to his message. "Yes, I know the data you're seeing might not show any reason for concern yet, but our experimental systems have been accurate in the past. I'm only asking that you keep a closer eye on the situation than usual. I thought it was important to convey a warning, given how serious the potential consequences are."

When he hung up, I leaned forward in the expansive back area of the limo. "Are they listening to you?"

Torrent glanced back with a grimace. "So far, all of the monitoring stations I've spoken to have been skeptical, but at least we're putting the possibility into their heads. They'll be primed to notice any concerning changes in the weather patterns or tidal behavior."

I blew out my breath in a huff, but that outcome might be the best I could have hoped for. We couldn't whisk *everyone* across the entire coastline away from the threat of a tidal wave, but there was more chance of saving lives if the people watching for problems had advance warning and could spot the signs of trouble sooner.

A distant rumble reached my ears. A jet appeared against the stark blue of the sky. As it soared toward us, dipping lower, I tensed in my seat.

It was right on time. I guessed Rollick hadn't had that much trouble getting my parents on board. I wasn't sure if that boded well for the methods he'd needed to resort to or not. I had a flash of an image of him working some demonic magic on them to knock them out, slinging them over his monstrous shoulders, and hauling them back to the plane like that.

Well, he couldn't have gone quite that far. I was at least sure that he wouldn't have walked around downtown Jacksonville in full demon form.

I still didn't know how I was going to explain any of this situation to them: my absence, my new companions, why they were in danger. The truth sounded totally insane, but there were no alternate explanations that sounded more normal. My general plan was to start out as vague as I could get away with and only get into details where Mom and Dad pushed for them.

They trusted me. They knew I'd never gotten into any significant trouble or made up wild stories before. But who knew how far that trust would get me, especially after I'd vanished on them for weeks on end?

The roar expanded until it filled my ears. Crag lowered his hand to wrap his fingers around mine. "Do you want us to stay with you for this or would you rather they didn't see us?"

I looked at him, nearly human but huge and with that jaw of literal stone, and at Torrent, with his tentacles braced on either side of his waist. Torrent could probably have sat reasonably comfortably without his extra appendages out for a short time, since he didn't need to put any significant weight on his lower legs in his current position, but I didn't like asking him to.

Anyway, even if they'd been totally human, I couldn't

imagine my parents being super comfortable with even more strange men taking part in the conversation beyond the one who'd essentially kidnapped them.

"I think it'll be better if I talk to them on my own first," I said. "But I might need backup at some point... if I need to prove the supernatural side of the story to them. So, I guess stick around in the shadows and follow along with the conversation, if you don't mind? If I need you, I'll make that clear."

"That's no problem," Torrent said without hesitation, shooting me a tight smile that seemed to say, *Good luck*. Crag nodded. As the private jet touched down on the runway with a faint bump of its wheels, both men slipped away into the patches of darkness within the limo. I knew Lance would rejoin us shortly too, heading our way from the moment he noticed the plane's arrival.

Not for the first time, I wished I could still sense them in the shadows the way they could track each other's presence. Even with all this supernatural power of my own, I was still nearly as unaware as any other human being.

The plane slowed to a stop only about twenty feet from where the limo was parked. The door swung open with a soft hiss, lowering into a short flight of stairs. Rollick appeared first, the sunlight gleaming off his tawny hair. He drew himself a little taller and beckoned behind him, and two other figures stepped hesitantly into view.

My chest constricted at the sight of my parents. It'd been more than a month since I'd last set eyes on them. Which wasn't *that* long in the grand scheme of things—I'd gone longer without visiting them in person while I was at college, although we'd usually video chatted once a week then. But so much had happened in the past several weeks that it might as well have been years.

And they had no idea about any of what I'd experienced yet.

The confusion was clear on both of their faces as they followed Rollick down the stairs and across the pavement to the car. I wavered for a second and then gave in to the impulse to push open the door and meet them outside. Let them see me sooner rather than later.

The moment I stepped out, Mom's eyes widened. "Quinn!" She rushed forward to meet me and flung her arms around me, hugging me against her compact frame.

Dad hurried after her on his longer legs, his pale hair unusually rumpled as if Rollick had pulled them out of bed for the trip. The second Mom had released me, he hugged me next, with a tight squeeze that had a bit of a tremor to it.

"We've been so worried," he said roughly. "Where have you *been*?"

"We tried texting and calling," Mom put in. "I don't like to interfere with your life on campus, but after a while with no response, I checked in with the college and found out you hadn't participated in any of your classes since last month. After that we filed a missing persons report, but they won't do much for adults. No one had seen you."

She sounded so relieved and frantic at the same time that my heart ached. I gripped her arm and Dad's and guided them toward the back of the limo. "I'm so sorry. There's been so much going on—I know Rollick will have told you a little about it—and I was afraid if I got in touch with you, I might send the wrong kind of attention your way. Put you in danger. Unfortunately, now you're in danger anyway. But we're going to get you someplace safe, and I'll explain everything as well as I can."

Mom balked a little at the car, peering over at Rollick, who'd stopped by the driver's side door with a mild expression. She turned back to me, lowering her voice to a murmur. "I don't understand. He said you've been helping against some group that wants to attack the country? Who even *is* he? How did you meet him? He isn't forcing you into some kind of cult situation or... or I don't even know what, is he?"

I swallowed hard and nudged them toward the car. "No. And that's a pretty good basic explanation. I want us to get going, but I'll try to give you the whole story while we're in the car."

My parents both hesitated for a few seconds longer, but then they climbed into the back of the limo with me following. They sat on the seat facing backwards, and I took the one across from them where I'd been sitting before. As Rollick started the engine and the car rolled forward, I could tell they were taking in the luxurious trappings of the vehicle with even more bewilderment.

"Rollick has a lot of resources," I said. "He set up this safe house for you too." I didn't have to mention it'd originally been for me. "But—let me start at the beginning."

It wasn't that simple, of course. At a halting pace, I laid out how I'd first been attacked back home in the park near their house, the way the group of men I was now with had come to my rescue, the discovery that my heart gave me unexpected powers, and a summarized version of the enemies we'd realized we were up against. With each additional piece of the tale, my parents' expressions shifted from confused to utterly bewildered.

"I know it sounds crazy," I said for what might have been the tenth time as I wrapped up the truncated version of events. "I'd think it was crazy too. But I've been living in this craziness for weeks now. I know the shadowkind are real. I know how much destruction the really monstrous ones can cause. Maybe you've even seen reports of the strange stuff that's been going on in L.A."

Mom and Dad exchanged a glance. "They said there've been attacks by wild animals," Mom said. "Not *monsters*."

"That's the best way they can explain it. No one would believe anything else, right?"

Dad was frowning. "You've always had a good head on your shoulders, Quinn. You have to be able to see that none of this fits with what you know about the real world."

"Yeah," I said with a humorless chuckle. "That's because there's too much of the real world that we weren't aware of. I... Let's wait until we get to the safe house, and then I can really show you." Somehow I didn't think they'd handle an encounter with my shadowkind men in the confines of the car all that well. Better not to freak them out too much while Rollick needed to concentrate on driving.

Mom leaned forward to grasp my hand. "Whatever's going on, we'll get through it together. I'm just glad you're here with us again."

I smiled back at her and was about to say something intended to be reassuring when a hitch in my chest stole my breath. The increasingly familiar pressure clamped around my heart, tight enough that my head momentarily spun.

I fought to keep my expression blank, but Dad's eyes flickered with concern. "Are you all right, kiddo?"

"Yeah," I lied, speaking slowly so that I could get out the words without my voice turning ragged. I pushed my posture a little straighter despite the urge to hunch in on myself, unable to stop my jaw from clenching briefly at the pain. A deeper discomfort wound around my gut.

I wasn't going to let them know that my heart was giving out on me on top of everything else going on. They didn't need worries about my shortened lifespan hanging over their heads when there was a much more pressing problem threatening all of us. If I still could spare them one little bit of anguish, I was going to do everything in my power to do so.

Mom's brow had knit. I forced my smile back into place, willing it to stay relaxed, taking careful breaths through my nose. The worst of the pressure eased off, but a prickling sensation remained, spreading farther through my chest and across my back and shoulders.

I was lucky all three of my other men hadn't sprung out of the shadows to make sure I was okay. They'd no doubt been able to tell my heart had acted up again. But it wasn't as if they could have done anything to help regardless.

"I'm really glad to see you again too," I went on, easier now that the vise in my chest had released. "It was really hard not being able to talk to you, knowing you'd be worried. I was just even more scared that the monsters that want to hurt me would realize they could use you to get to me. I didn't want to totally upend your lives the way we're having to now."

"Don't you worry about us," Mom said firmly. "Whatever you need, we'll figure out how to make it work. That's our job, sweetheart, not yours."

Sudden tears pricked at the back of my eyes. They had no idea how much I'd worked at keeping our family time happy and worry-free all through the past several years. How much responsibility I'd felt not to drag them down any more than my childhood illness already had.

When we reached the bunker, my parents climbed out of the car and peered around across the desolate desert. I led them over to the door in the small shack-like structure that was the only part of the building above ground. When Rollick unlocked the door, they halted, looking down at the stairs that would take them under the earth.

"This is all a little much," Dad said. "What exactly is going to happen to us here?"

"Nothing," I promised. "It's just a little apartment, basically, with everything you could need to stay comfortable. We've set it up with a TV and a computer so you can follow the news, and Rollick made sure there's a cell signal if you're near the top of the stairs so I'll be able to call you and touch base while we're... trying to deal with the rest of the problem. Hopefully you won't need to stay for too long. There's no way any of the creatures after us should be able to find you down here."

Honestly, the setup was a bit overkill since the silver and iron protections around the place were mainly there to prevent shadowkind from sensing my sorcery magic. Mom and Dad didn't have any of that. But the protections would also repel any shadowkind that ventured near here, and being under the ground would keep my parents completely out of view. I couldn't complain about them being *too* safe.

But I could see from the tightening of their faces that this was one step too far without further evidence. Sucking in a breath, I glanced at Rollick. He raised his eyebrows in question.

No. I didn't think a massive naked demon would be the best example of the shadowkind to present them with first.

"Lance," I said, knowing all three of the other men would be nearby. "Could you come out so my parents can see that shadowkind beings like you are actually real?"

Lance wavered into view a few feet away from us without hesitation, in his human-like form but with his hands held up, clawed fingers splayed to show them off. He gave my parents his usual jaunty, crooked grin. "Quinn is working very hard to protect you. And because you're important to her, we are too."

My mom blinked, taking in his talons, and Dad gripped her shoulder. Before they could make some excuse about makeup or prosthetics, I tipped my head toward Lance. "Show them your dragon form."

He bobbed his head and stretched forward, shifting effortlessly with a rippling of his jewel-toned scales over his now-reptilian body. He twined around on the dry earth and flashed a fanged grin at my parents.

Mom let out a little shriek and clapped her hand over her mouth. Dad was simply gaping. I walked over to Lance and rested my hand on his smoothly scaled neck, giving him a gentle stroke with my fingers. He turned his head to nuzzle my hip.

"I—I don't understand," Mom mumbled.

"I know," I said. "It's crazy. But it's also real. Wait until you meet the other friends I've made."

Both of my parents stared at me, momentarily lost for words. But I could see the change in their eyes as disbelief gave way to horrified acceptance.

CHAPTER TEN

Rollick

I let Quinn sit in silence for a good while after we'd gotten into the car before I glanced over at her. "I'd say that could have gone at least twice as badly as it did. Consider it a win."

She exhaled in a rush as if she'd been holding most of her breath for the past hour. "I know. I still don't like it. I don't like that I can't stay with them while they're wrapping their heads around all this. It's so much to lay on them at once."

In the back, Lance slid down to prop his feet against the back of my seat. "We take down the leviathan and his beasties, and then your parents won't have to worry about it anymore anyway."

Next to him, Crag let out a wordless rumble. "We don't

know how long that might take. But they'll be safe until then, even if they're still confused."

"Yeah." Quinn rubbed her face. "I just hope they stay there. I'll have to call them regularly to make sure they know I'm okay and everything's on track... as much as we have a track at the moment."

"They'd have trouble getting very far," I said. "Torrent's taking the limo back to where it belongs, and this car was the only other vehicle I had nearby. They seem like practical enough people not to attempt a hike across the desert when they have perfectly comfortable accommodations where they are—and their daughter's assurances."

My remark didn't appear to put Quinn at ease. She folded her arms over her chest, gazing broodingly out the window. "Do we even know for sure that any of Paisley's friends will be waiting for us? They might have gotten caught up in the wave of sorcery the leviathan sent out, just like she did."

"I expect we'll have a few new allies, and those will be the most eager ones of the bunch too. I told them to meet us at a spot near the New Mexico-Arizona border, which would have put them well out of range if they set off fairly quickly. Her mistake was glomming on to us so early."

I said the last bit flippantly, but even as I spoke, an icy jolt shot through my nerves. For just a second, my thoughts scattered as if they were dandelion fluff in a sharp gust of breeze.

My hands tightened on the steering wheel as I clamped down on the abrupt reaction. I trained all my attention on the road ahead and the steady, even breaths I was sucking into my lungs.

Quinn's head twitched toward me. No doubt she'd gotten a flash of the strange panic that'd come over me, through the blasted emotional connection I hadn't meant to forge. I hadn't minded it so much when it'd allowed her to trust my loyalty to her, but I wasn't pleased at all with her sensing my moments of weakness. Which had been happening far more often than I liked in the past few days.

I kept my expression relaxed and let out a light chuckle to follow up the remark, emphasizing how absolutely fine I was. From the corner of my eye, I saw Quinn's mouth tighten, but she didn't badger me about what she'd sensed. I was managing to convince her it wasn't a big enough deal to impinge on my dignity in front of the other beings in the car. Maybe she was being kind enough to wait until I was comfortable discussing it with her, as long as I wasn't at the point of driving us off the road.

If I *never* had to discuss what was plaguing me, I'd be satisfied. It should go away on its own, as randomly as the unwanted bursts of emotion had begun.

All right, their arrival hadn't been entirely random, but I'd prefer not to think about that fact either. The less I thought about it, the less likely I'd provoke another discomforting response.

I was a millennia-old demon with more power than the majority of beings in either realm possessed. I could handle this small problem on my own while we tackled the much larger one ahead of us together.

It was the physiological responses of the woman sitting beside me—the woman who'd come to matter more to me than just about anything in either realm—that I should be more concerned about. Especially when we pulled up at the wooden hut that was all that marked the meeting spot I'd picked and I sensed not just a few but dozens of beings lurking in the shadows around us.

"We'll want to go through the same test we did with the pixie on all of them," I said reluctantly as I parked the car. "Confirming that they're all free from any enemy's sway and joining us with the right intentions. But expend as little energy as you can get away with on each of them. And if you start to feel tired, I expect you to give yourself a break."

Quinn gave me a quizzical look. "I don't see why that should be a problem." She pushed open her door, stepped out onto the dry earth, and froze as the multitude of beings of various shapes and sizes rippled into physical form around us. Her breath caught with a hint of a gasp. "Oh."

"We do have an army!" Lance declared eagerly, springing out of the car and then leaping onto the roof of it in dragon form. I couldn't tell whether he thought he was offering them a warmer greeting by meeting them in his shadowkind appearance or attempting to intimidate anyone who might not give our mortal woman the respect she was due.

But our reluctant sorcerer knew how to handle herself just fine by now, initial hesitation aside. Her shoulders had already squared as she gazed out over the crowd of what I could now see was several dozen beings—and at least half of them higher, capable of more than just animalistic fighting. Twice as many as I'd spoken to yesterday. Many of the lesser shadowkind had wandered off since the pixie had first approached us, but the arrival of more thoughtful beings more than made up for their absence. They must have gathered more numbers like a snowball picking up new layers of frost as they'd moved across the country.

The leviathan's gambit might even have worked a little in our favor, despite what we'd lost to him. Any being that'd sensed what he was attempting to accomplish but managed to escape the sweep of his sorcery would be that much more motivated to make sure he never got the claws of his unnatural magic into their heads. More motivated than the various contacts I'd established over the centuries, most of whom still preferred to protect their own necks while they hadn't seen the full impact of the threat.

But then, how could I blame them when I'd taken the same tactic myself for so long? Too long.

"All right," Quinn said, moving to the hood of the car and propping herself against it. "Can you all get into some kind of line so we can be a bit organized about this? I just need to make sure none of you are under any compulsion from the shadowkind that wants to, y'know, kill me. I'm sure you can understand why I'd be cautious."

I'd already told the original bunch I'd talked to what would be required. They shuffled forward without argument, though they appeared to have some trouble with the whole idea of assembling in a line.

As Quinn got started, aiming a few sorcerous words at the first being to approach her to check for existing magic gripping its mind and then to question its intentions, Lance sprang back off the car. He and Crag prowled around the crowd like monstrous sheepdogs surveying their flock.

I stayed next to the car, within easy reach of Quinn should I need to yank her away from a troublesome being, though they seemed peaceful enough so far. Standing in one spot also made it easier to ride out the faint tremors of chill that rippled through me here and there as the odd syllables spilled from her tongue.

They reminded me too much of the commands the behemoth had hurled at me when he'd tried to force me into becoming his slave. The memory of that time was the deepest, darkest chill in the back of my mind.

I'd fought him off enough that I hadn't hurt Quinn or interfered with the trap we'd managed to set off. He hadn't gotten the best of me.

But he *almost* had. There'd been that moment, right before the trap had closed its metal jaws on him, that something had fractured in my self-control. There'd been nothing ringing in my head except his orders. I'd been about to attack Quinn.

Maybe I'd have wrestled control back and stopped myself, but I'd never know that for sure. And now I'd spend the rest of my ancient life living with that uncertainty.

As well as the uncertainty of whether another time, if a foe like that tried me again, I might lose myself altogether.

But that possibility didn't matter right now. Right now I held the most authority out of any being around us, and I wasn't going to let them forget that.

I stretched into my full shadowkind form, letting my hooves paw at the dusty earth and smiling to show off my jagged teeth. Any shadowkind who'd had the slightest inkling of turning on my woman had better think twice.

Quinn moved through each of the beings in just a minute or two, but I noticed when that time started to stretch a little longer. Once she'd spoken to maybe half of the crowd, finding them all honest about wanting to stand up to the leviathan, she exhaled so raggedly I was about to enforce a break. But then she got up herself and took a brief walk around to stretch her legs, drink some water, and eat a pear that Lance insisted on dicing up for her, show off that he was.

Even so, I wanted to tell her to give it a rest. That we would bring the beings we'd confirmed were trustworthy back with us and let the others linger here for another day or two until she'd recovered. But I could already imagine how well the suggestion would go down. I settled for eyeing her closely for any signs of deeper discomfort.

By the time she'd checked the last of the shadowkind who'd come to our aid, the sun had touched the horizon. Quinn sagged back against the hood with a sigh of relief.

"All good," she said. "Where do we go from here?"

I glanced to the east. "I was thinking we'd gather our forces and decide on our next steps in my badlands house—the one you visited briefly before. It's well out of the way of any ocean and also well-protected. Any beings in this bunch who can't handle the metal installations can stay outside them, and you'll go out to them when you need to make arrangements."

Quinn cocked her head but seemed to decide my strategy was solid enough. "Fine. Let's get going then."

I turned to the crowd around us. "There are plenty of shadows on and around the car. Hitch a ride if you like and can find room. The gargoyle will stay back with those who can't and show you the way. Stick to the gloom—we don't want to be spotted by any of that beast's minions who might have wandered this way."

A murmur mixed with grunts of agreement spread

through the mass of beings. I didn't know how much of an army they'd prove to be, but at this point, I wasn't going to be choosey. At least every shadowkind with us was one that the leviathan hadn't bent to his will.

As we got into the car, I settled back into the driver's seat and started the engine. Quinn pulled out her phone, equipped with the SIM card I'd newly restored to her. I thought she might be going to place a call to her parents even though we'd only left them behind hours ago, but instead she flicked at the screen. I didn't know what she was up to until a few minutes later when she sucked in a horrified breath.

My gaze flicked from the road we were cruising down to her. "What?"

"A big wave hit Jacksonville just forty minutes ago. Half of the city is flooded. A bunch of people who were near the beach drowned or were killed by wreckage in the currents." Her voice wobbled.

"It's a good thing we got your parents out of there, then," I said. "The rest... We did our best to warn them. There are probably fewer casualties than there would have been otherwise."

"Yeah. It's just scary thinking of how close a call it was. If we'd waited even another day..." She ducked her head. "And I'd bet the leviathan told his minions to start with Jacksonville because of me. If I wasn't involved in this—"

"Hey," I said, sharply only so I could cut through her self-recriminations. "He'd have had them hit *somewhere* no matter what. He's the one responsible for the deaths, not you. You're doing everything you can to stop him."

"I know. I know." She closed her eyes for a minute and

appeared to gird herself. Then she started scrolling through the news reports again. I kept most of my attention on the road, but I noticed when her frown deepened.

"It isn't just that one wave," she said. "There was another near Seattle. And people have finally figured out there's a huge one building off the coast of L.A. But it's not just waves either. There are strange cloud patterns in the skies where all the storms are happening. People are saying they're seeing faces there, glowing eyes, that sort of thing." She glanced at me. "I thought shadowkind like to keep a low profile. This is even more over-the-top than the attacks on the streets in L.A."

"They generally do lay low." A frown of my own crossed my face. What was the leviathan up to? "It's sounding more and more like our enemy wants to make his influence known. I guess he isn't scared of the Highest stepping in now that he's already faced off with some of their warriors and won. Maybe he's even rubbing his disobedience in their face for some sadistic reason."

Lance let out a short growl from the back seat. "Maybe he wants to scare all the other shadowkind who see it hoping they'll obey *him*."

"That's also possible," I said, but my stomach had knotted with uncertainty. None of those reasons quite added up with what I knew about my kind.

But if the leviathan was going for something beyond the obvious, what *was* he hoping to achieve?

And how the hell was our little makeshift army going to stop him?

CHAPTER ELEVEN

Quinn

It seemed like every time I glanced at the news feeds, the situation on the coasts had gotten worse. I woke up in the guest bedroom in Rollick's Texas badlands house and immediately grabbed my phone to find reports of more storm activity and a couple more tidal waves that'd crashed along the coastal regions. By the time I ventured out into the common areas, showered and theoretically refreshed for the day, my stomach was a mess of knots.

Lance was already in the kitchen, crisping bacon and frying eggs with his fiery breath. He motioned for me to sit at the gleaming central island and nudged the plate toward me before swiftly slicing an orange into crescents with his claws. I guessed he'd sensed as soon as I'd woken up and decided to be ready for me. I wasn't going to complain.

"Thank you," I said, and he beamed at me.

"You have to keep your strength up, baby girl. I'm always going to take care of you."

I couldn't bear to tell him that bacon wasn't exactly the best option for heart health. I doubted a little grease really mattered at this point when so many other things were putting much more strain on my transplanted organ.

As I dug in, my other three men wavered into sight around the island. Crag grabbed a bottle of water from the fridge and set it in front of me as if he was afraid I'd forget to hydrate. Torrent leaned against the counter with a pensive expression.

"We had a few more beings turn up overnight," he told me. "Wanderers who noticed the increased activity here and wanted to find out what's going on. They've opted to stay. You'll need to test them."

Rollick gave a tight grin. "For the moment, we have a few of our confirmed allies keeping watch over them to make sure they don't get up to anything nefarious. And the most competent beings standing watch at a farther distance to make sure no one else meanders close enough to see what's happening here without being vetted."

My gut clenched even more with that new worry. "Do you think the leviathan's minions will realize we've come out here—or what we're doing?"

"I expect we're reasonably safe," the demon said. "He's focusing his attention on the coasts, which are his natural habitat anyway, and he has no idea what our current plans might be or where we might have gone to. It's unlikely he has enough minions to spare to closely investigate every corner of the country. But the patrols will guard against any of those minions happening to stumble on our little army on the off chance that they do head this way."

"There aren't many beings hanging around out here at all," Lance put in. "Not much to do. Very boring. No people, no buildings, and everything is so flat."

Rollick shot him a light-hearted glower. "The boringness is what makes it safe. You always seem to find plenty of ways to entertain yourself no matter where you are."

"The storms are getting more volatile," I said. "I read that there's a major hurricane brewing in the Atlantic now, bigger than they usually see at this time of year. Will that be shadowkind-generated too?"

Torrent nodded. "There are definitely beings that can affect the weather that way, and I'm sure the leviathan has the reach to bring them under his sway."

"The humans have been evacuating many of the coastal areas—all across the country, not just in L.A. now," Crag said in an obvious attempt at reassurance. "They'll get to where it's safe for them too."

"If they can." I rubbed my mouth, forcing myself to finish chewing even though I couldn't take much pleasure from the food. Rollick might have had a general idea of the logistics after how thoroughly he'd involved himself in urban life, but I doubted the other shadowkind had any concept of how difficult it was to move entire cities' worth of people and keep them fed and sheltered.

Maybe it was the stress of that added concern or maybe it was just random, but a moment later, my chest contracted with a now-familiar vise. I braced my hands against the island, closing my eyes as I breathed through the painful sensation. My pulse skipped and raced, and a chill washed through me, deeper than the air-conditioned coolness.

A hand came to rest on my shoulder, rubbing it gently. I focused on that contact rather than the pressure in my chest. Lance let out a rough noise of frustration, but there really wasn't anything else any of them could do—as they had to be recognizing by now as much as I had.

When the pressure released, a sheen of sweat had formed on my brow. I wiped it away and stared down at my plate, a faint queasiness in my stomach making it hard to imagine eating more.

"We can put your food in the fridge for later," Torrent suggested, his even voice unusually soft.

"Yeah, that might be a good idea." I dragged in a breath and glanced toward the windows that looked out onto the house's yard and the desert terrain beyond it, where all of our new "army" was hiding in the shadows. "First I'm going to check in with my parents, and after that I'll confirm that the newcomers are above board, and then I think we should get on with figuring out who in this 'army' can actually do anything to fend off the leviathan."

I went back into the bedroom to make the call in private, my chest constricting in a different way at the sound of Mom's voice. She still sounded shaken but resigned. I didn't sense any sign of rebellion in her tone.

"It's good to hear from you," she said. "Are you all right? What we're seeing on the news is pretty frightening."

"I know," I said. "But I'm far away from it right now, and I'm making sure we're totally prepared before we try to fix things." As much as we could be prepared anyway.

"I feel so selfish staying here out of the way when so many other people are suffering."

A lump rose in my throat. I could have said the same thing. People were dying out there, losing their homes, struggling to survive, and I was living in relative comfort, even though I was one of the few people who had any chance of tackling the threat. I hated that we'd had to run away, as necessary as I knew that move had been.

"You're helping by giving me one less thing to worry about," I told her. "Knowing you two are okay makes it easier for me to concentrate on finding ways to stop this disaster that won't put *me* in too much danger."

I talked with her a little longer and then with Dad. After, I walked out of the room with my emotions in a muddle, pulling on my protective vest so I could go beyond the house's yard without fear of detection. Out under the searing sun, I pushed my worries to the back of my mind and went through the motions of making sure the new arrivals to our shadowkind gang weren't operating under enemy influence. Then I sat down on a bench in the shade of the pair of scrawny trees at the edge of the yard.

My men had followed me out to oversee the proceedings. "Let's find out exactly what we're working with," I said to Rollick.

Torrent leaned his forearms against the back of the bench, one resting next to my shoulder companionably. "The most important factor in tackling the leviathan is going to be making sure no one we send into battle will get caught up in his sorcery."

Lance clicked his tongue. "Quinn's magic shielded us from the behemoth. He didn't get into my head at all."

"Yeah, but the behemoth was only half as powerful as the leviathan is now," I pointed out. "And my sorcery has a stronger effect on you four because I know you so well. I don't know the beings that've joined us since then at all."

"And there are too many of them," Crag put in firmly. "Quinn would wear herself out if she tried to cast a powerful command that'd last long enough on all of us." He loomed over me with a concerned frown, not mentioning the possible consequences beyond simply making me tired.

I swallowed thickly, and Rollick let out a faint huff. "I doubt we'd want to send all the beasties right into the fray regardless. If we can pick out a few key allies, Quinn's magic would at least give them some protection. We can't decide how to proceed until we're aware of the possibilities."

He stepped forward into the sunlight, snapping his fingers. "All right, all of you who want to help stop the leviathan from carrying out whatever other horribleness he has planned, our sorcerer wants to speak with you. Let's start with the higher beings. Show yourselves a few at a time, and let us know any supernatural abilities or other skills you can bring to the table."

I raised my voice to carry across the desolate terrain. "If any of you have some kind of power that allows you to ward off other beings' supernatural abilities, that would be particularly useful. Or anyone who can manipulate water and weather, since that's what the leviathan is mostly using against us right now."

A slim woman with bluish skin materialized out of the shadow by a patch of desert grass. She approached me with her head bowed low. "I don't know about warding off, but

I'm a sea nymph," she said. "All of my powers have to do with water."

My spirits rose a little. This was a decent start. "Do you think you'd be able to push back against the tidal waves that are being summoned—maybe even break them apart before they reach the shore?" We could send her to the east coast or farther north on the west where she'd only be contending with the leviathan's allies, not him and his sorcery directly.

"I could try. The way they're stirring up the oceans, throwing the water around—it isn't right. It'll be hurting the other shadowkind who like to live in the water too."

Lance had perked up. "Maybe you have some friends who could help? That way you could push back more."

She offered a shy smile. "I'll reach out to whoever I can find. I don't know how many others like me would want to get involved. I know what it's like to be caught up by that awful magic... I don't want it to happen again. But when they haven't had their minds taken over, they don't realize what's at stake."

"Whatever you can do would be great," I assured her. "Let's see who else is here to help, and then we'll decide the best place for you to go."

A gangly man with shaggy yellow hair had appeared while I'd been talking to the sea nymph. As she stepped aside, he gave me a jaunty bow and brandished a gleaming flute. "I don't know about deflecting powers, but I have a sort of sorcery of my own that I can use on mortals. I managed to get away from the leviathan before his magic totally caught me, so maybe my own powers have given me a little resistance."

"Maybe" and "a little" didn't give me a whole lot of hope, but it was better than nothing.

I smiled back at him. "That's good to know. Is that your only supernatural ability?"

"I can work minor glamours, but I'm not sure how much use they'd be."

Neither was I, but I forced my smile to hold. "You never know. Thank you." I glanced around the terrain. No other beings had emerged yet. My temporary good spirits started to fade. "Is there no one else here who has abilities related to persuasion or water?"

When no other shadowkind showed themselves, I sat up a little straighter, willing myself to hold steady. "That's all right. I'd still like to know what the rest of you can do. Let's hear from all of you."

But if the ones I'd already spoken to were the best of the bunch... I wasn't sure we had a hope in hell of defeating the fiend we were up against.

CHAPTER TWELVE

Quinn

"All right," I said, staring down at the puppy-sized frog, which peered up at me with its round eyes. "I'm guessing that you prefer a watery home. Anything else you can show me?"

The lesser shadowkind simply croaked. I couldn't tell whether it'd understood my question or not, but then, most of the lesser beings hadn't. From what I could tell, they'd joined up with us more for their own protection than to help with ours.

I dipped my head to it in acknowledgment. "That's fine. Glad to have you with us."

As it bounded back into the shadows, I stood up and stretched. I hadn't been doing much other than talking for the past few hours, but exhaustion rolled over me as if I'd barely slept last night.

That was another symptom of a failing heart—getting tired faster. I gritted my teeth against that knowledge and headed into the house, moving slowly but steadily.

Though I'd stayed in the shade outside, stepping into the air-conditioned cool was a welcome relief. As I let out a little sigh, watching my men emerge from the shadows around me, Lance slipped his arm around my waist and nuzzled the side of my head.

"What do you think of our army?" he asked.

I made a face. "Honestly? It's not much of an army. If the sea nymph can convince some of her fellow nymphs and whatever other beings to help counteract the magic that's driving the tidal waves, that'll be great, but it won't do anything to stop the leviathan himself. None of them seem to have much hope of deflecting his sorcery."

Crag had headed into the kitchen, where he was now leaning into the fridge to grab one of the pre-made meals they'd stocked the place with for me. He was clearly determined to make sure I never went thirsty or hungry. "It's unfortunate that they can't all wear shirts like yours. Or some kind of hat to shield their minds? I don't know how it would work."

"It might not do any good even if they could tolerate the silver and iron," Torrent pointed out, dropping into one of the chairs at the kitchen table with his tentacles arcing on either side. "Those metals can deflect the kinds of persuasive magic shadowkind use on humans. There's no reason to assume they'd protect against human-based magic, even if it's being wielded by a shadowkind."

"That's true." I sat down across from him and rubbed my brow. "The only beings who'd be able to stand up to the leviathan without getting caught up in his sway are other humans like me. And the only humans like me who could do anything at all to affect *him* are other sorcerers. And apparently they're all just as selfish as the average shadowkind, since pretty much none of them responded to our request for help."

And the one sorcerer who had turned up had been promptly slaughtered. I had no illusions about the vulnerability of our human bodies, even those that weren't harboring borrowed hearts.

Lance hissed through his teeth. "That bunch off in their enclave tormenting beasties to make new sorcerers—but they can't be bothered to come when there's a shadowkind who actually deserves to be messed with."

"Well, to be fair, I haven't asked *them*."

Rollick propped himself against the kitchen island. "I think we'd better keep it that way," he said dryly. "If they found out where you are after you disrupted their rites— and brought a demon into their midst who murdered a few of their people—I suspect we'd have two sets of enemies to contend with rather than new allies."

"Yeah." So it still came down to me. I dragged in a breath. "If I could just control him enough to make sure he didn't enslave any other beings, maybe the rest of you could restrain him. Or if I could force him to admit what he's really planning, we could focus our defenses better." I paused. "There really isn't any way to completely stop him other than killing him like we did with the behemoth, though, is there? I mean, after everything he's done, there's obviously no reasoning with him or convincing him to give up his plans."

"I think that's a fair assumption," Rollick said. "So fair that I've already had my human contractors building another trap on the outskirts of L.A., since we had solid blueprints on hand for what that should look like. What we really need is a way to get our serpentine adversary in there, and then it'll be game over."

"I don't think we're going to trick him," Torrent pointed out. "Even the behemoth only came all the way into the first trap when Quinn compelled him."

I nodded, biting my lip. "But it took everything I had to manage that."

"And it hurt your heart," Lance said with a frown.

I didn't think that really mattered in the long run. If I died stopping the leviathan, that'd be a hell of a lot better than living another few months while watching it wreak havoc across my world. But I knew the dragon shifter wouldn't like hearing me say that out loud.

Crag set a ham and cheese wrap in front of me, and I picked it up gingerly. I was still wiped from the morning's activities, and suddenly all I wanted was a few moments away from the horrible problem looming over us.

"Thank you," I said to the gargoyle, and stood up. "I'm just going to check whether my parents have left me any messages and take a look at the latest news. Then we can talk some more, see if we can figure anything else out."

As I walked to my bedroom, the men's voices continued to murmur behind me. Their conversation fell away after the door shut in my wake.

I actually had my phone on me, so I knew I hadn't gotten any alerts, but I double-checked for new texts or voicemail anyway. Then I found I couldn't quite bear to look into what other disasters might be going on around the country that I couldn't do anything about yet. I sank down on the edge of the bed, grappling with my uneasiness.

And then a sharp jab of panic lanced straight through my chest.

I jumped up instinctively, my pulse racing before I recognized that it wasn't a more potent effect of my failing heart. It was a flash of emotion, and not mine—it must have come from Rollick.

I'd been catching flickers of what felt like uneasiness and even fear from him over the past few days, but none quite as intense as this. With all my nerves jangling, I rushed back to the kitchen.

The men were still poised around the room, Torrent in mid-sentence, his voice fading when I came charging in. Rollick had kept his spot by the island, his stance typically languid, but as I came through the doorway, my gaze shot to his hand gripping the edge of the counter. His knuckles had turned pure white.

His eyes darted to me, and I caught a whirl of tumultuous emotion there in the instant before he managed to will it away.

"What's going on?" I demanded. I knew he didn't want me bringing it up, but he'd refused to say anything to me all the other times that rush of emotion had come over him, even though he must have realized I'd been picking up on what he was feeling. And something about the conversation with the other men must have provoked it, so if he wouldn't give me answers, they would.

We were all in this together now. He shouldn't be

hiding something important enough to make him react like that.

Rollick offered me one of his movie-star smiles, as if that was going to distract me. "I don't know what you're talking about. We were simply having a conversation."

I folded my arms over my chest. "You do so know what I'm talking about. Something upset you—a lot. Something's *been* upsetting you ever since we faced off with the behemoth. If we're going to fight his partner, I think we need to know what's going on with all of us. If something's come up that makes the situation worse, we have to deal with it together."

Lance cocked his head. "What made you think something's wrong with Rollick? He didn't do anything."

I opened my mouth and closed it again. Not only had Rollick and I never discussed the emotional connection that'd formed between us with the other men, we hadn't told them about the incident that'd caused it. I'd been so relieved to have the three of them back, and I'd already been avoiding thinking about the way Rollick had forced his essence on me—and the way my body had responded to him in that moment. They'd been aware that my sorcerer powers had been developing in general. It hadn't seemed important.

But maybe I shouldn't have been hiding any of it.

Rollick stared me down for a moment, but it didn't take him long to figure out that he wasn't going to intimidate me into backing off. He sighed and rolled his shoulders. "Fine. The rest of you have heard about the rites we discovered at the enclave. It seemed obvious that a similar process could enhance our reluctant sorcerer's abilities too. So I took it upon myself to insist that she consume a significant amount of my essence."

Crag's brow furrowed. "'Insist'?"

The demon waved off his implied objection. "She wasn't totally on board, but she was mainly hesitating out of fear of harming someone, and I didn't mind making the offering. We've hashed it all out since then. In any case, along with heightening her magic, it also seems to have left her unusually sensitive to my emotional state. Unfortunately, I haven't figured out how to turn off that connection." He grimaced.

"It's a good thing, considering you like to hold everything that's going on with you so close to the chest," I muttered. "So, what *is* going on with you right now?"

He hesitated in a very un-Rollick-like way, another tendril of anxiety reaching me, although this one didn't have the same urgent flavor. Whatever it was, he didn't like the idea of how we might respond.

"She's right," Torrent said quietly. "We need to know exactly where we stand—with each other and with our enemies. It's not as if the rest of us haven't had plenty of problems of our own to work through."

Rollick let out a disgruntled sound, but the reminder that his companions weren't likely to get particularly judgmental appeared to spur on his confession.

"It wasn't at all pleasant when the behemoth tried to wrap his magic around my mind," he said in a voice that might have been breezy if not for the thread of tension woven through it. "I've spent thousands of years never bowing to anyone else's will unless I chose to for my own reasons, and the sensation of nearly being taken over has left me... unsettled. And in random moments, I get flashes of memories from that time that unsettle me even more all over again. That's all there is to it. No new villains to worry about or additional problems to heap on our plates."

A pang ran through my heart. It sounded like a problem to me. My fingers curled into my palms against the urge to reach out to him, not knowing if he'd appreciate a comforting touch or find it embarrassing.

"That makes sense," I said. "Is the effect getting worse? This time just now... it *felt* worse than before."

He shrugged as if his answer didn't really matter. "I'm keeping it under control. My emotional state doesn't affect anyone but me. I assure you that if you need anything from me, this minor issue won't get in the way."

As if I only cared about his mental stability when it affected my plans. "I don't like that it's happening to you at all—because I don't want you to be going through any kind of emotional pain. If it isn't getting better over time—"

"Then I'll just have to keep coping," Rollick cut in, sharper than before. He paused with a wince and continued in a gentler voice. "You don't need to worry about me, Quinn. I've survived far too much already for this little setback to bring me all that low. And we definitely have much *bigger* problems to contend with."

Lance let out a wordless grunt, glancing from me to Rollick and then to the other guys. "We do have lots of problems—but maybe this is also a way that we can solve them."

CHAPTER THIRTEEN

Lance

Quinn blinked at me, confusion clouding her pretty blue eyes. "What do you mean? How could Rollick's panic attacks fix anything?"

"Not that," I said quickly, with a flick of my gaze toward the demon. He had stood by her side when the rest of us couldn't—he had kept her safe. I didn't want him to think I'd want him to suffer, even if it would have helped us. "I meant taking in his essence and getting that connection to him. You could do the same thing with all of us."

Quinn's lips parted, but it took her a moment before she seemed to be able to speak. "You—you know that would make my sorcery stronger. You don't like that part of me."

It was true that remembering the magic she'd cast on

me to force me to leave her side sent a jolt of horror through me. My stomach turned at the thought of how much more easily she'd be able to work a spell like that even now, with the extra benefit of Rollick's essence. If she took a long drink of mine, she might be able to control me with a single brief word, with no effort at all.

But she wouldn't. She was my Quinn and I was her dragon, and she'd promised never to use her magic on any of us again unless we asked her to for our own benefit. She'd told me she was never going to use it on *anyone* again after we'd defeated the leviathan. She was as horrified by what other sorcerers did as any shadowkind was.

"I like that it could be what stops this unhinged leviathan from enslaving any more beings himself," I said. "Or hurting more mortals. That's a good enough reason. And—if you could sense how we're feeling, then you'd worry less about us, right? You'd know that if you're not noticing anything bad, then we must be okay."

Something in her face softened. "And if I did realize that you were in danger, I'd know to come help."

Well, that hadn't been exactly what I was aiming for. I'd rather Quinn stayed as far away as possible from wherever the danger was and let us deal with it when we could. But we couldn't always, and it was hard to tell her she shouldn't be allowed to help us when we were so determined to help her.

If I expected her to keep her promise not to force us out of harm's way, then I shouldn't try to force *her* to keep away from the danger we all faced either.

I let out a light huff. "Yes. But hopefully less of that. The most important thing is that we're all pretty strong, so if we give you some of our strength, the three of us might be enough to put you on the same level as the leviathan. Rollick's contribution made you powerful enough to control the behemoth."

Quinn's mouth twisted. "Not on its own. I—when I was trying to get the behemoth to come into the trap, it didn't work at first. I had to take in some essence from one of the higher shadowkind minions that'd attacked us before I managed it."

I shrugged. "Still. That was one and there are three of us. It could work. Maybe you could take a little more of Rollick's too."

The demon chuckled. "I'm not sure I want to give her even more of an open invitation inside my mind, as eager as you seem to be." He paused, and his voice turned more serious when he looked at Quinn again. "But I would offer more regardless if it could mean we can end this catastrophe for good."

"You're welcome to my essence, as much as I can spare," Torrent said. "It won't only boost your sorcery to tackle the leviathan. It'd also give you an even closer connection to us so that your commands can shield us from him better."

I clicked my claws happily. "Yes, that's good too." Torrent always thought of all the aspects of a plan. And if he didn't see any problems with my suggestion, it couldn't be a bad idea, could it?

Crag let out a rumbling sound. "You can take whatever you need from me, Softness. But will it tire your heart to absorb more power?"

Guilt flashed through me. I hadn't considered that possibility. But Quinn was already shaking her head.

"I didn't feel any effects like that when I consumed Rollick's essence," she said. "The symptoms only started after I exhausted myself controlling the behemoth. I don't think the process itself should affect me. Who knows what'll happen when we confront the leviathan... but I've got to try. Having more energy might mean it's less of a strain."

Crag dipped his head in a nod. "Then I think you should do it. I know you'll use the power well."

Quinn glanced at each of us in turn, her eyes wide and a little shiny, like they'd collected a few tears. She did cry sometimes when she was pleased as well as when she was sad. I hoped this was one of the happy times.

"I don't really like the idea," she said. "I don't like the thought of doing to you what other sorcerers have done to so many other shadowkind selfishly. But... in this case, it wouldn't be selfish. And you're giving me permission rather than having it stolen from you. So I guess it'd be silly to refuse. I don't want more people dying because I have hang-ups about the power in me."

"You've never tried to hurt anyone," I reminded her. "You're always protecting all the people and beings you can. I wouldn't say we should do this if I didn't know it'd be okay."

She beamed at me, and a warm glow lit up in my chest as I grinned back. It was such a miraculous sensation, this emotion of love. And when she was connected to me the way she was to Rollick, she'd be able to feel just how strong my devotion to her was.

Maybe I liked that more than any other part of this plan.

Quinn raised her chin. "If we're going to do it, I suppose we'd better get on with it right away. Rollick, you said you've already constructed another trap. All we need is a way to propel the leviathan into it. Let's see if we can't accomplish that and put an end to his reign of terror before he takes it any further."

"All right." I stepped forward, my heart suddenly thumping faster. "I'll go first, since I made the suggestion. Does it matter what form we're in? Where should we do it?"

"I carried out the process in my demon body, but that made it easier for me to inflict the necessary wound," Rollick said. "Your claws should do the trick just fine either way. It might be more reassuring for Quinn to look into that pretty face of yours while she's still feeling conflicted about the situation."

I snorted at him. "I'm a very pretty dragon too."

Quinn's mouth twitched with another smile. "Yes, you are. I think I'd be fine either way. How would you feel more comfortable? You're the one who'll be bleeding."

Of course she would think of my well-being first. I weighed the options and decided, "Like this. I want to hold you while we're doing it. We can sit on the sofa."

I headed into the living room, and the others followed. As I sank down onto the sofa's soft cushions, Quinn hesitated.

"When I took in Rollick's essence, I kind of lost my mind in the moment. Went a little wild, feeling all-powerful and like I should be roaming around, stretching what I was capable of." She arched her eyebrows slightly at me. "Knowing how energetic you typically are, I might get even more that way when it's your essence. Just so you're prepared. If I can't control the reactions, you'll want to hang on to me, make sure I don't go running off."

She was putting a lot of trust in me too, then. I motioned her over and collected her onto my lap. "I won't let you go, baby girl."

Quinn tipped her head against my shoulder, molding herself against me as if she belonged nowhere else, and even more affection swelled in my chest. I adjusted her position against me so my arms could wrap all the way around her, flexed my claws, and slashed through my forearm deep enough to open a vicious gouge.

Quinn flinched in my embrace, but she tilted her head so I could easily bring the smoking wound to her mouth. The pain that radiated through my arm was diluted by the thrill of knowing that soon we'd be merged in new ways I'd never imagined could be possible.

My essence streamed from the cut in rhythmic billows with the thudding of my heart. Quinn had opened her mouth wide, inhaling steadily, but plenty of the stuff wafted up from the edges of her mouth and dissipated into the air around us. I kept my own breath steady. If I started to feel unwell, I'd have to stop and seal the wound, but I didn't want that to happen any sooner than it needed to.

The lingering tension in Quinn's body gradually released. Her muscles relaxed against me, her posture slackening as she absorbed more and more of my essence. She barely moved. At first, I thought she'd been mistaken about the likely effects.

Then the first tremor ran through her limbs. Her legs shifted against my lap, starting to squirm. I couldn't hold them in place with one arm around her waist and the other pressed to her mouth, but Torrent stepped closer, resting a tentacle over her shins to keep them still. Crag and Rollick eased nearer as well, ready to step in if I needed more assistance.

We were all in this together even now.

That recognition might have pleased me if Quinn's muscles hadn't flexed in my grasp at the same moment. The restlessness seemed to be rippling through her entire body.

One of her hands clutched my shirt, her fingers tightening and easing in an erratic pattern. A disgruntled murmur emanated from her throat. Her eyes darted from side to side, barely focusing on me. I couldn't tell if she was all that aware of anything in the room anymore.

Should I stop now? I could keep going—I should give her as much as I could, shouldn't I? But as I watched her quiver and jerk against my and Torrent's hold, a sudden chill washed away the warmth that'd filled me earlier.

This wasn't my Quinn in my arms right now, not really. A wildness had gripped her—the wildness of her expanding sorcery. I was giving her even more power to enslave shadowkind to her will, and it was muddling her head, making her fight me. She didn't remember the intentions she'd come to me with.

What if I'd gone too far by making this suggestion? Was I betraying my own kind, all the beings like me, by giving her the power to perform even more sorcery?

I might not know until we'd seen this war through to its end.

CHAPTER FOURTEEN

Quinn

I woke in a daze, blinking and finding myself staring up at the white ceiling in the guest bedroom. In that first second, my body felt weirdly numb, giving me the impression that I was floating over the bed rather than lying on it. Then my awareness sharpened, and I felt the silky texture of the sheets wrapped around me. A waft of cool air brushed my cheek.

"She's awake!" Lance bounced right onto the bed but slowed down his movements as he reached for me. He gazed down at me with obvious concern and stroked his knuckles over my temple, brushing the hair away from my face. "How are you feeling, Quinn?"

I cleared my throat before speaking. "All right. A little disoriented. Did everything go okay? I remember getting kind of stir-crazy—trying to run off—it's a good thing you held on to me. But the rest is blurry." I had distinct impressions of drinking in Lance's essence but not whether the other men had managed to contribute theirs as well.

Torrent's voice spoke up from near the foot of the bed. "After a little while, you seemed to realize you weren't going anywhere and resigned yourself to the process, just testing us a little here and there. We offered as much essence as we safely could—even Rollick again. Do you notice any change in your powers?"

I focused my attention on the ripples of energy that often passed through my chest. I had a sense of my sorcery whirling around my heart, but it was vague. "I didn't really feel the difference the first time I took in Rollick's until I actually tried to use my magic. I'm sure it's done *something*."

"You should try it on us," Lance declared. "Come up with a command that'll protect us from the leviathan's magic. We're about to go off and do battle with him anyway, right? As soon as you're up to it."

He spoke easily and without any outward sign of concern about me using my sorcery on him, but a twinge of anxiety quivered into me that I could tell was his. It had a Lance-like flavor somehow, which was a relief, because it would have been a huge muddle if I'd been getting hit by emotions constantly with no idea how to tell who might need my help.

I pushed myself upright and knit my brow at him. "I don't need to start giving commands. Not yet, anyway. We've got to get back to California first."

Rollick appeared in the bedroom doorway. "We do, but we don't know how far the leviathan is extending his reach now or how often he's putting out a call with his power. I think it'd be better if we're protected as much as we can be before we venture anywhere near his chosen domain. You can top up our protections when we're closer, of course."

He didn't sound at all bothered by the thought of me using my sorcery on him, despite the distress he'd talked about experiencing leftover from the behemoth's attempt at enslaving him, and I didn't catch any flicker of emotion that undermined his tone. I guessed he didn't associate my magic with the power that monster had used on him. Small comforts.

Crag loomed next to the demon. "You wanted to go right away to confront him, didn't you, Softness? Are you well enough to?"

I sat up and stretched my arms. "I'm totally fine. Just must have needed some rest after the whole essence-consuming thing. But we need everything else to be ready too."

I gave Rollick a questioning look, and he offered a slightly crooked smile. "The trap is ready whenever we are. If you want to flex those extra-enhanced powers of yours and see if we can hook a sea serpent, I say we go give it our best shot."

"I guess we'd need to find him first," I said.

Torrent nodded. "I don't think that'll be much trouble. He's mostly sticking to the ocean now and sending his minions to do his inland work. I might be able to draw him farther up the coast toward the trap so you don't have to go quite as far into his territory. We'll have a better idea once we get there."

"Okay." I dragged in a breath, ignoring the knotting of

my stomach. I *had* wanted to get this confrontation over with. And I should make sure my powers were noticeably revved up before we took that step. Maybe I'd maxed out my potential with Rollick earlier and my other men's essence wouldn't have done anything other than forge those tenuous emotional connections. "What command should I give you that won't get in the way of anything you might need to do?"

"You had good phrasing last time," Crag rumbled. "It didn't cause any problems. You could stick to just the part about refusing orders from the leviathan for now, since we don't know exactly what we'll be doing out there yet."

"Yeah." Relief trickled through me at that thought. Protecting them really could be that simple.

I just had to hope my sorcery would be strong enough to fend off the leviathan's magic as well.

I turned to Lance, reaching to grasp his hand. "Do you want to go first again?"

No more tremors of anxiety reached me. He simply beamed. "Absolutely."

I fixated on the power I knew I held inside me, willing it to activate at my call. When I opened my mouth, it burst up my throat more like a bolt of lightning than a sizzle of electricity. The words flew out in its wake. "You will refuse any orders the leviathan gives you."

The command rushed out of me, leaving my skin tingling. Lance blinked and grinned. "That went in faster than before, and deeper I think. I can feel the magic wriggling around in my mind. But it's a good order. That's okay." He cocked his head at me. "Did it feel more powerful to you?"

A giggle bubbled my throat. Now that I'd stirred up the sorcerous energy inside me, it was jittering all through my veins. "Oh, yeah. You know, we might just be able to do this."

Torrent's lips curved in one of his rare smiles. "I like the sound of that. Then the rest of us had better receive our orders."

It was hard to maintain my optimism for the entire, long drive out to the L.A. area. Even with Rollick handling the car tirelessly and using some demonic power to ensure we didn't get caught speeding, night had fallen by the time he slowed at the edge of the terrain he considered reasonably safe.

He pulled off onto a smaller road and parked just beyond a desolate-looking gas station. Rain drummed against the roof, and wind warbled overhead. He glanced toward the back seat. "I think we'd better split up here. If any of you have concerns about your part in this scheme, you'd better mention them now."

Lance shifted impatiently. "I just want to see that big snake fall down."

"Well, you might not get to *see* it, but if all goes well, you can come watch the aftermath. One big bonfire of essence." Rollick chuckled darkly.

Torrent slipped a tentacle around my wrist to give it a quick squeeze. "You're stronger than him in the ways that matter most."

Then he and Lance vanished into the shadows.

The rest of us waited in the thickening darkness for half an hour, letting the two of them get a head start on us. The plan we'd come up with during the drive was that the dragon shifter and the tentacled man would create multiple disturbances across the city—making it look as if my supposed army was launching an attack. If it worked as intended, the leviathan would send a bunch of his minions to go deal with the threat but not bother going himself, which was his usual MO. That would leave much fewer lackeys hanging around guarding *him*.

We'd never come right to him or his partner before, not like this. I didn't think he'd be expecting it. The only question was whether I could pull off my part of the plan once we were close enough for me to cast my sorcery at him.

When Crag nudged me, I obliged his concerns by eating the rest of the drive-through meal we'd picked up for dinner. My stomach was still tight, but he wasn't wrong that I could use all the energy I could get. Whether it worked or not, the attempt was going to take a lot out of me.

I popped my pills at the right time, trying not to think about whether they were really making a difference at this point. At the ping of Rollick's phone, he started the engine. That was our signal that the other men's gambit was underway.

We didn't know exactly where the leviathan was. All Rollick's shadowkind contacts in southwest California had been swept up in the fiend's waves of magical influence. So we were going to go down as close as we could get to the most central beach and work from there. Knowing the leviathan's preferred habitat, Rollick had possessed the presence of mind to arrange for the second trap to be constructed not far from the coastline, in an old warehouse on the outskirts of the city.

The roads were eerily vacant even once we reached the suburbs. The streetlamps glowed off the rain-slick asphalt, and the only sound was the pounding of the rain and the distant thunder. The west-most end of the city had been totally vacated, flooded by the earlier smaller waves that we knew were just a precursor to the immense one the leviathan was building.

I wasn't totally sure how Rollick determined when we'd better leave the car ourselves. He parked outside a bar that was closed far earlier than I'd imagine it would have been under normal circumstances. "Out into the deluge we go."

I pulled on the ankle-length rain slicker he'd gotten for me, tugging the broad hood as far forward as I could so that it would shield my face. This wasn't going to be a fun excursion. But Crag's head had already lifted, his gaze focusing on something in the distance beyond his actual sight.

"He's close," he said. "Just a little farther north, out in the ocean shallows. I can fly out there in just a minute."

In just a minute, I'd be facing our ultimate foe. I swallowed thickly. "All right. Let's do this."

Rollick grasped my shoulder. "I'll be right there with the two of you. In this darkness, I can travel almost anywhere." He glanced at Crag. "If Quinn's sorcery isn't working and that serpentine monster comes at you, get her out of there as quickly as you possibly can. You know where we'll regroup."

Crag dipped his head in a brisk nod. He wrapped his

arms around me, and I adjusted my position against his chest in the way I'd learned was more comfortable for both of us. The vinyl layer of the rain slicker gave him another barrier of protection from the silver and iron threads woven into my undershirt, but they were thin enough that they didn't bother him as much as my old vest had even without that. He showed no sign of irritation as we lifted off together into the downpour.

The cool rain spilled over the brim of my hood and streaked across my rain slicker as well as Crag's granite-like gargoyle skin. My hands were immediately drenched. I kept my feet tucked under the hem of the slicker so my sneakers didn't end up sopping too. The drops battered us in waves with each sweep of Crag's wings, lifting us higher.

At least the weather hid us from view—and stopped many people from coming out where they might have been able to see us in the first place. And as Crag soared closer to the churning sea, the buildings beneath us looked totally abandoned, no lights gleaming in the windows. The only glow was from the streetlamps that hadn't been toppled by the earlier waves.

I fixed my gaze on the frothing water beyond the coast. Somewhere amid those currents, our greatest enemy was lurking. He must have been deep beneath the surface or hidden in the gloom for now, because I couldn't make out the monstrous serpentine form I'd watched devour his partner just days ago. He was too massive to hide his physical form very easily.

Crag's sensitivity to shadowkind presences guided him. He flew farther north along the coast, gripping me firmly. It would have been difficult for him to speak in the storm, but for the most part, my sense of *him* was steady and calm. Only a few brief, faint quivers of apprehension filtered through the connection we'd formed.

Finally, he stopped and swung around in mid-air. He ducked his head so his mouth came close to my ear.

"He's down there," he rumbled through my hood. "I took us a little past him. You see where that red car is halfway in the water? He's almost directly across from there, maybe a hundred feet out."

"Okay." Now I just needed to call the leviathan toward us—and keep calling him all the way to Rollick's trap farther north. No big deal. Ha.

I closed my eyes and trained all my attention on the whirling energy inside me, tuning out the damp and the chill and the battering of the rain. Just with that internal gesture, the magic spurted and sizzled, crackling through every nerve. I felt like a live wire, ready to zap anything I touched. My pulse thumped faster as I opened my eyes and my mouth.

As always when I aimed my sorcery at any beings other than the men I knew so well, the words that seared from my mouth came in a language I couldn't understand myself. But I knew the intent I was putting into the shout, the command I was hurling at the invisible being below.

Show yourself and follow me. Now.

My skin quivered and my tongue tingled as the energy rushed out of me. It rang through my body so intensely that my vision briefly whited out. I reached toward the monster in the crashing sea with every ounce of strength I had in me, as if the foreign syllables were talons I could dig into its flesh and yank it forward with.

Something twanged deep in my chest. Exhilaration flared through my veins in the wake of the sorcery. I'd snagged the beast; my magic had caught hold.

Crag grunted with a mix of uneasiness and approval as a sinewy blueish green form materialized below us, a few shades darker than the wild waters that swept over and around it. The creature raised its head, its smoldering orange eyes large and fierce enough that I could make them out even across the distance between us. But it pushed forward through the water, heading our way.

"Good," Crag murmured, propelling us backward with flaps of his wings. "Very good. You're doing amazing, Quinn."

I hugged his arm and braced myself before flinging the command at the leviathan again for good measure. My heart stuttered with the blast of energy that surged through me as the words left my mouth, but the massive serpent slid forward a little faster than before.

It was working. I'd really made it happen. I was controlling this immense fiend.

I couldn't tell whether it was exhaustion from the energy expended or giddiness at my victory that'd left my head spinning. Maybe some of both. My mouth had gone dry. I clung to Crag even tighter, doing my best to ignore the increasingly erratic thump of my heart and the prickles of pain that were starting to dig into my rib cage.

I had to concentrate on the leviathan. I had to reel him in all the way to the trap, or this whole effort would be for nothing.

He was still coming, weaving through the waves, more of his seemingly endless snake-like body revealed as I drew him into shallower waters. I wasn't sure exactly how much farther it was to the trap; I wasn't sure how far we'd already come. My sense of time had fallen away along with everything else other than the hitches of my pulse and the magic shivering between me and my prey.

The ache in my chest spread down my back and out through my arms. Crag nuzzled my head through the hood. "Halfway there, Softness. We've got him."

The reassuring words had only just left his mouth when the leviathan reared up. Seawater streamed off its dark scales. It shook its upper body from side to side like a dog drying its fur and then smacked itself down on the road right at the edge of the coast.

I flinched automatically at the impact, the thud of it carrying all the way to my ears. And then the jitter of energy inside me fizzled. I knew in an instant, with a gaping horror that stretched wide through my chest, that I'd lost my hold.

A cry burst from my lips. I grappled with the magic twined through my heart, willing as much of it as I could still summon up to my tongue, and hollered out another command so forcefully it turned my throat raw.

My pulse lurched. The constricting sensation squeezed harder, pushing the air from my lungs. I gasped and choked on a sob as the answering jolt of a successful command didn't come.

My efforts hadn't been enough, and I didn't know what else to do. My limbs felt like jelly; my heart was on fire. My head was spinning so fast that the leviathan seemed to double and triple before my eyes as he surged farther out of the surf.

He threw himself upright and shrank at the same time,

his body shifting into a mostly man-like form that stood at least seven feet tall. His wet, tangled hair hung halfway down his back, and his eyes glared up at us. A sheen of smaller scales dappled his bare torso and arms.

"You tried and lost, sorcerer and traitors," he bellowed at us. "Now you'll just have to sit back and watch. I'll bring the depths of the shadow realm down on this place and make it ours even if I have to summon them myself."

Then he whipped around and dove into the water. His body never resurfaced that I saw; he'd probably melded into the shadows there as he made his way back to his former haven.

I couldn't pay much attention anyway. My lungs were heaving and my breaths rasping as I gasped to fill my chest. I couldn't tell if I was suffocating or having a heart attack— maybe both.

"Quinn," Crag muttered in a mournful voice with a flash of fear that rushed from him into me. He whipped around. "Relax now. You can't do any more. Just—just breathe, and I'll take you someplace safe."

As he soared onward and I grappled for control over my body, one clear thought penetrated the growing haze in my head.

There *was* nowhere safe. Not in the entire world. And from what the leviathan had said, even if I didn't know exactly what he'd meant, soon our home would be even more dangerous for all of us.

CHAPTER FIFTEEN

Quinn

By the time we made it to the meeting spot and the new car Rollick had arranged to have waiting for us there, breathing was no longer a fight. The vise in my chest had eased off enough that I wasn't afraid I was going to die right this moment. But an ache still gripped my sternum, prickling more sharply when I moved. If I turned my head too quickly, it started spinning again.

Crag yanked open the back door and set me down on the seat with the gentleness he could offer in contrast with his hardened body. Rollick immediately emerged into physical form next to him.

"Do you need water?" the gargoyle was already asking, flicking on the overhead light. "More of your medicines? Should we get you to a hospital?"

I shook my head—slowly so that I didn't set off the

dizziness. My voice came out with a rasp but not too wobbly. "No. There isn't much they'd be able to do anyway. I think if I just rest a little, I'll recover like I did before. It's already getting better."

"Get her that water," Rollick instructed, and Crag leapt to the front of the car to grab the bottle. With shaky fingers, I peeled off my rain slicker and tossed it on the floor. Here beyond the reach of the storms, the air held only a hint of dampness.

As I tipped back on the seat, letting out a relieved sigh as soon as I was lying on the firm cushions, the demon leaned through the doorway. He peered down at me, his concern for me rolling through our collection to mingle with the jolts of fear I was picking up from Crag.

"I almost did it," I muttered. "I got him halfway there. I wasn't strong enough." A sense of hopelessness swept over me that was far more uncomfortable than the physical pains.

Rollick's mouth twisted. "You're plenty strong. The leviathan is a menace beyond anything any of us has ever had to deal with. Including the Highest, I suspect, or they'd have..."

He trailed off with a furrowing of his brow, his gaze veering away from me. The emotion that wafted from him next was a mix of shock and horror that set my own nerves jangling.

"What?" I gasped out, moving to push myself upright again.

Rollick jerked out his hand to nudge me back down. "All you need to focus on right now is recovering that strength of yours. We can talk about everything else once you're back to your regular self. I want you contributing to the full extent of your abilities." He managed a tight smirk.

I grumbled inarticulately at him, but he'd dampened his emotional response down to a faint, dull current of uneasiness that reassured me a tad. It didn't seem like whatever had upset him was an immediate emergency, anyway.

Crag got into the back seat at the opposite end so he could help me drink some water without my having to get up. I leaned my head against his now human-like thigh, still pretty damned solid but a little less rocky than his gargoyle legs would have been, and he stroked my hair with careful fingers. *His* worry for me had barely ebbed.

Rollick must have called Torrent to let him know that no further distractions were needed. Several minutes after an engine rumbled by on some distant road, the tentacled man and Lance appeared by our car, presumably having hitched a secretive ride with that other lone traveler.

By that point, the pressure in my chest had eased off enough that it didn't hurt at all when I sat up. My muscles still felt jellified, but I figured that was regular exhaustion more so than any kind of symptom. It was pretty late, and I had pushed myself hard.

Could I expend that kind of magic even once more without pushing my heart past its limits? I really wasn't sure. What I'd experienced tonight had been at least twice as bad as any of the fits I'd experienced before. I was speeding my borrowed organ toward its end faster than any medical guidelines could account for, that was for sure.

"Quinn!" Lance exclaimed, and sprang past Rollick to dive into the back, yanking me into his arms. I nestled in his embrace with the contentment of knowing he'd survived creating his "diversions" without any significant problems.

I glanced past the dragon shifter to Torrent, who didn't look any worse for wear than he normally did either. "The minions didn't give you too much trouble?"

He shook his head, though his expression was even grimmer than usual. "We knew what we were doing. They weren't difficult to dodge when that was always the plan." He glanced to the west. "You weren't able to compel the leviathan?"

"I did," I said, with a twinge of shame as I remembered my failure. "I got him to follow us part of the way to the trap. But it wasn't enough. He managed to throw off my sorcery before we made it there. And he sounded like he was sure that now that he'd figured out how to, I'd never be able to conquer him again."

Crag frowned. "He said other things too. About summoning the shadow realm *here*. That doesn't make any sense."

Rollick sighed. "Actually, I think it does. If I'm right about what he was hinting at, it's the first bit of information we've gotten that ties all his actions together into a coherent picture."

I lifted my head from Lance's shoulder. "What do you mean? You understood what he was talking about?"

"The pieces only clicked together after I'd had a little time to think about it." Rollick folded his arms over his chest, unable to keep up his usual nonchalant expression. In the darkness beyond the interior of the car, his blue eyes glinted sharply. "He said he was going to bring 'the depths' of the shadow realm here—that he'd summon 'them.' He's been expanding that one rift. And he's been carrying on for the past several days as if he doesn't care whether the chaos he's causing here gets noticed."

Torrent sucked in a breath, the chill of his surprise reaching me. "You don't *really* think—how could that even be possible?"

"What?" I demanded, looking from one of them to the other. "The rest of us would like to be completely filled in, please."

Rollick glanced away for a moment before meeting my eyes. "I've told you before about who the Highest are—that they're the most ancient and powerful shadowkind in existence, and to some extent they monitor what happens here in the mortal realm through their underlings to make sure no one gets out of hand. They live in the deepest parts of the shadow realm. The trouble the leviathan has been stirring up is exactly the sort of thing I'd expect to draw their notice."

"But they couldn't stop him before," I said. "He and the behemoth overpowered the warriors they sent."

"They may have sent more since then. Or after that initial defeat, they may be waiting to see how far he'll go and if he'll betray any clear weaknesses before making another attempt. But I believe the fiend wants *them* to come. The Highest themselves, entering the mortal realm."

Lance let out a startled sound. "They don't go anywhere! They stay in their cavern and let beings come to them."

"But maybe the leviathan thought that if he disrupted the mortal world enough and subdued their underlings, they'd have to venture out," Crag put in, his expression still gloomy.

Torrent nodded. "It hasn't worked. I'm not sure how easily the Highest even *could* come through a rift at their size and how strongly they're tied to our home." He glanced at Rollick. "But you figure that's why the leviathan has continued expanding the rift. It's not to allow *more* beings to come through. It's to ensure that it's large enough for the largest of us all to fit."

"Yes. And believe me, I'd love to be proven wrong." Rollick sighed. "But it makes an unnerving amount of sense when you have that piece of the puzzle. Even the sorcerer-killing—why the leviathan has amassed so much of that human-based magic."

A chill of my own washed over me. "He's going to summon these Highest beings right out into the mortal realm? *Can* he do that?" Could he really have gotten that powerful?

"I don't know," Rollick admitted. "I'd imagine it'd take a tremendous amount of sorcery—possibly more than anyone could gather. But he seems to think he has a chance."

I shivered. "And from the way he talked about it, he figures that bringing the Highest here will make the mortal realm belong to shadowkind. Would it really change things that much?"

"It might," Torrent said quietly. "They might bring a lot of the shadow realm's energies through with them, whether they want to or not. And their very existence contains so much power that there's no way of knowing what impact their presence will have on this world. I can't imagine it'll be good."

Lance drew a breath through his teeth with a hiss. "The leviathan thinks it'll change the mortal world to be better for shadowkind. That's what he was telling his minions— that we'd own this world when he's done. I don't *want* to own it. I like it the way it is."

"Me too," I said, my heart thumping faster. "What can we do? I tried using my own sorcery on him. There's not much chance we'd be able to come up with another trick to get him into our trap, is there?"

We all sat in silence for a minute, pondering. "Well," Rollick said slowly, "I believe if he's hoping to summon the Highest, he'd need to put every shred of sorcery he has to that task. So he'll have to let the magic he's cast on all his minions fade rather than continuing to hold them bound to him. And while he's actually doing the summoning, it's unlikely he'd be able to enslave anyone else without risking his whole scheme falling apart."

A flicker of hope lit in my chest. "Then we'd have a chance once he actually makes a move. The shadowkind who've come to help us—they'd be able to intervene without getting swept over to his side. And I wouldn't have to worry about protecting the four of you quite as much, maybe. Then I'd have a little more of my own magic— maybe enough to overwhelm him after all."

Rollick rubbed his chin. "We can't be sure of that. And I doubt that our current motley crew of beings would have much hope of making an impact on him. But we can gather more, call on every shadowkind we can find in the mortal realm who'll have seen what's at stake. The damage he's causing is becoming increasingly obvious." He paused. "We should also make another appeal to the Highest. Let them know our suspicions. If they could send more of their underlings to join us, that'd give us even more of a fighting chance."

Crag bared his teeth with a brutal smile. "If Quinn can't compel him to the trap, we'd get together and drag him there."

Lance chuckled. "Yes. I'd like to see him squirming."

"Or even better," Rollick said, "we could bring the trap to him. If we know where he'll be, there by the rift, maybe my mortal contractors can work out a somewhat portable version. All we need is to fling a lot of iron and silver into him. He'll have to be in physical form to use his sorcery, since it requires a voice. I'll get them at the ready, since we can't put anything in place near the rift ahead of time or he'll notice and destroy it."

A spark of hope lit inside me. "All right. We do have a chance then." Even if it was a small one. I tipped my head toward Rollick. "Will you go appeal to the Highest again?"

He grimaced. "I'm not sure that would be the most ideal option. They might not be very pleased with me if they feel I didn't sufficiently prepare them for what their warriors would face."

"And you're needed here to continue appealing to your own contacts, as much as you can convince them to take part in the battle," Torrent said. He raised his chin with a resigned but determined expression. "I'll go. I'll be the least useful here. Any beings we could reach out to as potential allies who are strong enough to be much help will look down on my weaknesses—they won't see me as someone worth banding together with. The rest of you can focus on building our army and our weapons, and I can go to the Highest. They might not respect me, but they don't much of anyone. I don't need their respect to deliver a warning."

A pang shot through me at the thought of Torrent going off on his own again. "Are you sure?" I asked. "You've taken on so many of the jobs like that." And, selfishly, I didn't like how little I'd gotten to see him in the past several days.

He offered me a small but warm smile. "I've got to take the jobs I'm best equipped for. I'll speak to the Highest as quickly as I can manage and then come straight back."

Rollick clapped his hands together. "It's settled then—the start of a new strategy, anyway. Let's get back to the house, ensure Quinn gets a proper rest, and begin some real recruiting."

CHAPTER SIXTEEN

Crag

As I soared over the depths of the Atlantic, I couldn't help thinking that this was really Torrent's domain. I might have spent many hours coasting on wafts of wind over ocean waves, hunting for marine life and enjoying the scenery along various coastlines, but he was most at home in the actual water. I'd rarely dipped in other than a brief dive to snatch a particularly tasty looking fish.

But he had his own task to see through, and I couldn't say I'd have done a good job of making a verbal appeal to the Highest. I'd probably have ended up offending them with whatever blunt comments slipped out. There was no reason I *couldn't* travel through the darkness beneath the waves nearly as easily as he could. The currents barely tugged at our shadowy bodies.

It turned out, though, that I didn't have to plunge in just yet. In the distance, I spotted a few sleek heads poking from the water. Their short gray fur gleamed wetly under the early morning sun. They looked every bit the seals they were pretending to be, but real seals wouldn't have swum out this far. I could tell from that and my growing sense of their presence as I approached that these were shadowkind. Selkies.

I slowed as I came up on them, starkly aware of how my gargoyle bulk might unnerve them. "Hello," I called out, wishing my voice wasn't quite so rumbly. "I was hoping—"

Two of the four dropped beneath the waves with barely a ripple, vanishing from view. The other two bobbed farther away from me at the surface, their faces transforming into human-like ones: a man and a woman.

The man flashed animalistic teeth. "What do you want?" he hollered.

The two of them were clearly tensed, ready to swim away at any second. I stopped where I was, still twenty feet distant, hovering with swift flaps of my wings. "I'm not with the one who's been stirring up the seas," I said quickly, figuring it was important to make that point first. "I assume you've seen some of his minions riling up the waves near the coasts."

The frowns that crossed both the selkies' faces confirmed it without either of them speaking. "This could be some trick," the woman spat at me.

They seemed awfully hostile despite the leviathan's watery schemes not reaching this far out. How had it even affected them?

"Why would I want to trick you?" I asked, honestly

puzzled. "The leviathan is making the beings under him do what he wants with sorcery, but he's the only shadowkind who's grabbed that kind of power. Many of us are working out a way to stand up to him and end the destruction, but I don't see how I could force you to do anything you don't want to do."

The words might have come out a bit gruffer than I'd have preferred in my confusion, but to my relief, I thought the selkies relaxed a little rather than becoming even more defensive. The man pushed a little higher amid the lapping waves, raising his chin. "What are you doing here then? Why are you talking to us?"

I would have thought that was pretty self-explanatory after what I'd just said, but apparently not. And this was why it was a good thing Torrent was doing the talking with the Highest, not me.

I cleared my throat. "Those of us who want to stop the leviathan are trying to gather as large a group as possible. He's so strong that it'll take a lot of us to overpower him. Beings comfortable at sea like yourselves would be particularly useful to the cause, since you can work against him in his natural habitat."

The woman let out a disgruntled-sounding huff. "Why should we? We don't even know you or this group you're gathering. You could be just as bad as him."

I could picture Quinn rolling her eyes at the statement. I restrained myself to a brief grimace. "I think that would be awfully difficult, considering that he's made himself the biggest menace I've ever seen in the centuries I've been in existence. You *have* seen what he's forced his slaves to do, haven't you? The way they're churning up the ocean along the coast, the waves they're hurling at the mortal cities. It's even worse on the Pacific side. And what he plans to do next…"

I trailed off, abruptly uncertain of whether I should mention what Rollick had deduced about the leviathan's ultimate plans. I didn't know how much I could trust *these* beings. What if they ended up reporting back to the villain somehow? It was better if he didn't know we'd figured out his end game.

The woman's eyes narrowed. "What's that?"

"Nothing that would be good for any of us who enjoy the mortal realm," I settled on as my answer. "He wants to turn this place as dark and dreary as our original home. I don't want that, and I doubt you do either. But if not enough of us are willing to take a stand, that's what we'll get."

The two selkies glanced at each other. The man's expression tightened. He looked at me with narrowed eyes. "We're not built to fight like you are. I doubt there's much we can do. One of our own was already badly injured in the recent storms."

My heart sank. So *that* was why they'd reacted so fiercely. "I'm sorry to hear that. If there's anything I can do…"

Both of them gave me a skeptical look. Then the woman said brusquely, "There's a particular kind of seaweed that's helpful for sealing our sort of wounds—for holding in the essence. I don't suppose you know anything about it?"

Her statement tugged out a memory from ages ago, when I'd chatted with an elderly merman while we shared the meat of a shark that I'd caught while it was in the middle of attacking him. He'd gathered some ocean plant to wrap around the wound on his arm.

"Reddish with broad leaves?" I asked, bringing up the faded image in my mind.

They couldn't keep their surprise from their faces. The man nodded. "That's the one. It's usually closer to the shore, but with all the churning of the waters, we haven't been able to get close. We've been searching for strands that were torn up and drifted farther out, but there hasn't been much. If you want us to help you, maybe you should help us first."

His caustic tone suggested that he expected me to disagree, but my spirits lifted at the opportunity to take concrete action. "I'll see what I can do. Where will you be if I find some?"

The woman waved toward the east. "There's a small island several miles that way. We're using it as a temporary camp."

Without another word, they both slipped under the water, transforming into their seal bodies as they did. I had the sense of a dismissal—that they assumed this was the last time we'd ever speak.

My jaw clenched. I could battle storms just as well as I could fight any creature.

I flew in the opposite direction, keeping low to the water, scanning as far into the depths as I could for a telltale hint of red. As I got closer to the coast, still well out of view of any mortals who might have dared to brave the storm on land, the waves grew choppier, forcing me to lift higher overhead. Rain first pattered against my hardened skin and then pelted me.

I swerved to the side and followed the angle of the shoreline, sweeping a little farther east again to avoid the worst of the storm. The leviathan must have enslaved a lot of seafaring beings to his cause for them to be stirring up this much turmoil on the opposite side of the country for him. My teeth gritted with frustration.

Just as I started to think I'd have to give up the search, that I'd wasted too much time on it already, my gaze snagged on a flash of a ruddy leaf tossed by one of the waves. I dove without hesitation, my hands shooting out to snatch at my target.

It was a lot more than just one leaf. A huge clump of the weed had been uprooted from its coastal grounds and floated out here. I bundled enough in my arms to have wrapped around an entire human body and, with a small smile of triumph I couldn't suppress, soared out of the storm toward the selkie's island.

Trickles of salty water streamed down from the mass of seaweed to patter against the ocean, and its pungent herbal scent filled my nose, but it wasn't difficult to carry. I had lots of practice flying around with Quinn in my arms by now, and I had to worry a lot less about the seaweed's well-being.

It was a matter of minutes before the little island came into view up ahead. The place was barely more than a cluster of boulders poking out of the water with some sparse bushes sprouting from the bits of dirt that'd managed to catch in the cervices between the rocks.

Several seals were gathered on the stones, most of them

forming an attentive circle around one of their number, who was lying limply in the most sheltered area of the island. As I drew closer, I made out trickles of essence gusting from the prone body. However that one had been caught up in the storm's violence, the wounds hadn't fully healed yet. No wonder the others were worried.

One of the seals noticed me and barked an alarm. All the others' heads swiveled my way. I couldn't easily wave while holding the seaweed, but two shifted into human forms that I recognized. They leaned toward the others, their mouths moving hastily with words I couldn't make out.

As I swooped down toward them, a few scooted to the edges of the island, their teeth bared. But a couple of the seals and the two I'd spoken to before stayed with their injured companion, braced protectively around the slumped body.

I landed on a bare rock. "This is the weed you wanted, isn't it?"

The woman took in my cargo, and her eyes widened. "You found so much!" Her head whipped toward her partner. "We must wrap her up quickly. She's lost so much essence already."

They both darted forward, their stances still wary. I shoved the clump toward them so they didn't have to get too close to me. Then I watched from my rocky perch, feeling more fully gargoyle-like than I had in decades, as they bandaged up the injured seal. I'd have offered to help, but my thick fingers wouldn't be able to handle her wounds with as much care as their slimmer ones.

They layered the slick leaves over the wounds, and the

trickling essence faded away. The unconscious seal let out a shuddery breath. The woman who'd bandaged her sat back on her heels and swiped her hand across her forehead, looking weary but relieved. I understood the kind of anguish she was going through better than I would have even a month ago.

"She means a lot to you," I observed in as subdued a tone as I could manage.

Her gaze flicked to me. "All of my pod-mates do. We stick together—we look out for one another, both here and in the shadows."

Her voice came out taut, as if she thought I'd been criticizing her. I did my best to form a sympathetic smile. "I'm glad I was able to help stabilize her then. It looks as if the seaweed helped. I hope she has an easy recovery from now on."

"We'll see," the man said, frowning. "She hasn't woken since she took those blows in the storm. There was so much wreckage floating in the waves."

I glanced around. "I passed a rift a few leagues from here. If you wanted to bring her back to the shadow realm so she might recover faster, I'd be happy to carry her—and I could probably manage one or two others—to get her there right away."

The woman blinked at me. "Why would you offer that?"

I knit my brow. "For the same reason I found the seaweed. I'd rather she isn't suffering if she doesn't need to be. And the same for all of you, worrying about her. It's... it's good to find some of our kind looking out for each other, supporting each other, after everything I've seen recently."

I meant the statement totally honestly, without any ulterior motives. It seemed unlikely that they'd volunteer to dive back into any kind of battle regardless of what I did now. But maybe because of my honesty, something softened in the woman's face.

"Yes," she said. "It is good. And maybe we shouldn't only think of our pod. Maybe *for* our pod, we should do more. How is it you think we can help stop the one causing these storms?"

A jolt of startled joy shot through me. I paused, grappling for the right words to show how much I appreciated her response, and it occurred to me that it hadn't been my strength that'd convinced her. It hadn't been my ability to take the storm either.

It'd been the kindness I'd offered, even though kindness wasn't a trait I'd ever thought of as my own.

Possibly I was more than just a monster after all.

CHAPTER SEVENTEEN

Quinn

Of all the places to ride out the intensifying symptoms of a failing heart, Rollick's badlands house was probably one of the best. I had innumerable softly cushioned surfaces to stretch out on when my chest clenched up. There was a salt-water pool to take a refreshing dip in while I shook off the effects of the latest attack. And all the food and drinks I could possibly want were on hand, regularly replenished by Crag and fried or sliced up by Lance as need be.

Most other places I could have ended up would definitely have been *worse*. But I couldn't say I was enjoying my stay all that much regardless.

None of the spasms in my chest had hit me as hard as the pain right after I'd compelled the leviathan, but they were coming frequently enough that my men had insisted I stay here while they did their recruiting—and from a practical standpoint, I couldn't really argue. It wasn't as if the average shadowkind being was going to respond better to overtures from a human sorcerer than from one of their own kind anyway.

So I was doing my best to recover more fully and to not go stir-crazy from boredom. When I felt steady enough, I went out into the yard and chatted with the newer beings who'd come to join us, getting a feel for their strength and skills. When I didn't, I paged through my sketchpad, looking at the designs I'd set on paper with pencil and fighting the constricting of my throat.

I wasn't going to see any of those plans to fruition. My chances of seeing my career through to any kind of real accomplishment had always been uncertain, and now it was pretty much impossible. I suspected I'd be lucky to have as much as another month or two before my borrowed heart crapped out on me completely, and that was if I didn't put any more significant strain on it. I wasn't on any waiting lists; my medical team didn't even know I might need a replacement. Even if I had been, the chances of getting the right match at the right time were always iffy.

That was the way it was. I'd resigned myself to my probable limited lifespan before, and I could deal with it now—as long as I knew I'd stopped the threat to everyone else's lives before I went.

Today, there hadn't been a whole lot that I could accomplish toward that goal. I'd talked with several new shadowkind arrivals in the morning, and no other beings had turned up since then. Walking around had left me feeling faint enough that eating a proper lunch had been a bit of a struggle.

I'd dug my trusty multi-tool out of my bag in the hopes it might give me a sense of purpose, but as far as I could tell, Rollick kept his property in such good repair that there was nothing for me to fix even a little. And anyway, when I thought about it, making some tiny tweak to a fixture or piece of furniture seemed so pointless now compared to the vast problems looming over me.

Finally, I went out onto the inner patio around the pool in the hopes that soaking up some sun—after a careful layer of sunscreen, as if I really needed to worry about minor precautions like that at this point—would rejuvenate me, and ended up drifting off in a brief nap.

I woke up feeling annoyed with myself for dozing when there was so much to do, even if *I* couldn't really do any of it at the moment, and headed inside to see if there'd been any news I'd missed. I was just coming through the patio door when a pressure like a massive hand digging its fingers into my ribs squeezed around my chest.

My breath hitched. I stumbled and caught my balance on the back of one of the living room chairs. A chill washed through me from head to toe.

"Quinn!" Crag appeared by my side out of the shadows, sliding his arm around my shoulders.

I opened my mouth to tell him I'd be okay, but all that came out was a choked gasp. Making a rough sound of dismay, the gargoyle swept me up in his arms and carried me into my bedroom.

Inside, he set me gently on the bedcovers and then seemed at a loss for what else to do. I gritted my teeth against the pain that was gripping me and jerked my hand toward him in a vague beckoning gesture.

Crag eased onto the bed next to me as gingerly as a man that large could manage. He tucked me against his massive form, brushing his fingers over my hair and humming in what I could tell he intended to be a soothing sound. "I've got you, Softness. You'll get through this. I know how strong you are, even if you shouldn't have to be strong enough to endure this pain."

I managed a ragged chuckle and nestled myself closer against him. The warmth of his body radiating over me and the tenderness of his attentions melted the worst of my discomfort. I breathed in and out as steadily as I could, and gradually the tightness released me. My heart thudded on, if with a beat that was a little erratic.

"Thank you," I said. "I'm all right now. No big deal."

Crag grunted. "Of course it's a big deal. I don't like to see you hurting." He pulled away from me just as tentatively as he'd gathered me against him, and I felt his nervousness about hurting me *himself* through the connection between us. "Is there anything else you need? Would you like help getting back to the living room—or wherever you want to go now?"

I rested my hand against his chest, where the planes of muscle were covered in human-like skin that now felt not quite as familiar as his rocky gargoyle form. Now that my body was no longer fighting itself, a different sort of heat was tickling through my veins.

Lance had needed a particular kind of assurance that my health problems hadn't made me totally fragile. And Crag had always been the most worried about how his monstrousness might damage me.

And I had even less time than I'd had before to make the most of the life I'd gotten. The love I'd discovered in that life.

"I think I'd like to stay right here," I said, looking up at him through my eyelashes. "As long as you're here too."

Desire flared in the gargoyle's eyes even as I caught another tremor of uncertainty from him. "Are you sure that's a good—" he started to ask in a tone that showed his reluctance at balking, and I answered him the fastest and most effective way I could: by slipping my hand around his head and pulling him into a kiss.

As our mouths melded together with the delicious friction of Crag's rocky lower lip against mine, he let out a groan that reverberated through his chest. More desire licked at me like flames through our emotional connection. He sank down again to slide closer to me, but the hand he rested on my waist still felt too careful.

I ran my fingers over the sheen of black hair on his scalp, curling them to tease my fingernails over the bronze skin in an imitation of claws. An eager quiver passed through Crag, and he kissed me harder. The bulge behind the fabric of his shorts was already stiffening.

A rush of wildness caught me up. I wanted him. I wanted every part of him. He needed to know that.

I tore my mouth from his and met his eyes, my cheeks flushed from the passion we'd already kindled between us. "When you've been with other shadowkind, it wasn't just with your gargoyle size. You brought the gargoyle fierceness too."

A whole lot of other parts of Crag stiffened at those words. He frowned. "They could handle it. They—"

"They didn't have delicate human bodies, I know." I cupped his cheek. "But I'm not that delicate either. I've taken Lance's claws and Torrent's tentacles. I don't want to be just pampered, as nice as that can be. I want to be ravished too."

Crag's tongue flicked over his lips in a way that sent sparks right down the center of me to my cunt. "I don't need to let out that side. You shouldn't have to witness any more of my brutality than you've been forced to before."

I stroked my thumb over his prominent cheekbone. "I love your tender side *and* your brutal side, Crag. I appreciate your hardness as much as you enjoy my softness. And what I'd really like right now is for you to rip the clothes right off me and take me like you can't stand to wait another second without us fucking."

A guttural sound emanated from Crag's throat. His eyes flared with a hotter light as his body expanded into his full gargoyle form: skin turning rock hard, horns jutting above the sharper angles of his face, wings extending from his back.

With a growl, he flipped me onto my back and loomed over me. The claws that had sprouted from his fingers were much shorter than Lance's but no less deadly. He raked them down the front of me with a swipe of his hand, shredding open my tee and shirts without doing more than grazing the skin.

That prickling, not quite painful touch woke up even more desires in me. I trembled with giddiness, a gasp tumbling from my lips. As Crag shoved the tatters of my clothes aside, I raised my arms to pull him closer, rising up to seek out his mouth. He needed to see just how into this I was now that he'd accepted my demand.

He let his lips crash into mine with a force that left my head spinning with a heady pleasure that was echoed through our connection. His forceful hands swept aside the last fragments of my panties and the cups of my bisected bra. He gripped one breast, massaging it firmly and pinching the nipple between his thumb and forefinger with a jolt of bliss. I whimpered eagerly against his mouth.

Crag raised his hand to scrape the tips of his claws over my breast the way he'd have seen Lance do a dozen times. I pressed my lips against his while holding the rest of me still so that he didn't sever anything important with his thrillingly dangerous touch. Then he reached farther down, trailing his claws over my sternum and belly until he reached the mound between my legs.

When he cupped my pussy, I arched to meet him, my lips parting to let him devour me even more fully at the same time. With a heated rumble, Crag swept his long gargoyle tongue into my mouth and flicked his claws up over my slit to my clit. I moaned, shuddering against him with nothing but enthusiasm for all he was offering.

His mouth wrenched from mine as he teased his fingers over my sex at an aggressive pace. My head tipped back into the pillow, my breath breaking into pants. Crag let out another growl as he gazed down at me.

"I want to make you mine in every possible way. I want to plunge into you so hard it knocks every other thought from your mind. I want to feel you shaking with delight."

An impatient noise formed between my ragged breaths. "Then what's taking you so long?"

He snarled and heaved my hips up to meet him with one hand. I knew how large he was, but I was used to him now—and the savagery of his foreplay had left me drenched and ready. I hefted my ass a little higher to show just how on board I was, and the next thing I knew he was thrusting his entire thick shaft into my pussy.

The giddily searing friction had me gasping for more. I shook in his arms like he'd asked for, clutching him and pressing closer. With a flurry of noises that were half growl, half groan, Crag pounded into me. I bucked to meet every thrust with all the hunger scorching through my veins.

"So soft," he muttered, "but so strong. I love you, Quinn. Always. Always."

"Always," I gasped in agreement, and lost my voice completely with the next plunge of his cock. I was seeing stars, pleasure blazing through me like a flashfire, burning away everything but this moment. Me and one of the monstrous men I loved so much.

His claws dug into my thigh with a flash of pain that I knew meant I'd need a quick swipe of Lance's tongue later, but in the moment it brought nothing but a deeper shock of bliss. I cried out, a tremor wracking my body as the building ecstasy exploded in a final, epic firework. But even in the haze of my pleasure, I kept rocking my hips to meet Crag, wanting more, wanting him to come with me.

"Want to feel you come," I muttered, and Crag slammed into me with a roar that shook the walls. His cum flooded me, perfectly hot and thick, his cock pulsing with the effort he'd expended.

He eased me down on the bed and held himself over me on his hands and knees, his chest heaving, his fiery gaze seeking out mine. I beamed up at him, a little delirious in the afterglow, and only then did he relax. A smile crossed his lips that was broader and brighter than anything I'd seen from the usually solemn gargoyle before.

"I satisfied you well," he said with a hint of pride in both his voice and the emotions traveling between us.

I couldn't restrain a giggle. "Very well. But then, you always do. My stony gargoyle."

He leaned in to nuzzle the side of my face with a gentleness that was the total opposite of the beast he'd brought out on my request. "My soft-but-strong mortal. The leviathan is a fool if he thinks he can beat you."

My smile faltered just slightly. I sure hoped my lover was right about that.

CHAPTER EIGHTEEN

Quinn

"So your idea is that you could distract him?" I said to the pair of impish demons who'd just carried out a demonstration in how they could belch puffs of smoke. "Obscure his vision with the clouds so he can't tell what else we're doing?"

One of them nodded eagerly. The other emitted another burp, which honestly barely contained enough smoke to obscure *my* sight, let alone a giant sea serpent's. But I wasn't going to say that to their faces when they were trying so hard to be helpful.

Instead, I jotted it down on the notepad where I'd been keeping track of our allies and their abilities and shot them a grateful smile. "Thank you. I'm sure that'll come in handy when we confront the leviathan."

From an indistinct noise behind me, I thought Lance

might have muffled a skeptical snort. He came up behind me and kissed the back of my head. "I'll find more useful beings to bring back," he murmured. "If I keep searching, there've got to be more who won't turn their backs on the rest of us."

"You've been doing your best," I reassured him, knowing it was true. He, Crag, and Rollick had only been back at the desert house for an hour or two at a time in between ushering new recruits here. For the first little while, they'd insisted that one of them had to be present at all times to watch over me, but now that we had enough loyal beings prowling around the house that they really could be considered an army, I'd persuaded them that all of them working toward stopping the leviathan was better for my well-being than acting as additional bodyguards.

That didn't mean I didn't miss them while they were gone, though.

I gazed out over the desolate landscape where I knew hundreds more shadowkind lurked in the patches of gloom at the bases of the straggly vegetation, around stones and boulders, and everywhere dips and cracks had formed in the dry earth. They were keeping out of sight when they weren't talking to me, but enough of them surrounded me that my sorcerer energy vibrated in my chest with the sense of their presence.

Unfortunately, the majority of them were lesser creatures or not particularly powerful higher beings who couldn't contribute much more to a battle than nipping at the leviathan's heels... or blowing puffs of smoke at him.

A burly, man-shaped being with small tusks jutting from beneath his square jaw appeared in front of me. He flexed his bulky arms and swung his fists a few times through the air. "Maybe I can help pummel him unconscious. I might not be able to do it alone, but if enough of us go at him..."

"We'd have to make sure he falls where the new moving trap can hit him," Lance pointed out. "Hard to move him anywhere once he's out."

I sucked my lower lip under my teeth. "That or just weaken him rather than knocking him out completely. Getting him out of sorts, dizzy and disoriented, would make it harder for him to fight back. And maybe easier for me to use my sorcery on him if I need to." I tipped my head to the man, who I thought Rollick had told me was a troll when he'd escorted him in earlier. "How hard can you hit?"

He grinned. "When the behemoth had my mind, they only saw half of what I was capable of. I was fighting them the whole time inside, dragging against their commands. Watch this."

He marched over to a narrow boulder that stood beyond the edge of the yard's protections, cracked his knuckles, and slammed his fist into the rock. A crack opened up from the top about halfway down the middle of it.

Lance let out an approving whistle. "A leviathan skull is probably stronger than that," he couldn't help saying, though. "Also, it'll be moving, not standing still for you to punch."

I swatted him. "It's a start. Don't become a pessimist now." But something the troll had said was niggling at me. I studied him as he walked back over to us. "You said that you didn't use as much strength when the behemoth ordered you to do things. He couldn't make you put in your full effort?"

The troll grunted. "It *felt* like a full effort by the time it happened. Just pushing back against the influence meant I used up some of my strength on that. Like punching through water rather than air—the drag holds it back."

I wasn't sure I totally followed his explanation, but it sparked a flicker of excitement in me. "Do you think... if you were ordered to do something you *wanted* to do... that the magic might add more to your effort instead of taking away from it? If it was propelling you forward instead of you fighting against it?"

The troll's eyebrows rose. "I don't know. I didn't like anything he wanted me to do... mostly because *he* wanted me to do it and didn't care how I felt about it." He paused, seeming momentarily wary of me. "I guess we could try and see what happens."

I swallowed thickly, knowing what an expression of trust it was that he'd even offered. "Are you sure? I know that having any kind of sorcery worked on you would probably bring up bad associations."

He shrugged, lifting his chin as if in defiance of his own worries. "We've got to find out what's possible. I'd rather have you in my head than the beast that's tearing up the coastlines."

I couldn't argue with his logic, and I didn't want to. Jittery anticipation was already tickling through my nerves —jittery because I was afraid I might be wrong and my hopes would be dashed all over again. But he had a point. We needed to know if my suggested strategy would work, and as soon as possible.

We had no idea how soon the leviathan might be able to carry out the final stages of his plan and actually drag the Highest beings through the rift he was preparing.

"All right." I stood up. "I'm not going to exert full control on you or anything like that. I'll just command you to punch that boulder again, and as soon as you have, the magic should wear off. Nothing permanent."

The troll nodded, his eyes gleaming. He looked like he was starting to get excited about the possibilities too. Lance hummed thoughtfully, watching us both with a growing smile. I had the impression that an awful lot of the eyes in the shadows were fixed on the unfolding scenario.

I dragged in a breath and drew on the magic twined through my heart. It took no effort at all to throw just a flash of it at the being in front of me. *Punch that boulder as hard as you can*, I thought as the odd syllables spilled from my lips.

The troll's muscles twitched, and for an instant I was scared he was going to react to the sorcery with panic or anger after all. Then his grin came back. He strode across the dusty earth without hesitation, heaved back his arm, and flung his fist at the boulder like he had before.

Except it wasn't exactly like before. This time his knuckles slammed into the stone surface with so much force the rock split right apart. It tumbled over in jagged chunks, nothing left but a stump no higher than the troll's knees.

He let out a triumphant laugh and spun to face me. "I could feel it! The magic, flowing through me, and I moved with it instead of straining against it. And it was like it was *my* magic, making me more powerful. How else can you use that power?"

Hope was expanding through my chest, light and fluttery. "I don't know," I admitted. "But it seems like it should help with just about anything we want to do."

The impish demons might be able to produce more smoke. Lance might be able to lunge faster, Torrent wrench harder with his tentacles. The magic that most sorcerers used to constrain the shadowkind might also be capable of boosting their supernatural abilities, transforming them into even stronger versions of themselves. The irony of it provoked a giddy chuckle of my own.

I might have continued the experiment, called for more volunteers to see what other ways we could make this new discovery work for us, when a few beings wavered into sight about a half a mile from the house, one of them letting out a shout of warning.

"Hey! We've got a sneaky one here. What should we do with him?"

Three of the figures I recognized as beings who'd volunteered for the security patrols: a svelte guy I believed was some kind of large cat shifter, a skinny harpy woman with slate-gray feathered wings and taloned feet, and the beefiest member of the selkie clan Crag had sent our way. It was the selkie who'd hollered. I didn't understand what he was hollering about until he tugged a much smaller figure in his grasp into better view.

The petite man whose neck he was clutching didn't stand much higher than the selkie's waist. But it was the reddish-gold curls and his forest-green suit that made him instantly identifiable.

I stiffened where I stood at the same moment as Lance hissed through his teeth. "The leprechaun," he snarled.

The small, spritely man who went by the name Goldie had been a friend of Torrent's. *Had*, because not long after I'd first met him, he'd sold us out to the villainous duo's minions. I'd never expected to see him again, and I couldn't say I particularly wanted to.

But he must have come out here looking for us for a reason.

"Are you sure he's alone?" I called across the scrubby field. "And no weapons or anything dangerous on him?"

"Just him," the harpy confirmed. "I flew around to scan the area and make sure of it before we brought him over. He says he has an important message, but he wouldn't give it to anyone except you or the kraken and his friends."

I gritted my teeth but waved them over. "Keep him at a distance, but I'll talk to him. I'd rather not have to scream the whole conversation. All three of you, stay on guard around him."

Lance shifted into dragon form to encircle me with his scaled body like a living shield. I rested my hand on his shoulder, feeling the distrust and protectiveness radiating off him as our patrollers led their prisoner closer.

"He's been in with the leviathan and his lackeys," I said in an attempt at reassuring him. "He might know something useful. He did *use* to be Torrent's friend."

Lance's growl told me exactly how little that fact warmed him to the new arrival. I didn't disagree with him. But I could admit that Goldie hadn't seemed totally *happy* about the whole betrayal business. He'd been risking us killing him where he stood by coming out here. His reasons had to be important. We'd just be careful about the conversation.

I held up my hand when the group was about twenty feet away. Crossing my arms over my chest, I stared Goldie down. His face looked ruddier than I remembered under that heap of curls, and now that he was closer, I could see that his suit had gotten scuffed and torn. The best smile he managed was tight and pained-looking.

"Thank you for giving me a chance to speak," he said, looking right back at me without flinching. "It's been a long time, with a lot happening in between, and I know we left things on a very bad note the last time you saw me."

"The last time I saw you, you were arranging for me to be kidnapped and eaten," I replied. "I think 'a very bad note' might be understating the situation a little."

His smile pulled into a grimace. "Yes. Well. I'm free of those degenerates now. I wish they'd never gotten a hold on me. I don't like what I've seen of them since at all. You seem to be doing *something* to make their lives harder, so I figured if there was anyone to tell what I know, it'd be you."

"And what do you know?"

Goldie rubbed his mouth, wincing when the selkie tightened his grip on his neck. "The big serpent doesn't think he's got enough power to pull off his plan yet," he said with a cough. "He's figured out that there's a bunch of top sorcerers living in Norway. He might be headed out there already to look for them. I don't want to think about how it'll tip the scales if they're really out there and he finds them."

The blood turned cold in my veins. *I* knew for sure there

was an enclave of powerful sorcerers in Norway—and that they wouldn't have a hope in hell of defending themselves against a creature as ancient as the leviathan. It was possible he wouldn't find them, but Rollick had managed to locate their home with very little information to go by, so I didn't think we could count on the monster failing.

I'd hated what I'd seen there. Those sorcerers were monsters too. But having the leviathan chow down on them and absorb their magic was just about the most horrible outcome I could imagine.

He might not be quite strong enough to summon the Highest yet, but after that grand feast?

I tensed against the nausea rising through my abdomen. "Why should we believe you?" I asked, and then remembered I didn't even need to get into those kinds of questions. I could confirm the truth of his statement in a matter of seconds.

Squaring my shoulders, I gathered my own magic and opened my mouth. *Tell me why you're really here.*

My voice pealed across the terrain in those strange sounds of the sorcerous language. The energy smacked into Goldie's head without any resistance—he wasn't under the leviathan's control.

The leprechaun shivered, and his mouth popped open. "I'm afraid of what'll happen to this world if the leviathan gets what he wants. I was hoping the warning might help you stop him. And that maybe I'll be a little less likely to get killed if I'm on your side instead of his."

The selfish admission at the end fit what I knew of his character. And I didn't think he could have lied while my magic was compelling him. But that didn't mean what he believed he knew was the truth.

"How did you find this out?" I asked him in my regular voice.

Goldie spread his hands. "After our last encounter, those brutes hauled me off to the leviathan, but I managed to keep a very low profile among his minions. And he didn't have much use for me. He forgot I was there, and his magic wore off eventually. He also didn't notice me around when one of his other slaves gave the report about the Norway sorcerers. I saw how interested he was. It's not like it's a secret what he's done with other sorcerers and why."

No, I supposed it wasn't. That didn't sound like a staged conversation. I bit my lip.

Even if it wasn't guaranteed to be true, I needed to warn the enclave. If they got out of there in time, holed up in some other country where the leviathan didn't know to look for them, maybe he'd never find them.

But how in the world was I going to send that warning —across the ocean, to people who'd enslave or slaughter any shadowkind that crossed their paths?

CHAPTER NINETEEN

Torrent

Lingering in one place in the shadow realm had a similar effect to soaking in the depths of the ocean, getting lulled by the rhythms of the currents. It was a lot less enjoyable without the more varied textures of the water and the endless tastes and sights that would pass by, but the sensation of time passing without my being able to track it was familiar.

Had it been hours since one of the beings standing sentinel at the entrance to the Highest's vast hollow had told me to wait there and that they would speak to me when they were ready? Days? I hoped by all the water in the oceans that it hadn't been weeks.

My only small comfort was that the leviathan clearly hadn't gone through with his final plans yet if the Highest were still there in their home, immense presences that I could sense with an uneasy quiver through my essence even from a distance.

I'd told the lackey that this was an urgent problem that directly affected the Highest. Had she not bothered to pass on that part of the message? Did they not care? I adjusted my position in the shadowy currents restlessly, my tentacles twisting and twining.

I'd never spoken to the beings that were so old they were practically part of the realm itself before. I had no idea how they typically handled appeals from unexpected visitors. Rollick hadn't suggested it was likely to take very long, though.

A more prickly thought rose up in the back of my mind that maybe it *hadn't* taken them anywhere near this long with him. The lackey would have been able to evaluate me and report what kind of being had come calling. I was decently established, but not as ancient as the demon—and he had all his limbs in full working order. My physical disabilities had certainly worked against me before.

It wasn't difficult to imagine that the most potent beings in existence might assume a being like me couldn't possibly have anything all that important to say.

I drifted a little to the left and then to the right, pushing those self-recriminating thoughts away. I was what I was. I'd probably still been the best choice to make this trip out of the four of us. The realms only knew what Lance would have gotten up to if we'd sent him here and he'd been left to contend with this seemingly endless boredom. Or how gruff the gargoyle would have become by the time the Highest welcomed him in.

I'd be ready, whenever they got around to giving me the

time of day. Or night, as the case might be. Neither really existed in this world.

How could that monstrous serpent really think it'd be better if the mortal realm was *more* like this one? All his years wandering the seas must have pickled his brain.

More time passed without any ability to measure it. Then a different being, one I hadn't noticed before, glided over to me. He bobbed his head with its elephantine ears to me and gestured for me to follow him without saying so much as a word.

I moved through the gloom after him. My awareness of the gargantuan beings ahead of me expanded as I approached the deeper, thicker depths of their shadowy home. I couldn't tell how many of them there were, other than there were definitely at least a few. I got the impression that their attention had fixed on me, so weighty it dragged me down like an undertow.

"What business have you come here with, kraken?" one of the beings demanded in a voice that echoed right through my bones. I had to tense my limbs to avoid wincing. "What is so important?"

So they had heard that I'd insisted I needed to see them quickly. Apparently they hadn't believed my claim.

I drew myself up into as authoritative but respectful a pose as I could manage. "Thank you for seeing me. I've come because of incredibly severe troubles in the mortal realm. As you may already be aware, a leviathan has been openly slaughtering mortals, taking in human sorcery and using it to enslave his fellow beings, and—"

A different, equally impactful voice let out a huff. "We are aware. Our loyal servants are monitoring the situation."

Then why the fuck hadn't they done more about it already? I bit back the bitter question and forced a brisk nod. "Good. But what you might not know, because a few of us only found out about it right before I came here, and only because we've managed to observe a lot of evidence and talk to the leviathan himself briefly—"

"Get on with it," another Highest said with a warbling growl that made every nerve in my body vibrate like a struck funny bone. My most recent deformity, the mangled end of my tentacle that Lance's teeth and breath had damaged beyond repair, started to throb.

It took all my effort to hold an ingratiating if thin smile on my face. "His ultimate plan seems to be that he'll compel *you* into the mortal realm using the sorcery he's stolen. He believes he has or can accumulate enough to force you through a rift against your will—and that your arrival in that realm will permanently alter it to be more to his liking. There's no telling how much destruction he might cause if he manages it."

One of the Highest let out a sound that might have been a rumbly laugh. Another sneered in a harsh voice, "You think another being could command *us*? That is what you've come here to jabber about?"

I swallowed, willing my voice to stay steady in the face of their disdain. "I have no idea if he's really capable of it. But I thought—we all thought—that you should be warned so you're prepared in case he attempts it. And maybe you'd want to take some action against him, to ensure that there's no chance you would ever come under threat."

The next sound that emanated from the gathered

Highest was more of a hiss, with a definite angry edge to it. "It sounds as if *you're* threatening us. Trying to force us to deal with this being the way you'd prefer by telling us how we'll be harmed if we don't."

Shock hit me in a chilly smack. "What? No. Of course not. I'm not making any demands. I'm just passing on the information to—"

"Information about how frightened we should be," another bellowed. "We will not stand for this kind of insult. You bring these threats to our faces and try to bend us to your will yourself, and you think we won't realize?"

"That's not at all what I intended," I said in what was more of a babble now. My body instinctively pulled backward, away from them. "I promise you I—"

"And now he tries to run. Don't let him! Show him what happens to anyone foolish enough to attack we who own the shadow realm."

"No!" The protest burst from my mouth unbidden. I whirled around, panic overcoming rational thought, my mind whirling with no idea whether I'd be better off running or attempting to prove my peaceful intentions by holding my ground.

I didn't get a chance to decide. Bodies hurtled at me from multiple directions. Claws raked into me—horns gouged me—hooves battered me.

In our shadow forms, the pain didn't radiate through solid nerves the way it would have in the mortal realm. But their presences tore at mine all the same. Agony spread all through my essence as the Highest's guards shifted in turn without letting up their assault. Their ephemeral forms had enough friction against mine to choke and smack and pierce. My being frayed, life gushing out of me in billows in all directions.

Shadowkind couldn't die in the shadow realm, but we could come awfully close.

I hurled myself away from the onslaught with every fragment of will I had left in me. Again and again, nothing in my mind but the searing pain and the need to get away. Onward, onward, dragging myself inch by broken inch...

I wasn't even sure when the beating ended. By the time I realized no new blows were reaching me, my awareness of myself was so scattered and wrenching that they might as well have still been tearing me apart. With a guttural groan I couldn't hold in, I forced myself to crawl farther.

Just a little more. Just a little more. In case they decided they hadn't done enough. Get away. Get away.

Then I couldn't move any farther. The agony simply short-circuited my brain. I curled in on myself, pulling together all of my essence that I could still hold on to, and held there as the particles of my being started to ever-so-slowly knit themselves back together.

More aches jabbed and sizzled through me. I had the sense of gritting teeth I didn't currently have. But even through the pain, I willed myself to come back together, to heal, as quickly as I could, even if the speed amped up my anguish.

I had to get back to the others. I had to let them know that the Highest didn't believe us—that they'd scoffed at the idea of the leviathan as a threat—that they knew what he was doing and were looking the other way in their pompous over-confidence.

I had to get back to Quinn. I didn't even know how she

was doing right now, whether her heart was failing faster, whether the leviathan had managed to launch another attack against her.

If I couldn't make it back in time to stand by her side at least a little longer, to hear her bright voice and revel in her touch, to bask in her determination and affection, I'd rip *myself* apart. There was no pain I could imagine that would be worse than that.

The truth hit me then like a glowing beacon shining fiercely through a storm: I loved her. I did, with every shred of my being. The fact of it felt so true and obvious that I could have smacked myself for not acknowledging it sooner, for shying away from the words as if they were somehow dangerous rather than a statement of devotion. As if she'd be disappointed in me if I somehow didn't make good enough on them.

She wouldn't, and that was part of the reason I loved her. Quinn had embraced all of me—man, kraken, injuries, past, and all. The statement wouldn't be a promise or a guarantee. It'd only be three words that she deserved to hear back after how freely she'd offered them to me and how deeply I felt them resonating through me now.

I had to get back to her and let her hear them. Let her understand that *I* understood just how much she meant to me. I wouldn't let those hulking assholes with their even more inflated egos stop me from reaching her in time.

With that resolve coiling around me, I braced myself and pulled my essence together even faster than before, ignoring the torment of the sensation.

CHAPTER TWENTY

Quinn

I gnawed on the lid of my pen and stared down at the piece of paper I'd only managed to add a couple of sentences to in the past hour. Writing my message to the enclave by hand had seemed like the best option. A printed note would come across as much more detached. But deciding on the actual words had been even more of a struggle than I'd anticipated.

I wanted to warn them. I didn't want the leviathan to eat them for dinner. That said, there were a pretty large number of other uncomfortable fates I couldn't say I'd have minded them meeting. What I'd seen during my time there had shown me those humans were more monstrous than most of the beings they called monsters. I was more concerned about stopping the leviathan from getting a power boost than saving the enclave from destruction.

It was kind of hard to figure out how to convey my concern in a way that'd sound like I meant it—and not grudgingly.

Rollick appeared at my bedroom doorway with a glass of lemonade in hand. He set it on the night table next to me and glanced down at the paper I had braced on the cover of my sketchpad on my knee. "Not going so well?"

I made a face. "I don't think 'Please don't let a huge sea serpent eat you, but if you wouldn't mind falling off a cliff during your escape, I'd appreciate it' is going to go over the way we'd want."

The demon chuckled. "That's a sentiment I fully agree with, though. Do you want me to handle the letter? I've conducted an awful lot of negotiations in my time. I know how to keep my less helpful feelings under wraps."

"No." I scowled at the paper. "I should do this. I was the one who lived with them for a little while. Who knows if they have some way of telling that a shadowkind wrote it, and then they won't pay attention at all. I'll figure it out."

"Have it your way, sweet sorcerer." He rumpled my hair teasingly and left me to it.

I scowled at the lemonade too, but gulping some of the sweet-and-sour liquid did revive my spirits a little. I squared my shoulders and forced myself to keep going.

To the members of the sorcerer enclave,

I'm sure you're aware of the murders of sorcerers that've been happening around the world, most recently across the United States. You might also have noticed the news about storms and tidal waves that've been battering the coasts here.

All of that destruction has been caused mainly by one vicious, ancient monster who's set on further ruining our world. I've heard from a source I trust that he's discovered that there's a group of powerful sorcerers living in Norway and he intends to hunt you down. I have no idea how likely it is that he'll find you, but for everyone's safety, I thought you should know so you can relocate before he even has the chance.

We're doing whatever we can here to stop him and make sure he can't hurt anyone else. If you hear that the storms have ended, you'll know it's safe.

"And then I'll be heading over there to stop all the crap *you're* doing too," I muttered to myself. I hesitated, and then simply signed the letter as "A concerned ally," as much as the "ally" part made me wince. Then I added my phone number for good measure with a note that they could call me if they wanted to ask questions to confirm my story. The more opportunity I could give them to believe what I was saying, the better.

And hopefully they'd never realize that their "ally" was the same woman who'd crashed their rites and called a demon straight into their midst a few weeks ago.

I folded the letter and tucked it into the small protective case Rollick had given me for that purpose. We were going to have to send the letter to the enclave in the hands of a shadowkind, because one of them could travel to Norway nearly instantly, way faster than me going by plane and car. And anyway, if I'd shown up at the enclave's borders again, they'd probably shoot me on sight. They'd already tried to shoot me before, and that was before I'd called on Rollick for help and he'd killed at least two of the sorcerers while rescuing me.

But sending the letter with a shadowkind meant the messenger might face a similarly hostile greeting. It was a dangerous mission, and we didn't want to risk the message being burned up or shredded in whatever defenses the enclave raised against a supposed intruder. A protective case had seemed like an important precaution.

When I'd decided to take this course of action, I'd asked the beings hanging out around the house for a particularly speedy volunteer. A few had offered their services, and when I stepped out into the yard, the hawk shifter I'd chosen shimmered into human-like physical form. He bobbed his head to me in a distinctly bird-like motion, his sharp eyes fixing on the case. "It's ready to go?"

"Yes," I said. "I know Rollick's already gone over the directions to the enclave with you. Remember, don't linger there. Just drop the message off at the edge of the boundary, set off the flare, and get away from that place as fast as you can."

He gave another bob. "I'll have no interest in sticking around. Shouldn't take any more than an hour. Happy to be able to pitch in."

He took the case from my hands and vanished back into the shadows faster than I could blink.

I dragged in a breath and resigned myself to a tense, uncertain wait.

It didn't take even a fraction as long as I'd anticipated.

In less than an hour, as promised, the hawk shifter reappeared at the house. His hair was slightly singed, and a scrape marked his jaw, but he'd made it back in one piece.

"They had a lot of beings lurking along the borders," he reported when I hurried out to meet him. "I couldn't even get all the way to the edge of their territory. But I flew the letter as close as I could, dropped it, and shifted for long enough to yell at them to bring it to their masters. Hopefully someone listened."

"Thank you," I said emphatically, meaning it. "That's the most I'd have asked from you. If it doesn't work, it's their fault, not yours."

But it'd be the whole world paying for it, not just the enclave.

I paced through the house, wanting to be focusing on figuring out battle strategies but too wound up and distracted to make much progress. I was just simmering down and getting my focus back when my phone rang.

My pulse stuttered. No one had that number who'd be calling in any situation that wasn't important. I yanked it out of my pocket, took in the unknown number on the screen, and hit the answer button. "Hello?"

"Who is this?" said the caustic male voice on the other end without any preamble.

My throat closed up. I inhaled deeply, groping for my inner calm. The man who'd spoken didn't need to introduce himself for me to be sure he was one of the enclave's sorcerers.

"That's doesn't matter," I said. "What matters is that I know about the enclave and about the monsters who come out of the shadows, and I know that everything I wrote in my letter to you is true. What you do about it is up to you, but I hope you protect yourselves."

There was a rustling sound and the murmur of breaths, and I realized he wasn't the only one following this call. "It sounds like her," someone else muttered in a firm female voice I thought I recognized as belonging to Vera, the sorcerer who'd mentored me during my brief time at the enclave. I hadn't known for sure that she was even still alive.

She'd been with the bunch who'd caught me at the rites and then tried to hunt me down before Rollick had rushed in to retrieve me.

"Quinn?" she demanded now. "That is you, isn't it? I can't think of who else would have known where to send a message like that—or be friendly enough with the fiends to have one deliver it for you."

I wasn't sure there was any point in denying it, but her tone didn't make me particularly inclined to confirm her suspicions either. "Like I said, it doesn't matter. If you need any more information about what's happening here in the States or the monster that's searching for you—"

"As if we'd listen to anything you'd say after what you already put us through," she interrupted. "This is probably some new conspiracy with those murderous beasts to get us away from our protections. We're fine where we are. You can't scare us into fleeing."

My spirits sank. "You've never dealt with any being like this one before. It's thousands of years ancient, and it's already consumed the power of dozens of sorcerers, maybe hundreds."

"It can't turn that sorcery on us. We'll fend the thing off if it makes it here. We aren't leaving our home. And if we ever find out where *you* are, you'd better believe you'll pay for the havoc you already caused."

The line went dead with a swift thump as if she'd slammed the phone down. I lowered my own from my ear with a heavy heart, my stomach knotting.

Was there some other way I could have delivered the message that they'd have received better? Was the leviathan going to get his potentially world-ending meal *because* I'd betrayed the enclave already?

Of course, if I'd never gone out there to investigate them, I'd never have known where to send the message to begin with. And witnessing their sick practices had taught me how to increase my own powers to use them for good. So I couldn't say it would have worked out better the other way.

I'd done the most I was capable of. Now I just had to hope that clearer heads would prevail over there. If they didn't leave right away, hopefully they'd at least ramp up their security even more. Maybe if one of their enslaved shadowkind sensed the leviathan approaching soon enough, they'd be able to make a run for it and get away before he reached them after all.

Those hesitant hopes didn't do much to dislodge the lump of uneasiness that'd expanded in my gut. I went back to my laptop, going over the chart I'd created of our main allies and their abilities. I'd been working out possible strategies for keeping the leviathan's minions busy while Rollick's human associates put the weapons that would make up his portable "trap" in place.

If we'd had the enclave's sorcerers on our side for this one thing, between me and them, we probably could have compelled the leviathan straight into the trap and ended all of this. But they wouldn't even leave the enclave to save their lives. There was obviously no way in hell they'd cross the ocean to purposefully face this creature beside me.

I was still ruminating on the problem when a shout went up outside. Panic jolted through my body. I was up and running to the door, snatching up my crossbow as I went, before I'd even had time to think about what the problem might be.

When I reached the yard, I still couldn't tell at first. Several of the shadowkind had emerged into physical form, crouched in a ring around something I couldn't see. Thin wafts of smoke rose up from their midst.

As I hurried over, a few glanced over their shoulders at me. The nearest eased to the side so I could join their circle.

"The injuries are already sealing," one of them said. "We'll do what we can to help him recover."

Those last words reverberated through my head as I found myself gazing down at Torrent: his eyes squeezed shut, his body halfway between its human- and octopus-like forms, twisted in agony. The smoke I'd seen was the essence seeping from multiple breaks in his flesh, drifting away into the open air.

CHAPTER TWENTY-ONE

Quinn

The fae woman leaned over Torrent's crumpled form on the bed. The flowers attached to stems that seemed to grow right out of her scalp swayed with her silvery hair. She pressed a hand to his side just above where one of his tentacles was twisted around his human-like torso and murmured. I caught a faint ripple of energy in the air.

His wounds had finished sealing as a bunch of the shadowkind outside had carried him into the bedroom. No more smoky essence dissipated into the air around us. But he was still unconscious, his limbs tensed at awkward angles as if braced against some internal pain.

At the fae woman's attentions, at least some of the stiffness in his expression had faded. She moved her hands to his shoulders and murmured again, and the final furrow smoothed out of his brow. Her lips pursed as she looked down at him.

"He should have stayed in the shadow realm longer to properly heal. But I've done what I can for the internal damage. The rest will have to knit together on its own over time."

I swallowed thickly. "How much time?"

She shook her head with a rustling of the flowers. "I don't know for sure. But he should wake up."

That didn't sound like a promise.

I tucked my legs up onto the bed where I'd perched next to Torrent's feet, hesitant to even touch him in his potentially fragile state. A couple of the beings who'd been gathered around him when I'd found them outside eased closer.

"He must have come through the rift that's about twenty miles from here," the hunched goblin said. "That's the closest one. I don't know how he managed to make it as far as he did from there on his own. We found him on our patrol about halfway here already, crawling along through the shadows but barely able to talk."

The fanged man next to him nodded. "He conked right out when we went to help him. We had to carry him back. Someone really wasn't happy with him, wherever he ended up." His gaze slid to Torrent with a sympathetic grimace.

"Thank you," I said. "For bringing him back so quickly. It sounds like... it sounds like he'll probably be okay." I was afraid to say anything more certain like that, as if I might jinx his recovery.

They dipped their heads and wavered away, leaving me alone with Torrent. None of my other men had returned from their most recent expeditions yet. I had no idea what else I could do.

Gingerly, I sank down on my side facing Torrent. I'd never seen my tentacled man really sleeping before. Shadowkind didn't technically *need* to sleep as part of their regular routine, and he'd tended to slip away into the shadows when he wanted to take a break.

His scarred chest rose and fell with slow but now steady breaths. His mouth twitched and then stilled. I wanted to reach out to him, but I had no idea how much internal damage might be healing beneath his skin.

Taking in the bruises and scars that mottled his body and remembering the battered state I'd found him in sent a wild rush of emotion searing through my chest. I could make sure that didn't happen again. I could send him away from all of this, from every being that might hurt him, like I had before. How the hell could I be so selfish to keep the men I loved in this fight?

Especially when at the end of it, there'd only be more heartbreak even if we won. Because I was becoming more and more certain that I wasn't going to make it past the final battle with my heart still beating.

I closed my eyes against the wave of anguish, hot tears welling up at the corners. As much as the ache inside wrenched at me, I knew I couldn't give in to it. I *had* taken that approach once before—and I'd seen how much pushing my men away had hurt them too.

There was no getting out of this scenario without some pain along the way—for any of us. But the sweet parts of life, the thrills and the beauty, had made the hard parts worth it for me. I knew all of my monstrous men would have said the same.

We were as connected as any beings, human or shadowkind, could become. And that meant we'd stand together through whatever happened next.

The body next to me stirred. As my eyes popped open, one of Torrent's tentacles flexed. It slid across the sheets to loop around my waist, looking instinctive in its movements.

His jaw flexed. His brow knit, and he blinked. His gaze fixed on me blearily and then with increasing focus. A whiff of confusion and then another of relief passed from him into me.

"Quinn," he said in a ragged voice.

With a leap of my heart, I sat up. "Can I get you anything? There was a fae who helped heal you—if you think you need more of her powers—"

"Quinn," he repeated, a little steadier, and tightened his grip on my waist. "I want you here. That's what I came back for. Don't go running off on some new mission, Ms. Fix It."

The old nickname brought a lump to my throat. I lay back down, letting Torrent tug me closer. When I rested my hand on his chest, his eyelids lowered to half-mast with an expression contented enough to absolve my guilt about not insisting on doing more.

"What happened?" I asked quietly. "Who did this to you? Was it the leviathan's minions—did they catch you on the way to the Highest—"

Torrent's dark laugh interrupted my question. "It *was* the Highest. Or their underlings, anyway. They took my warning as a threat, an attempt at manipulating them, and they were deeply displeased."

An icy jolt lanced through my chest. "You told them what was happening, and they attacked *you* for it? What the hell is wrong with them?"

"A very good question." He sighed and rolled toward me with a wince at the movement. "They've been holed up in the deepest parts of the shadow realm for so long I wouldn't be surprised if their minds are as muddled as the leviathan's seems to be. Which is all the more reason it'd be a very bad thing if they were dragged into the mortal realm. They didn't think it was possible."

"Which means they're arrogant and over-confident as well as being vicious jerks," I muttered.

A soft smile touched Torrent's lips. He raised his hand to my face and stroked his fingers over my cheek. "So angry on my behalf."

"Of course I am. They practically *killed* you. The beings who found you said you should have stayed in the shadow realm longer to heal. Did something else happen that we need to be ready for?"

He shook his head slightly against the pillow. "No. That was just— I didn't know what was going on here. I was worried—" He cut himself off, holding my gaze so intently that my pulse stuttered.

A warm wash of emotion carried with his next words. "I love you. I want to be here with you for as much time as I possibly can. If that means it takes a little longer for my wounds to heal, I don't mind."

He'd never said those three words before. He'd specifically told me he wasn't sure he'd ever be able to. I hadn't minded, but hearing them fall from his lips so emphatically set off a swell of answering emotion in my chest.

I scooted even closer to him and wrapped one arm around him, hugging him as tightly as I dared. "I love you too. So much. I'm sorry— You went through so much and they didn't even listen—"

"It wasn't your idea for me to go," Torrent said gently. He kissed my forehead. "It was the right thing to do. We had to try. Now we try something else. I'm sure you and the others can bring me up to speed on where we're at now."

I thought of everything that we'd learned since he'd left, and my stomach started to ache. I was going to need to tell him about all of it, but first I raised my head so I could meet his mouth for a lingering kiss. The quiver of joy that passed from him into me through our connection confirmed just how worth it this moment was to him.

Afterward, I sucked in a breath to gird myself. "There's been a lot. And the humans we've had to reach out to are being just as stubborn as the Highest. This is what you've missed..."

***

When Torrent drifted back into the sleep-like state that seemed to be helping him recover, I eased off the bed and went back to the bedroom where I'd been sleeping. The words he'd said and the devotion he'd offered me were still humming through my body. There were so many things wrong with the world, but that brief conversation had made everything feel a little more right.

I'd spent so much of my life trying to protect everyone around me from the impact of the problems I was facing. Going it alone. Keeping them at a distance or shoving them completely away. Suddenly I couldn't help wondering if I'd actually accomplished anything close to what I'd hoped to that way.

I couldn't do anything about the friends I'd pulled back from or never let in to begin with, but there were two other people I loved who I hadn't been fully honest with in a long time. I might not see them again before I died. Maybe they deserved my honesty more than my attempt at protecting them.

With my pillow propped against the headboard, I sat back and dialed Mom's number. Beyond the guestroom window, evening was falling, pink and orange streaking across the clouds with the setting sun.

We'd survived another day. That counted for something.

Mom picked up on the second ring. "Quinn? How are you, sweetheart?"

So eager to get an update on my well-being before anything else. The affection and concern in her tone decided me.

"Right now, okay," I said. "Are you two hanging in there all right still?"

"As well as can be expected, I suppose. I don't like staying here rather than being out there helping stop what's happening... but I can admit I have no idea how I would help."

"Staying safe helps," I reminded her. "It means I can focus more on fixing all this."

"I know. But I wish it didn't come down to you. I still don't understand how any of this could be true."

"Yeah, it doesn't make a whole lot of sense to me either. But it is what it is." I paused and raised my chin in defiance of my own hesitation. "Is Dad up? Could you put the phone on speaker so you can both hear me? There's—there's something else I'd like to talk to you about."

"Of course." Mom couldn't disguise the tremor of worry in her voice as she clicked the phone over.

"Hey, kiddo," Dad said from somewhere slightly more distant.

"Hi, Dad. It's good to hear your voice." But beating around the bush would only leave them to wonder anxiously longer. Better to rip off the bandaid.

I closed my eyes. "I didn't tell you everything the last time I saw you. I didn't want to make you worry even more. But I feel like you should know. I'm not sure if it'd have happened anyway or if it's because of all the supernatural stuff that I'm wrapped up in now, but I'm getting symptoms like my heart is starting to fail."

"Oh, sweetheart." Something about Mom's voice wrapped around me like an invisible hug. "How long has that been happening? You know there are medications that are supposed to moderate—"

"I know," I cut in, unable to listen to her offer up false hope. "One of my friends was able to arrange for me to get some. And it's only been for a couple of weeks. But it seems to be getting worse quickly even so, which is why I think the supernatural stuff is probably a factor. I'm okay. I always knew it could start to go at any time. I knew I wasn't going to live to eighty or something. I just—I didn't want to keep that from you. I wanted you to be able to prepare, and to tell you that you really did everything you could for me. You were exactly what I needed as parents."

"Quinn." Dad sounded choked up. He paused before continuing hoarsely. "You've been everything we ever wanted in a daughter. Isn't there some way that these... creatures, whatever they are... I mean, some of them have something like magic...?"

I let out a rough chuckle. "This seems to be beyond anything they're capable of fixing. Believe me, they'd be doing it if they could. But I'm happy. I've been happy. I still had a lot of great things in the life I did get. And there's nothing I'd rather be doing with the rest of it than making sure as many people as possible get more life too."

"You've always been so strong," Mom said. "I know you haven't liked to talk all that much about anything you're worried about. I'm glad that you told us. You have to know how much we love you. Our thoughts are going to be with you the entire time. And if you can come back here and see us again, I hope you will."

Her voice wavered, but she didn't let herself beg to see me, even though I had the feeling she wanted to. My eyes teared up all over again. "I definitely will. I don't know if it'll be possible, but if I can, I'll be there."

A nostalgic note crept into Dad's tone. "I still remember the time when you were fourteen and you insisted on going on that new rollercoaster at Busch Gardens, and you were laughing the whole time while your mother and I hung on for dear life."

A bittersweet smile crossed my face. "That was a fun trip. We had a lot of good times."

"We did," Mom said softly.

We reminisced back and forth for a while longer, until my heart felt full and my gut heavy. When I hung up, I slumped back into the pillows—and a tall form wavered into being just inside the doorway.

Rollick had returned. He studied me with his incisive gaze. "I didn't want to interrupt your call. It sounded important. You told your parents about your health?"

I nodded. "It seemed like the right thing to do. Now the fact that I haven't isn't hanging over me." Then I pushed myself straighter, my melancholy falling away under a sharper wave of apprehension. "What's happened? Has something changed?"

He held up his phone with a twist of his mouth. "Unfortunately, yes. There's breaking news out of Norway."

CHAPTER TWENTY-TWO

Quinn

I sat on the sofa with my computer poised on my lap, staring at the article on the screen. My stomach felt as if it'd plummeted right out of my body, through the floor, and possibly all the way down to the center of the earth.

Massacre in Isolated Commune, the headline read. The rest of the report went on to describe how the bloody bodies of nearly thirty men and women had been found in a tiny community in the wilderness of northern Norway just a few hours ago.

"Each of the bodies was brutally mutilated," Rollick read aloud. "I think we can guess what those mutilations involved."

"All their vital organs torn out as if by some kind of

wild beast," I muttered, and let my head drop back against the sofa. "I tried to warn them."

Crag came up behind me to rest his hand on my shoulder. He'd made it back to the house shortly after Rollick had arrived with the bad news. "They might not have had time to escape anyway. We only found out about the threat this morning. The leviathan must have already been over there searching for them."

Of course he had been. As soon as he'd realized he had such a simple opportunity to expand his powers, he'd have wanted to jump on it before there was any chance of it slipping through his fingers... or talons, or whatever exactly leviathans had.

I rubbed my forehead. "I didn't like the enclave. The things they did were sick. But now the result of their psycho behavior is helping an even bigger psycho. How the hell are we going to stop him now?"

"We don't know if this will be enough to allow him to carry out his ultimate plan," Rollick said, though his tone wasn't all that confident. "Even taking in the behemoth's essence wasn't enough."

"But this is so many more sorcerers' powers, and they were strong sorcerers too." I groaned. "We don't have much time. We have to figure out some kind of plan to counteract his, or we might not be able to do anything at all before he's hauling the Highest through that rift."

Rollick got up, tucking his phone into his pocket. "I have human associates watching that area from a distance. As soon as there's any change in activity there, we'll know."

"We don't know what we'll do when that happens.

We've got all these shadowkind here, but most of them won't be able to do much against the leviathan, especially now that he's got even more sorcery to wield. We can't get close until he's focusing it on compelling the Highest, and then it'll be almost too late. Are your weapons using the materials from the trap even ready?"

The demon gave a curt nod. "Everything's prepared. They're almost like a larger version of your crossbow." He aimed a tight smirk at the weapon lying on the coffee table between us.

"But we still have to figure out how to get them in place without the leviathan or his minions destroying them first."

Crag squeezed my shoulder. "We've got a lot of allies on our side now to push them back, and you have your own magic that can strengthen the rest of us. He won't be prepared for that. Maybe we should give you more of our essence. If—"

I shook my head to cut him off. I didn't want to say it, but there wasn't any avoiding the truth. My hand rose to press against my clavicle. "At this point, I don't think a lack of magic is holding me back. It's whether my body—my heart—can handle having that much magic moving through it. It doesn't do any good making yourselves weaker if I can't even use all the power you've given me."

Rollick let out a rough sound and started to pace. "We won't give up. There are a lot of us willing to stand against the leviathan, even if the Highest are too arrogant or cowardly to."

His words echoed through my head. *A lot of us willing to stand against him.* There was someone like that who we hadn't called on yet, wasn't there?

I sat up straighter, fumbling for my phone. "We have to ask Sorsha for help. She and her friends—you said they're really powerful, didn't you? It seemed like they'd want to stop this from happening."

Rollick frowned. "We talked about this before. She's unstable. I don't know the men she runs with at all. And a phoenix isn't going to be much help against a being of water anyway."

I glowered at him. "If her fire won't be much use, then there isn't any chance of her burning the world down either, is there? She'd be able to do *something*, even if it's just helping keep the other shadowkind organized. And— you told me that she's some kind of hybrid, right? Part human? Maybe she can handle silver and iron. Maybe the leviathan can't compel her any more than he can me. That would count for a lot."

Rollick and I stared each other down. Crag seemed to decide it was wisest to stay out of the argument and let us duke it out on our own. The demon's mouth twitched, and then he sighed, dropping his gaze. "I don't even remember why I was so adamantly against her involvement. Fine. Call her. You're right—we need all the help we can get, and quickly."

"I'd imagine the whole 'nearly destroyed the world' thing was a pretty legit reason before we got to the point where the world was probably going to end anyway," I said, to be fair. "Also, you have issues with letting anyone in on your plans or even giving away that you *have* plans. That probably had something to do with it too."

Rollick went back to glowering at me. Wielding my phone, I marched into my room where I could figure out what to say to the phoenix without my monstrous men distracting me. I'd only talked to her briefly a couple of times in the past.

Once I was in the solitude of the bedroom, apprehension settled over me. I had trouble letting people in on *my* plans too, even if that hesitation came from a different place than Rollick's.

I was asking Sorsha and her friends to risk their lives to help us. My men wanted to stand with me because of their feelings for me—and because they'd seen the destruction the leviathan was causing. The allies we'd gathered so far had come of their own accord. To reach out to someone who'd already helped me more than once and ask her to stick her neck out again...

I grimaced at my phone—or really at myself. My stomach was all knotted up over something Sorsha had specifically told me to do. I'd met her because she was investigating the sorcerer killings. I knew that she'd want to hear what we'd discovered and have the chance to contribute, didn't I?

And we did need the help.

I just didn't like the feeling that it was my responsibility if something happened to her. But she was just as much a being with her own free will as Torrent and the rest of my men were.

My jaw clenching, I hit the call button and raised the phone to my ear.

It took longer for the phoenix to pick up than it had with my mom. I guessed Sorsha probably had more on her plate than the average human in general, and definitely more than my parents did in their little underground bunker. But just when I was starting to think I'd end up going to voice mail, there was a click and a voice that sounded a bit breathless, as if she'd been running. "Hello?"

"Hey, um, Sorsha, it's Quinn—"

"Oh!" she said, her voice brightening and steadying at the same time. "Sorry. I really need to remember to label my Contacts better. What's going on? Got another kid you want to shoot my way? That's not actually an invitation. We do have plenty."

Her irreverent tone set me at ease before I'd realized I was relaxing. A small smile even crossed my lips. "No kids this time. But—this is a much bigger ask."

"Please tell me you know what asshole shadowkind are behind the mess we're seeing with all these storms, because I'd really like to kick their asses."

A relieved laugh spilled out of me. It suddenly seemed absurd that I'd hesitated to reach out to her. "That is actually why I'm calling. It's not so much a they but a he. A leviathan. Well, there was a behemoth involved too, but we dealt with him... sort of. It's a long story. Anyway, the leviathan is basically trying to destroy the mortal world as we know it, and we're having some trouble making sure that doesn't happen, so any ass-kicking you want to bring to the table would be totally appreciated."

"You've got it. We've already been on the go trying to figure out what the hell is going on. Where exactly are you? We'll have the Everymobile out there as fast as its supernaturally enhanced engine can take us... Maybe faster if we decide to risk a rift. That's always a gamble."

"Whatever you think is best," I said. "Here, let me get—

this isn't actually my house—the demon who owns it will be able to give you clearer directions."

"A demon house, hmm. Keeping even more interesting company than before these days."

I couldn't tell whether Sorsha was just amused or being suggestive, but my cheeks flared anyway. "That's a long story too. I'll tell you when I see you—when we're not busy with the whole saving the world thing. Just a sec."

I hustled back out into the living room. Rollick gave me a look that suggested he knew exactly what I was there for— which, considering the keenness of shadowkind hearing, he quite possibly did. I handed the phone over. "Be nice and tell our very helpful friends how to find your super-secret house."

He huffed, but he said his hello with his usual charming drawl, so I figured it was safe to leave him to it.

I found myself heading into the guest room where Torrent was recovering rather than to my own bedroom. The tentacled man was still out cold since our earlier conversation, but the deep, rhythmic murmur of his breaths reassured me. I lay down on the bed next to him and imagined telling him that soon we were going to be bringing a phoenix and... whatever the rest of Sorsha's friends were into the fray. I thought he'd understand better than anyone else how hard making that ask had been for me.

For now, I closed my eyes and let myself revel in my victory over my self-doubts for a minute. Maybe Sorsha and her companions would be a big enough force to turn the tide. If Rollick hadn't been such a stick-in-the-mud about getting them involved before, I'd have thought to reach out sooner.

We were getting so close to having a real army. If the leviathan just allowed us another few days to finish preparing—

The attack came on me so suddenly I didn't even have time to catch my breath before the clenching sensation squeezed all possibility of breathing out of my lungs.

My lips parted with a silent cry of pain. My shoulders went rigid as I braced against the pressure, trying to think about anything other than the vise clamped around my chest.

But it wasn't just the pressure that I had to endure. A hot flash rippled through me, followed by a chill as if someone had doused me with icy water. A shiver ran through my limbs. Sweat had broken out on my forehead. The thud of my heart rang loud in my ears, sounding too slow and then too fast, thundering erratically like a train about to rattle right off the tracks.

It was impossible to say how long it took before the symptoms eased off again. Finally, I became aware of my hands balled in the fabric of the sheet beneath me, my breath coming again—now with a faint rasp. An ache lingered around my ribcage after the worst of the effects had subsided.

I dragged in a deeper breath and blinked hard, staring up at the ceiling. I was relieved that my fit hadn't woken Torrent from the healing rest he needed, but I was also feeling so very alone.

A few more days. Maybe we had that. And then we'd need to face the leviathan, and I was going to have to put every bit of power I had into winning that fight for my parents, all the beings who'd put their faith in me, and everyone else in this world.

And then, I was now surer than ever, my heart would give out completely.

But that was just how it was. At least going this way I didn't leave millions of others to go down with me.

CHAPTER TWENTY-THREE

Rollick

These days, the house that'd once been a sanctuary to me rarely offered much peace or solitude. The heaps of shadowkind who'd joined our crusade stuck to the yard and the areas beyond the ring of protections depending on their tolerance for silver and iron, but I was always aware of them nearby. And more often than not, if I was here, at least one of my mutinous former employees was too.

But I couldn't say their presence was necessarily a bad thing, because at least having other beings around kept me a little distracted. Kept my mind from veering in directions I'd rather it didn't go but couldn't seem to prevent.

Five in the morning was about as quiet as the place got. I wandered into the kitchen, having just finished a call with a few old associates overseas, wheedling them to the limits my pride allowed to join this fight and gritting my teeth as they balked. They saw the current disaster as a distant problem, nothing for them to stick their necks out over.

When I'd told them what we believed the leviathan intended to do next, they'd laughed. But they hadn't seen him in action.

None of us had seen him in action since he'd devoured the entire enclave's worth of sorcerers. That much more magic now hummed through his veins—

My pulse lurched, and I found myself clutching the edge of the island as if it were the only thing holding me upright. My thoughts had scattered, my heart hammering at my chest so hard I half expected to feel a rib crack.

I closed my eyes, clenched my jaw even tighter, and breathed evenly in and out until the rush of panic receded.

So ridiculous. The being that'd bound me was gone, dead. The other fiend that could wield as much power was hundreds of miles distant. I wasn't even *thinking* anything when the fear took over. It was pure, random emotion.

I didn't let emotion dictate my life, especially not irrational fears. Why the hell didn't this after-effect wear off already?

What if it never did?

The discomfort that came with that consideration brought a milder chill but one that lingered longer. I tried to walk away from it, ambling back to the living room where the solar lights still glowed dimly around the pool, and soft footsteps reached my ears.

"Hey," Quinn murmured, coming up beside me. "Is everything okay?" She winced as soon as the words came out of her mouth. "I mean, no more horrible than things were a few hours ago."

"I know what you meant. There's been no news." I also knew exactly why she was asking—that damned connection I'd inadvertently forged. Every time the panic hit me, she felt it too. "I hope I didn't wake you."

She shook her head, peering past me over the rectangle of dark water rippling with a breeze. "I woke up a while ago and haven't been able to get back to sleep. I figured maybe taking a break from trying would help."

"You need your rest," I couldn't help telling her. Her face definitely looked paler than it had when I'd first met her, with a sallow tone creeping into her normally peachy skin that I didn't like at all. And she moved a little slower these days, as if her usual briskly determined pace would have worn her out too quickly.

"I'm fine," she said emphatically, fixing me with a sharp look. In that moment, I was more annoyed than ever that the connection between us didn't flow both ways.

How was she really coping? She could be as stubborn as I was. I wasn't totally sure how much she'd admit to struggling, especially with all the responsibility that'd been piled on her shoulders.

"Well, so am I," I retorted.

She narrowed her eyes at me. "The flashbacks have gotten stronger. They're hitting me harder through you, which means they've got to be hitting you harder too."

"And I keep living through them just like you keep living with your heart."

Quinn frowned. "They might get even worse when we

go out to confront the leviathan, though. I don't know if I can protect you enough."

The fact that *she* was worried about protecting *me* when I was the all-powerful demon around here rankled me. I slipped my hand around her head to turn her to me and tucked her against my human-like frame. "I've survived just fine being near one enhanced sorcerer. I'll manage the shadowkind one out there too."

Quinn's body went still, not tensed but as if she were trying to listen hard to something she couldn't quite make out. She glanced up at me, close enough now that her breath brushed across my neck in a ghostly sensation. "You said it was having the behemoth work his sorcery on you that set this off. The idea of losing control again is what makes you panic."

"Something like that." I didn't really want to talk about it at all.

Thankfully, my lovely mortal seemed to have decided she'd had enough talking too. She curled her fingers into my shirt and tugged me with her, and I followed willingly. The spark that had lit in her eyes promised something interesting to come, whether I ended up liking it or not.

When she led me through the doorway to her bedroom and kicked the door shut behind us, I decided that chances were good that I'd approve. As she drew me over to the bed, I raised my eyebrows at her. "If you're in need of some carnal satisfaction, you only needed to say so."

Quinn hummed low in her throat, a sound that sent a heady shiver straight to my cock. But the heat in her gaze was as much determination as it was desire. "I think we can do a little more than that in here," she said, and hopped onto the bed, pulling me with her.

When I clambered after her, she shifted to the side and pushed me onto my back. I sank down without complaint, watching her curiously. She obviously had something specific in mind, and I saw no need to rush her.

Quinn gazed down at me, wetting her lips. She straddled my waist, her ass settling against my groin with enough pressure to bring a groan to my lips even with at least three layers of fabric between us. Her hands splayed against my chest.

"Maybe being commanded doesn't have to be a painful thing," she said. "Maybe it'd help your mind stop freaking out about it if you got to experience a more enjoyable enchantment."

A quiver of anxiety wound through my growing sense of anticipation, but I resisted giving it much attention. I'd seen how distraught Quinn got over even the thought of hurting any of us. I didn't fear her intentions at all.

"What did you have in mind?" I asked, keeping my voice languid.

She leaned forward, her hair falling like a golden veil on either side of her face, until her nose nearly touched mine. Then she spoke at a volume barely above a breath. "Touch me."

Magic resonated through the words and wound through my mind. My body stiffened against it instinctively —but there wasn't anything brutal about this sorcery. It was tentative enough that I could have thrown off the order if I'd wanted to.

I didn't, though, did I? I could play along with her little

game and see where it led us. If I wasn't strong enough for that, then the leviathan might as well kill me now.

I unclenched my muscles and let my hands rise as they'd itched to do at her words. My fingers stroked up her back and twined in her silky hair. I pulled her the last few inches down so our lips could meld together the way I'd been hungering for since she'd mounted me.

A soft noise worked from Quinn's throat. She kissed me back just as eagerly. I tilted her head to the side with a twist of her hair so I could delve my tongue into that hot mouth, and earned my first whimper in return.

It wasn't bad. No, it was absolute fucking paradise going along with her vague instruction. After a few minutes, the tendril of magic that'd gripped my thoughts gradually eased away, barely enough to direct my will, and I felt a sudden, strange thrill at the idea of continuing on this course.

I tipped Quinn's head even farther and pressed my mouth against her neck. A swipe of my tongue and the scrape of my teeth drew another gasp from her. Then I eased back just enough to speak, my lips grazing her smooth skin. "What does my sweet sorcerer want from me next?"

A tentative smile crossed her face, as if she'd been waiting for the confirmation that I was on board—and still wasn't totally sure she could accept it. She gave her next order in the same whisper with its faint whiff of compulsion. "Uncover me."

I sure as shit didn't object to that request. Even less anxiety twanged through me as I reached for the hem of the tank top she'd been sleeping in and peeled it off her. She'd used broad enough wording that I didn't feel overly controlled. It was like the gentlest sort of bondage, restraints I could have slipped in an instant but that gave a little jolt of excitement having them in place.

Somehow I doubted the sorcerers who'd developed and spread this magic had ever intended it to be used like this—and knowing that only made the moment more delightful.

Quinn wasn't wearing a bra under her shirt. I cupped my hands around her breasts and tweaked the peaks before pushing up on my elbows so I could suck one into my mouth. The feel of her nipple stiffening beneath my tongue made me growl. I hadn't been able to do this the first time we'd come together on our own—she'd had to wear that damned protective undershirt the whole time.

Quinn's hands traveled down my chest, making quick work of my button-up shirt and sliding across the planes of muscle beneath. It felt as if she were drawing flames across my skin with her touch, but only the most blissful kind.

Her command still tingled through me. I knew that I hadn't completely uncovered her yet. I could have fought the pull, but why would I want to when it aligned so well with my own interests?

As I suckled her breast, teasing the nipple with my teeth until she started to pant, I glided one hand down her body to her pajama shorts. As soon as I grasped the waist, her hips lifted to allow me better access. I dragged the shorts off her as quickly as I could manage, and then I couldn't stop myself from tucking my fingers between her legs.

She was so wet already, her pussy slick with arousal, that I groaned against her breast. As I stroked her from clit to slit, a matching moan spilled from her lips. She rocked against my hand, and another command tumbled out of her. "Let me see the demon."

I knew what she meant, even if I could have satisfied the tug of the magic by simply blinking in and out of my shadowkind form for a brief glimpse. She was after a more extended experience.

With a growl, I flipped her over on the bed, letting my demon form stretch my body at the same time. The cool air washed over my abruptly bare back while the front of me seared with the heat we'd already generated between us. My second cock jutted below the first, equally hard already.

I claimed Quinn's mouth again, letting my sharp demonic teeth nick her lower lip. She whimpered encouragingly, squirming beneath me until our bodies were almost perfectly aligned. My upper cock brushed against her mound, and she swayed up to meet that contact. The need to fill her burned through me—but the tension of waiting for her orders had become increasingly delicious.

"What should your demon do for you now, my lovely mortal?" I murmured.

Quinn made a needy noise and ran her fingers along the curves of my horns, sending a tremor of pleasure down them and through my scalp. "Take me—however you'd most like to."

Somehow I hadn't even been aware of my deepest urges until her sorcery unlocked the answer inside my skull. All at once, I was picturing her on all fours, crying out in ecstasy as I slammed into her from behind. A rumble carried from my chest, and without thinking I was already flipping her over and yanking her ass against my groin.

Quinn gasped, but there was nothing fearful in the

sound. I knew without any supernatural bond necessary just how much she trusted me. That thought caught at the base of my throat, stalling me in my tracks as I bowed my head to her shoulder blades. My hand delved between her legs again to tease even more pleasure out of her. But this bodily unification wasn't all I was craving.

"You are mine," I muttered against her back, and kissed the faint bumps of her spine. "*Mine.*"

"And you're my demon," she said, so happily I couldn't suppress the affection that swelled from my heart. I hugged her tighter against me, and in that moment, the most important thing was her knowing how much this "taking" meant to me.

"I love you. My sweet sorcerer. My defiant mortal. Everything you are."

She'd helped me find the parts of myself I'd buried so far within me that I'd started to forget they existed. The only other partner I'd ever said those words to had shunned that side of me, the side that could be generous, that cared about making the whole world better. But Quinn didn't reject the selfish, vicious side of me either. She accepted them all together, everything that *I* was.

And that was why I wouldn't let anything defeat her, not that leviathan, not her treacherous heart.

Quinn shivered beneath me, but the emotion that thickened her voice told me her reaction was all joy. "I love you too. My wicked fiend. My reluctant hero."

I chuckled at that second label and finally gave in to the other longing twined through my body. My fingers traveled up the crease of her ass to her other opening, smearing my own growing arousal with them.

My lover pressed into my fingers as I stretched her, her breaths fragmenting even more. It was the sweetest torture waiting until the give of her inner muscles convinced me I wouldn't cause her any pain—at least not any that would do more than heighten the pleasure that came with it.

With my first thrust into her, filling both her openings at once, she buried her face in the pillow with a strangled moan. I spread her legs farther apart so I could plunge even deeper into her slick channels and braced myself on one arm so I could fondle her breasts at the same time. With each smack of our bodies colliding, she rocked back into me, the gasps and moans escaping her in a chorus electrifying me.

The craving for release was already building in my balls. I rolled her nipple and then trailed my hand down to circle her clit with a careful claw, matching the movements with the pounding of my cocks.

Quinn broke, her body shuddering and clenching, the cry I'd imagined bursting from her in a peal even more beautiful than what my mind had conjured. The passion of her welcome unraveled what remained of my self-control. I thrust into her faster, harder, and felt a second release ripple through her as I tumbled over the edge myself with simultaneous surges of cum inside her.

"Fuck," Quinn mumbled as she sagged onto her side beneath me.

I grinned down at her. "Yes, that's the word for what we just did."

She swatted me with an amused wrinkling of her nose at the joke. Then a hint of somberness touched her expression. "Was that okay? The way I brought my magic into it—"

I eased myself down next to her and pulled her against me. "I enjoyed it quite a bit. And I don't think I'll ever be able to think about sorcery quite the same way again, so thank you for that."

She smothered a guffaw. "Just don't get any ideas about romancing the leviathan."

"Believe me, there's no chance of that," I said dryly, but as the words left my lips, a flicker of hope darted through me.

The mention of the ancient beast and his magic hadn't set off even the slightest flicker of panic this time. I couldn't say for sure that this creative interlude had completely cured my lingering fears... but maybe my precious lover's touch had been the salve that'd healed the worse of them.

If only I could heal her troubles just as quickly.

CHAPTER TWENTY-FOUR

Quinn

"These ones can move the earth," Lance said proudly, pointing to two beings he'd identified as ogres, who looked just as rocky as Crag's gargoyle form but were much more... lumpy about it. They squatted on the dry earth in the desert outside the house with their heads cocked curiously atop their stocky bodies. But at least they were here.

"That could be useful," I said. "For pushing the leviathan around or holding him in place if he's near the shore. Or even if he's not. There's earth under the ocean too."

Both of them nodded in jerky motions. "Yes, yes," the one on the right said. "We'll do our best. Mostly we crack things, but we can also make them collide."

And my magic should amplify whatever effects they

could normally accomplish. I gave them a weary but grateful smile. "Thank you for coming."

As they waddled off, I turned to Lance, who was beaming. "They were a good find. I'm starting to feel like we might actually have a proper army here." If we could get them all working together in unison without having their powers collide with each other. It wasn't as if we could easily practice our strategies without any leviathan around and on terrain pretty much the opposite of the coastline.

The dragon shifter grinned even wider. "I think so too." Then his good humor dimmed. "Crag said the biggest wave hit Rollick's city."

I grimaced with a lurch of my stomach, remembering the images I'd seen from the news websites this morning. "Yeah. The leviathan finally threw that tidal wave he'd been building at L.A. Thankfully they'd already gotten a lot of people evacuated, but there were still some deaths, and it destroyed a bunch of property. The storms are still battering the whole area... It's a mess." I couldn't help feeling guilty that I'd been able to escape to someplace so comfortable and, well, dry.

"We should go challenge him right now," Lance said, rolling his shoulders as a fierce light sparked in his violet eyes.

"And that'll just add to *his* army," Rollick said dryly, coming up behind us. "I'd rather not make a contribution to his cause. You know we need to wait until he's focusing his sorcery elsewhere before we have a real chance."

Lance grunted with annoyance, but he didn't have any more solution to that problem than the rest of us did. I swallowed thickly, folding my arms over my chest just shy of hugging myself. "I guess now that we know he's accumulated all the sorcery he's likely to, we should get ourselves closer to California again so it's less of a trek when we need to reach him. Do you have any houses that—"

Before I could finish my question, a clanging like a warning at a train crossing split the air. I spun around to see a familiar RV in the distance, roaring along the narrow road that led to the house and kicking up dust under its wheels. A figure I could barely make out appeared on the top of the vehicle, heedless of its speed, and brought his arms down on something protruding from the roof a few times. Whatever he'd smashed, the clanging sound cut out.

Rollick sighed, but my lips twitched with a smile. Sorsha's vehicle might be unusual, but she and her companions were the last definite allies we'd been waiting on. It'd be better to start moving toward California with them already with us.

As the RV approached, my other two men emerged from the house, Crag striding over from the doorway and Torrent only wavering into physical form when he could stand with us. The tentacled man had all four of his supporting tentacles out, his posture still a bit unsteady.

I moved to him, grasping his arm. "Are you sure you shouldn't keep resting?"

Torrent slipped his arm right around me, the damaged hand on that side resting against my waist, and pressed a gentle kiss to my temple. "I get the sense that final plans are being made. You're not leaving the cripple out of them."

I narrowed my eyes at his self-derogatory wording, but he'd said it lightly enough that I wasn't too worried about his emotional state. All the same, I had to say, "Don't beat yourself up. The jerks back in the shadow realm already had that job more than covered."

A startled laugh tumbled out of Torrent, and he tightened his sideways hug for just a second with a ripple of affection through our connection. "As I'm well aware."

I had the sense that all of the shadowkind gathered around the house were watching the vehicle's arrival, even though most of them remained in the patches of gloom beyond my sight. It was hard not to find the RV kind of momentous with its various streamers and spinning accessories. I'd gathered that most if not all of those were the result of previous trips through rifts, which would explain why Sorsha might not have been super keen to travel by that route again.

The so-called Everymobile jerked to a halt just shy of the garage that held Rollick's multiple cars. The door chimed as it opened, and Sorsha strode out with the unflappable energy I was starting to expect from her, her appropriately fiery red hair swinging in its wavy ponytail. The four shadowkind men who I suspected were more than just friends of hers followed more cautiously. They flanked her with a mildly protective air that seemed a little absurd if Rollick was right that this woman had enough power in her to destroy both realms all on her own.

They were certainly a varied assortment of beings. One loomed as tall and brawny as Crag, his pale blond hair contrasting with his burnished brown skin. He'd had wings at least once before, but darkly feathered ones, so he definitely wasn't a gargoyle. At the moment his only obvious monstrous feature was the crystal-like surface of his knuckles. I didn't think it'd be fun to get punched by that guy.

An equally tall but much slimmer guy rested his hand on Sorsha's shoulder, his golden curls as sunny as his smile. A forked tongue darted briefly from between his lips. I had no idea what kind of being he was either.

The dark-haired guy, who had his leanly muscled frame clothed in a posh button-up and slacks combo like he was about to head to a fancy nightclub, eyed us all with a faintly amused expression that didn't seem to fit the situation. Sorsha had mentioned he was an incubus. Two short horns poked from his chocolate-brown locks.

And then there was the well-built, tawny-haired man who didn't show any shadowkind features at all, though I knew he had to have one somewhere. His mouth was tight as if he was holding back a growl, and I had a flash of a memory to seeing him transform into that human-like shape from that of a monstrous, glowing dog. A hellhound, one of my guys had said.

Seeing them all in front of us, feeling how much more powerful they were than the vast majority of the beings who'd already joined our "army," I couldn't help finding it twice as ridiculous that we'd only just called on them for help. Rollick and that stupid shadowkind hesitation to ever depend on each other.

The demon himself stepped forward with an air that was all polished charm and a wariness I could sense underneath it. "Welcome to my humble home. Although we've just been talking about leaving it."

Sorsha nodded with a swish of her ponytail and a flex of her toned shoulders. "I heard about the tsunami that hit L.A. overnight. The leviathan's still out there, you figure?"

"That's where his favorite rift is, so that's where he'll be."

She glanced around, and I could tell she was aware of the beings lurking around us too. "Quite the motley crew you've assembled. We were talking on the drive down about how we could best pitch in. Feel free to make suggestions, since you've all dealt with this prick firsthand and we haven't. Ruse is probably best on crowd control." She motioned to the incubus. "He can make sure all mortals steer clear of the battle grounds, if there are any around."

I hadn't even thought about random mortals getting caught up in the clash. "That would definitely be useful."

Sorsha patted the slim guy's hand on her shoulder. "Snap can use his 'tasting' skill to see if he can pick up any useful impressions that would tell us more about the leviathan's plan of action, what steps he'll take next, so we can anticipate his movements. And also figure out if there are any deadly surprises he's arranged. Unfortunately the whole devouring souls skill seems to mainly work on mortals, not other shadowkind."

Rollick raised his eyebrows. "It sounds as though he'll be quite helpful all the same," he said, while I re-evaluated the cheerful-looking guy.

Sorsha jabbed her thumb toward the big dude. "Thorn can give the leviathan a shove if you need him on the move and generally distract him with a good pummeling. His wings allow him a lot of maneuverability."

Crag let out a grunt and dipped his head to the other hulk. "We'll coordinate our attacks, then."

Thorn nodded in return, his expression even more solemn than the gargoyle's. "It will be an honor to fight alongside such courageous beings."

I decided not to ask what century he'd come from. The sentiment was appreciated.

Sorsha gestured between herself and the hellhound shifter last. "Omen and I should be able to have some impact with our fire, even against an enemy who's all about the water. We can boil the area he's hanging out in. Flambé any minions that come at the rest of you."

"As long as you don't flambé the rest of us too," Torrent said evenly.

The phoenix flashed him a smile. "Don't worry, I've got much better control over my powers now that I've had more than a couple of weeks to figure out what the hell I even am." She paused. "None of us have gone up against anything quite as ancient and powerful as this leviathan before. But we'll do all we can. Between everyone here, we should be able to kick his butt."

I realized with a jolt that I hadn't told her one important part of our plan. "We've actually found that we can, er, rev up the powers everyone already has. Well, I can, anyway. Using my sorcery. If I order shadowkind to do something they already want to do, it seems to amplify their strength."

Sorsha's eyebrows shot up. "Fascinating. And very handy."

Omen snorted. "Maybe with beings like *this*," he said, tilting his head toward the shadowy crowd around the yard, his voice slightly disdainful. "I doubt it'd do much for us."

I wavered, not sure that arguing with him was the best

idea, but Sorsha clearly had no such qualms. She spun toward him with a sly grin. "There's an easy way to find out, isn't there? I think you've just volunteered yourself as a test subject. After all, you're the most ancient being here, except maybe our demonic host. If it works on you, it should work on anyone."

The man glowered at her, his tawny hair ruffling even though I didn't feel any breeze. "I'm not sure I can burn things even more to a crisp than I'm already capable of."

"Ah, but maybe you can burn them even faster!"

"Er, I don't actually have to use my powers on any of you," I said quickly. "It's totally fine if you'd rather not."

"No, no, our Disaster wants a demonstration, she'll get a demonstration." There was a weird fondness to the words despite Omen's grouchy expression. "Let's work with water, since that's what we'll be dealing with out there. Someone want to bring out a couple of glasses?"

Lance bounded into the house and returned moments later with two large tumblers brimming with tap water. Omen rolled his shoulders and then hunched over into his hellhound form—which was even more massive and unnerving than I'd remembered. He did look like a hound —one whose shoulders came up to the top of my head and whose charcoal gray fur was streaked through with magma-like currents of fire. Lance let out a whistle of approval.

Omen lashed a paw at the first cup, I supposed to establish a baseline. Even as the glass smashed into the hard terrain, the water was sizzling away into steam. Not a dribble touched the dirt. It was pretty impressive.

He looked at me impatiently with eyes that glowed just as searingly as the streaks in his fur. My pulse skipped a beat, but I tamped down my nerves and focused my sorcerous energy on him. A short string of syllables burst out of me. *Destroy the other glass.*

Omen lunged at the second cup. He smacked at it just like the first—but this time the vessel didn't shatter. It hissed alongside the water.

We all stared down at the blob of melted glass that now lay on the dirt. A giddy quiver raced through my chest.

I'd helped make that happen. Maybe we really did have a chance against the monster who meant to upend both our worlds.

Ruse started to laugh. Sorsha clapped her hands with a chuckle of her own as Omen returned to his human form. He ran his hand over his ruffled hair and gave me a warier glance. "All right. There's something to it. I mean, I *could* have melted the first one too if I'd been trying to. But I did the second without even trying."

"Yes, yes, you're very great and powerful," Sorsha teased. "Now that we've gotten the testing out of the way, how about—"

Rollick's ringtone interrupted her. The demon frowned and snatched his phone out of his pocket. "What?" he said smoothly, and then his expression tensed. "*What?* When did this start? Yes, yes. Just keep me updated."

He hung up, his jaw clenched, and glanced around at the rest of us. "We have to get going, *now*. The leviathan's gathering an even bigger mass of beings around the rift and has started slaughtering them faster than before. It looks like he's making his final bid to bring the Highest through —and he's not going to wait around for us to arrive before he makes that call."

CHAPTER TWENTY-FIVE

Lance

Watching Quinn disappear past the door of the phoenix's huge vehicle wrenched at me more than anything had since the time our sorcerer had sent us away from her with her magic. My limbs twitched, and I almost threw myself after her, but Torrent caught me with a tentacle around my wrist.

I halted instantly, knowing that he was still weak from the beating he'd gotten in the shadow realm—not wanting to hurt him worse.

"This is the best way to get her there with enough time for her to make a difference," he reminded me. "She can't travel through the rifts, and that vehicle is enhanced to go faster than any of Rollick's cars can."

I grimaced at the RV as the engine roared to life. It tore

down the dusty road so fast it wavered against the desert landscape. "I know. But I don't like her being away from us. We won't know what's happening to her. And we hardly know those shadowkind with her."

"We know they fought enemies the Highest refused to tackle before," Rollick put in, though he didn't look much happier than I felt. "I may have concerns about their specific methods, but I don't think we have to worry that they'd suddenly take the leviathan's side." He motioned to us. "Come on. Let's lead this army of ours to the battlefield. We'll get there well ahead of our woman, which means we can make sure her arrival is as safe as possible."

I didn't think there was any way that approaching the rift the leviathan wanted to bring the Highest through could be *safe* for Quinn, but Rollick couldn't have picked an argument more likely to motivate me. I whirled around and dove into the shadows. Winding through the patches of gloom scattered across the sun-drenched terrain, I snapped my teeth at and nudged my dragon shoulders against the ephemeral bodies I brushed past.

"Let's go, let's go. It's time to stop that watery fiend from ruining this entire realm. If you're with us, come along!"

Now that the fight was actually in front of us, something real they'd have to face in the very near future, I tasted a ripple of hesitation spreading through the crowd. A growl reverberated out of me. "If we don't stop him right away, there won't be *any* stopping him! He'll turn us all into slaves, cage our minds. All the wonderful mortal things will be gone. But there are a lot of us, and only one of him.

And our sorcerer is going to help us stand up to him. We can do this."

Many beings were already moving toward my three companions, who merged with the shadows as well. Rollick led the charge, continuing to beckon everyone as he headed toward the nearest rift that we could use to take a shortcut across the country. Crag and Torrent fell back near me, herding the more reluctant beings along with the crowd like shepherds.

"We could use all of your help," Crag boomed through the sporadic shadows. "But if you aren't willing to fight, we won't force you to come. *He's* the one who treats beings that way. We need everyone who's with us to be committed to stopping him. There's no shame in being scared."

I suspected the gargoyle thought there was plenty of shame in it, especially when it came to his own emotions. But his words seemed to rouse the slower beings, as if prodding them to action. They didn't want to be seen hanging back, cringing in fear, while their companions raced off to risk their lives defending everyone else. A hint of a smile touched my lips.

We ran on, darting through the narrow shadows in the cracked earth and leaping across stretches of sunlight when we needed to. The mass of beings condensed until we were all surging forward together like one creature.

I felt the vibration of the rift up ahead. Rollick was still leading us, a powerful presence at the front of the pack. He hurtled all the way to the patch of earth just below the rift, which hung several feet above the ground, invisible to mortal eyes.

"Keep following me," he hollered when the whole

crowd was close enough to hear him. "I'll find the route that'll take us to California—but not so close that we should be within range of the leviathan's sorcery. If you lose track of the rest of us, try to get yourselves to a spot northeast of Los Angeles and look for us nearby."

He spun around and sprang up into the rift. We leapt after him in a flood, rushing through into the dull but familiar gloom of the shadow realm, tracing his presence as he hustled past other rift openings, ignoring the beings who stopped to stare at the mass of us charging by. There was no time left to do any more recruiting—and anyway, beings who liked to hang out on this side of the boundary between the realms probably didn't care that much about what happened on the mortal side anyway.

When Rollick paused at a rift up ahead, my spirits lifted. The force of his nod carried through the gloom. He waited a moment for the beings around us to register the spot he'd marked, and then he jumped through it with the forerunners of our army right at his heels.

We burst out into much less pleasant conditions than we'd had back at his house. Storm clouds smothered the sky and spat fat raindrops down on us. Thunder rumbled in the distance. When I pulled myself out of the shadows into physical form, the grass squished beneath my feet. I wrinkled my nose, swiping my wet hair back from my forehead.

The demon clapped his hands together, somehow looking perfectly composed even with rain dripping off his own hair and soaking into his suit. "We've still got a trek ahead of us, but we need to be wary from here forward. My friends and I will take the lead. We've gotten the sorcerer's commands to deflect the worst of the leviathan's magic. The rest of you should keep at least half a mile of distance from us. If we sense that he's trying to send out more manipulative magic, we'll signal all of you, and you'll need to back away as quickly as you can. Through another rift if need be. But we're hoping that he's focused on conserving his energy for now."

So that he could use all his sorcery to compel the Highest into this world. My fangs itched in my gums at the thought. Those hulking brutes in the depths of the shadows had bashed around Torrent for nothing other than trying to warn them. I didn't want them in *this* world for any reason, even if they'd been coming of their own accord.

I hurried over to join Rollick alongside Crag and Torrent. We melded back into the darkness, which there was a lot more of here, to begin the final stage of our journey.

I scanned the damp, dreary landscape, finding that none of it looked particularly familiar. "What about the weapons you had the humans making? To throw the metal blades at the leviathan. Will we be able to use those?"

"We should," Rollick said. "But we have to be even more careful with the timing when it comes to them." He sighed, an uneasy sound that he'd been careful not to make when the rest of our allies were closer by. "I don't think it's even the leviathan we need to worry about the most for now—at least, not what he'll do from here on. It's what he's already done. I'm sure he'll have gathered all the minions he could call on to guard the site of his grand display."

A quiver ran through me. All those beings he'd

enslaved, many—probably most—of whom hadn't wanted this fight any more than we did. But we couldn't let them stop us from stopping him. They'd suffer even more if he went through with his plan.

"Do your mortal workers know we're coming?" Torrent asked.

"Yes. They've been building the contraptions in the warehouse that was originally meant to be the trap, so they aren't far from where we need them to end up. But I'm not calling them to cart the things into position until I'm sure we have a clear route for them. If they're attacked and cut down... none of us will be able to haul those things around."

"Quinn could," Crag pointed out. "And maybe the phoenix as well."

Rollick hummed to himself. "True, but I expect them to be busy with other equally urgent concerns. And I gather these things are heavy. I'm not sure they'd be able to move them *out* of the vehicles very quickly, just the two of them. Let's try not to get my mortal assistants slaughtered is all I'm saying."

I let out a huff. "I can agree with that."

I peered through the haze of rain. I'd expected it to pelt us harder as we approached the coastline, but if anything, it was tapering off a little. I shook my body even though the drops did no more than tickle through my essence while I was in the shadows. "The rain's letting up."

"The leviathan must have brought in the elemental spirits he had amplifying the chaos to join him by the rift instead," Torrent said grimly. "He thinks their energy, like his, would be better spent on making sure he can carry out his plan."

I decided to look on the bright side. "At least it'll be easier to see!"

Rollick chuckled. "Yes, that is a minor benefit."

I kept my senses on the alert for any hint of sorcerer energy. Quinn had given the four of us quick but careful commands before she'd climbed into the RV—to resist the leviathan and refuse his commands. That magic was already humming through my head, ready to deflect any attempts the fiend made to conquer our thoughts. But it was looking increasingly certain that he meant to aim whatever magic he had left in just one direction.

What if he still couldn't summon the Highest at all? Would he go looking for more sorcerers to devour?

I guessed it didn't matter. Whether he could have accomplished his goal today or not, we meant to destroy him before any of us had to find out.

The landscape became more uneven, rising into the low rolling hills I remembered around the coast where we'd seen the leviathan and the behemoth working on their rift. How many beings was he eviscerating in his final attempt to open it as wide as possible? How wide would it *need* to become?

I had no idea what the Highest's physical forms might look like, or how big they might be. I wasn't sure they'd ever taken on a true physical shape before. I'd never even gotten near them in their shadowkind form, but I'd passed close enough to the deep place where they lived to know their presence stretched far and felt uncomfortably heavy.

Rollick slowed and then stopped. The rain had eased off to a mere drizzle, but the clouds overhead still shut out all but a faint glow of sunlight. He pointed to a road that wound between the hill we stood at the base of and the one farther north. "Quinn and the phoenix's people should come along this route. Keep a close watch for any patrolling minions."

I stretched my long body, tension twined through my limbs. "Should we start harassing the leviathan now? We don't know how soon he might be ready to call on the Highest."

"If we send our allies in now, they won't have the benefit of Quinn's sorcery strengthening them," Crag pointed out.

"We'll wait as long as we can," Rollick said definitively. "Better to hit them as hard as possible all at once than to get into an extended battle that'll wear us down. You wait here and rally the troops as much as you can. Destroy any of the leviathan's lackeys that come near. And flag down the RV when you see it. I'm going to venture a little closer to see how much progress he appears to have made."

"On your own?" Torrent asked quietly.

Rollick raised a haughty eyebrow. "I've never needed a babysitter. I'm the one with the easy task." Then he raced off into the shadows stretched across the hill.

As we'd talked, the beings who'd followed us this far had amassed a short distance away, waiting for a signal one way or another. Rollick hadn't told them what to do if we stopped moving. Crag and Torrent motioned for them to join us.

Voices carried from the restless crowd. "What now?"

"Is he already calling the Highest through?"

"Should we attack?"

"Rollick has gone ahead to get a read on the situation," Torrent told them all. "We'll wait here for the sorcerer and our other allies who were traveling by road. Quinn will be able to enhance your powers so you're even better equipped to take on our enemies."

I was surprised by the uneasy murmur that spread through the swarm of beings. They'd seen what Quinn's help could accomplish, how it could make us stronger instead of restraining us. Why would they hesitate?

The answer came to me without needing to think. Because it was sorcery. It was the stuff meant to twist our wills and overcome our minds. *I'd* balked the first time Quinn had been going to use her magic on me as a shield, and I'd been the one to suggest the idea.

But since then, I'd fed her my own essence to increase her powers. And while I'd wondered if I was betraying my kind at the time, I found that I didn't have a single doubt left in me.

Quinn was good. What we were doing here was good. Somehow we'd worked together to transform something evil into something amazing.

I'd helped make that transformation happen—by thinking of the possibilities, by trusting Quinn enough to let her try.

Not that long ago, I'd have said the best thing a being could do to a sorcerer was cut them down. But changing their magic into something that fueled our own powers rather than binding them was even better.

I could show every being here how true that was. I could lead them just like Rollick had led them here.

I scrambled partway up the hill and turned to face them

again. "She'll be here soon. And as soon as she is, I'm going to be the first to accept her magic. It's going to make me faster and stronger and the flames in my breath burn hotter. She isn't just *a* sorcerer. She's *our* sorcerer. She's more ours than that beast of a sea serpent ever will be."

Not everyone in the crowd had been hesitant. A chorus of approving shouts rose up—the beings who'd been freed when Quinn had killed the behemoth, the ones who'd already experienced how her magic could protect and empower them. I even spotted Goldie, who'd hung back with obvious discomfort among the others after his arrival at the house, pumping a fist in the air.

With that rush of whoops, more voices rose with increasing eagerness. "All hail our sorcerer!"

A grin stretched across my face, but my heart sank a little as I looked down the road. There was no sign of the RV yet.

Our sorcerer might be beloved, but she still needed to make it to us in time.

CHAPTER TWENTY-SIX

Quinn

The Everymobile didn't feel as if it was moving faster than a regular car. The engine's thrum sounded strangely soft within the steel walls, and the floor only swayed a little with bumps and turns of the road. But when I eased back the curtain to peek out through one of the windows, the blur of the passing landscape made my mind whirl and my stomach flip over.

As I yanked the curtain shut, Sorsha came up beside me. "I find it's best not to look out there when we've got the special boost going," she said with a wry smile. "Unless you enjoy car sickness."

"Ah, that would be a no." I flopped down in the C-shaped seat around the RV's table and willed my queasiness down. "How much longer do you think it's going to take to get to the coast?"

"We're pulling out every possible trick we can. I don't know how long we can keep this speed up for, but if the Everymobile holds together, we're on track to arrive in the area your demon friend indicated in a little more than an hour."

My mouth pulled into a grimace that wasn't only because of my lingering nausea. "It'd be a lot easier if I could travel through rifts."

Or if my shadowkind allies had left me behind in Texas, I thought but didn't say. But maybe I didn't need to express that doubt out loud for my current companions to pick up on it. Ruse appeared in the short hall between the living-dining-kitchen area and the driver's cab where Omen was at the wheel. The incubus cocked his head at me.

"We all have our flaws. Our phoenix still isn't great at navigating the shadow realm herself."

"The fact that the rulers of that realm spent most of my life trying to *kill* me doesn't exactly bolster my motivation," Sorsha muttered.

Ruse shot her an amused glance before turning to me again. "It's good that you'll be out there with the rest of us. And not just because of the benefits you can obviously offer to us shadowkind going into battle. You've given those beings a heroic leader to focus on. Shadowkind aren't great at working together. I think we need a focal point even more than mortals do."

"Yeah." And I knew that the increased strength I could offer our allies with my sorcery might make the difference between stopping the leviathan and not. It was just that with every passing minute we were on the road while I knew the others had to be gathered and waiting for us, my gut clenched tighter.

Sorsha dropped into the seat kitty-corner from me. "We can do this. It doesn't matter how powerful that asshole is —there's just one of him and tons of us. The fight will determine how many lives continue or end in the process of stopping him, and I don't think there's any way every being with us will make it through alive, but we *will* stop him. I promise you that."

Her confidence eased my nerves just a little. I nodded. "Good." There wasn't any point in mentioning that I was pretty sure *my* life was forfeit no matter what else happened.

Maybe that was the other reason for the heaviness in my gut. Sorsha and her guys were perfectly fine company, but I wished I was spending my last hours with the men I loved. I didn't know how much I'd even get to see them or talk to them once we leapt into the fray. The brief embraces we'd exchanged before I'd hurried onto the RV might be our last. My emotional connection to them only seemed to work when they were nearby—I couldn't sense anything at all from them now.

A lump rose in my throat. It didn't matter. I couldn't let it matter. I'd gotten a lot out of our short time together. If all this craziness hadn't happened, I'd never have gotten to have them in my life at all. I couldn't lament the events that had brought us together, as horrible as those events might be.

The alarm on my phone went off. I startled, almost having forgotten that constant reminder of my mortality. Sorsha didn't comment as I popped my pills, including the new one from Rollick's doctor that didn't appear to be doing a whole lot to stave off my heart's impending failure.

Okay, that might not be fair. For all I knew, I'd already be dead without the new medication.

But Sorsha and her friends were aware of my transplant. They knew it was the reason for my powers. I set my hand against my chest, feeling the shudder of energy rippling from behind my sternum all through my limbs and up across my scalp like a static charge. It was hard to imagine that it was completely contained in that one organ now.

"I don't know if my magic will work on you," I said to Sorsha. "Because you're part human. The things that work against shadowkind don't normally affect you, right?"

"They don't," she agreed. "And shadowkind powers that work against humans often do affect me if I'm not taking steps to protect myself. But in this case, that works in our favor, because the leviathan isn't out to brainwash mortals. We'll see how he likes a boiling bath."

Her smile turned sharp. I guessed a phoenix with enough power to burn down two realms didn't need any sorcery to amp up her strength.

Snap slipped into view, peering at me curiously. "Do you want anything to eat? We didn't have time to pick up much before we left, but we always have fresh fruit."

Sorsha grinned. "Because this one is a fructose addict."

I raised my eyebrows at the golden-curled man because the question sounded so like one I'd been getting repeatedly from my own men. "Is this typical hospitality or did someone tell you to keep me fed?"

He dipped his head, abashed. "The rocky one said I should make sure you keep up your own strength."

Well, that was totally on brand for Crag. And he wasn't even wrong. My stomach gurgled right then as if to join their conspiracy.

"I probably *should* eat something," I said in resignation. "Thank you."

I picked from the broad assortment of fruits Snap brought out and also accepted a yogurt cup he exclaimed over when he found it in the fridge, still a few days shy of its best before date. By the time I'd eaten as much as I could handle in my anxious state, I got the sense that the motions around us, dampened as they were, had started to slow. I perked up, glancing toward the front of the RV. "Are we getting close?"

"Almost there," the hellhound shifter called back in his curt voice. "Don't get too excited yet. I still need to figure out—oh, wait, there they are. Of course."

There was a faint lurch as the RV veered to the side. I gripped the edge of the seat cushion. It seemed like only seconds before we were jerking to a halt. My pulse stuttered, and I propelled myself toward the door automatically.

Sorsha stepped ahead of me with the athletic swiftness she could bring out in an instant that transformed her into something a little more than human. She poked her head out the door, peered around, and then bounded out with a motion for the rest of us to follow her.

When I stepped onto the shoulder of the road to find all four of my men waiting for us, a deeper relief than I'd ever felt before swept through me. Quivers of the same happiness reached me from each of them. I couldn't stop the smile that was stretching across my face, even though it probably looked manic, even though we were about to enter a battle to the death.

We'd made it this far. We were in it together.

"The leviathan is at the rift," Rollick said without preamble, grabbing my hand to give it a quick squeeze of welcome. "Carving up dozens of beings by the hour. The rift has grown noticeably just since we've arrived. But he hasn't cast any more sorcery since then, and his minions are clustered pretty tightly around him."

I dragged in a breath. "That's all what we were hoping for. So we follow Plan A. Divert the minions, make sure the path is clear for our souped-up crossbows to get in place, and harass the leviathan enough that he can't summon the Highest while keeping him in about the same place for when the weapons are ready."

I raised my voice, ignoring my tremor of nerves at the thought of the responsibility I was taking on by acting as the leader of this group. Ruse had said the shadowkind might need a figurehead to look to even more than mortals did, and humans liked their figureheads a lot.

I could be that for this group. I was going to need to speak to all of them anyway.

"Come to me in the order we discussed yesterday," I said to the crowd I had to imagine waiting in the shadows beyond my mortal vision. "As soon as I've given you your command, get started with your part of the plan. We have to move quickly. We don't know how close the leviathan is to taking his final steps."

Lance sprang in front of me as the last words passed from my lips, shifting into dragon form as he did. *That* wasn't totally according to plan. We'd discussed starting with Rollick and Omen, since they were the most ancient of the shadowkind on our side. But Lance would have come soon after, and something about his haste and the way he dipped his gleaming reptilian head to me told me that he was making some kind of point, something he felt was important.

My sorcerer energy crackled at the base of my throat. I urged it into my words. "When you attack the leviathan or his allies, let them feel your speed and strength and the heat of your dragon fire."

Lance flashed a dragonish grin at me and leapt away. He showed no sign of discomfort, but my stomach twisted anyway. We'd agreed on the "When" part of the command to allow room to maneuver if, for example, it wasn't a great idea for any particular being to be attacking at some specific moment. If I'd just told them outright to attack, I wasn't sure if they'd be able to do anything else. But I still didn't totally understand how the magic worked. I didn't want to inadvertently cause more of the lives around me to be lost.

We'd been as careful as we could, and it was too late to re-think the plan. Rollick stepped forward next, stretching into his full demonic form. He held my gaze with total trust in his darkened eyes, and the anxiety inside me loosened a little. Another sizzling sentence traveled over my tongue. "When you're attacking the leviathan or his allies, let them feel all the demonic force you can aim at them."

He inclined his horned head, and then he was vanishing into the shadows. Omen was already stepping forward to take his place. I squared my shoulders, willing more magic into my mouth to give a similar order.

I drew up more and more energy, giving command after

command with sparks of electricity dancing through my nerves. The beings were soon flickering in and out of view in front of me so swiftly I barely had time to think between each jolt of sorcery. But I'd prepared well. On sight, I knew which of our allies was meant for which part of the plan and what powers I was supposed to enhance in them.

Even as my voice grew hoarse, a sense of exhilaration spread through me that came from more than just my magic. There *were* a lot of us. We were powerful in ways most of the leviathan's lackeys couldn't be when he was ordering them to fight a battle they didn't want to be in. We had our weapons; we had a human-shadowkind hybrid on our side.

Maybe we really could win this.

Suddenly there were no more beings to cast my sorcery on standing in front of me. My head was spinning, exhaustion and excitement mingling. Sorsha grasped my shoulders from behind with gentle fingers. "Let's get you in position now."

I lifted my arms slightly so she could lower her hands to grip my waist. Then, with a strength that was shocking even after everything I'd already witnessed from her, she lifted me with her into the air. Wafts of heat washed over me from the blazing wings that flapped at the edges of my vision.

I'd seen them before, but only very briefly and before I'd known anything else about her. They'd almost seemed to be a trick of the light. There was no denying their existence now.

"You really are a phoenix," I said inanely.

Sorsha laughed. "So they tell me."

We flew over a few low hills. The sounds of the battle

reached me before I could see it, penetrating the warbling woosh of Sorsha's flaming wings. Grunts, snarls, and cries of pain carried through the air. I willed my body to stay as relaxed as possible, knowing that tensing up would make me more difficult cargo.

Sorsha landed on the crest of a hill right over the coastline—the hill where Rollick's human accomplices were meant to set up the oversized crossbows—and I stared down over the mix of grass and rocky terrain below leading to the frothing ocean waters. In the dwindling daylight, smoky essence gushed from hundreds of forms, some of them still moving, others lying crumpled. I couldn't tell how many were from our side and how many the leviathan's.

The leviathan himself had been forced into physical form. The giant sea serpent, as tall as a low-rise apartment building, thrashed and roared as smaller shadowkind lashed out at him from multiple sides. They were doing exactly what we'd planned, keeping him too occupied to carry out his own plan but not letting him stray from this spot.

As we touched down, a ring of guards wavered into being around me. Sorsha wiped her hands together with an air of a job well-done and gave me a jaunty salute. "Off to see about boiling a snake," she said, and launched herself back into the air.

I had the urge to sit down on the grass now that I wasn't needed for at least a little while, but I had the sense that position would be undignified. Figureheads could stand on their own two feet, right? Even if those feet were attached to increasingly wobbly legs. Even if both a fever and a chill seemed to be trickling through that figurehead's veins.

But maybe I wouldn't have to extend myself any farther. Even though the minions must have spotted our arrival—the blazing wings were a pretty clear giveaway—none even made it far enough up the hill to challenge my ring of guards. Flickers of emotion reached me from my men, but they were all determination and fury, no fear or pain so far.

I couldn't see any fighting near the road that was the key to our plan. And as I looked along it, headlights gleamed in the distance through the dusk.

The trucks transporting our weaponry. They were on their way—they'd be here in a matter of minutes.

A smile that was outright joyful crossed my lips. We were so close. Somehow, everything had worked out the way we'd imagined it. Now all we had to do was—

A surge of thicker darkness barreled toward the approaching trucks so abruptly I barely had time to yelp in warning before the vehicle in the lead swayed on its wheels with the impact—and tipped onto its side with a thunderous crash. The other trucks screeched to a halt. Bodies whipped back and forth across the road: a mass of attackers we hadn't been prepared for racing into the fray and my allies charging to meet them.

Another shadowy surge hurtled toward the leviathan—but not to assault him. The minions who'd either been told to hang back in reserve or who'd only just arrived flung themselves at the beings who'd been harassing their master.

I caught the flash of Lance's scales as he snapped and slashed at them with a flare of hotter rage. Sorsha soared around the turbulent ocean shadows, sending a being here and there up in bursts of flame—but she had to be careful not to light up our own people, who didn't look particularly different from the leviathan's slaves. My knees locked as I watched the struggle in horror, torn between the urge to tell my guards to race down there to help and the fear of what might happen to me without their protection.

Before I could decide on the best course of action, the leviathan shook off the majority of his attackers and reared up even higher toward the spot where the rift must be. Either he'd already been ready to take the final step, or he figured he might not get another chance.

His monstrous voice tore through the night, a feral bellow that reverberated right into my bones. Syllables somehow foreign and familiar at the same time shook every cell in my body. He roared his sorcerous command again, its meaning smacking me in the face with the force of it.

Come to me. Come to the other realm.

Then he plunged his enormous snake-like head right into the rift.

CHAPTER TWENTY-SEVEN

Quinn

The top of the hillside trembled beneath my feet. I gaped at the leviathan's immense serpentine form, looking deceptively headless with the wavering darkness I knew was the rift around its neck.

I couldn't hear its bellowed commands anymore, but somehow my nerves still vibrated with them, as if he were putting so much energy into them that the air leaving his lungs was setting off tremors through the atmosphere. It wasn't hard to imagine that his call might be felt all across the shadow realm. All the way to its intended targets in the deepest depths.

My skin turned to ice for reasons that had nothing to do with my physical health.

We had to stop him. We had to turn the tide back in our favor before we had even bigger monsters to grapple with.

If we could kill him—if we could take our shots while he was totally immersed in his scheme—that would solve everything. Any sorcery he'd cast would die with him. This could all be over.

But the battle was still raging around the vehicles that'd been carrying our weapons. With the lead truck toppled and shadowkind rampaging all around the road, there was no way for them to reach this hill where they'd have a clear trajectory. No way for Rollick's people inside to try to shoot the leviathan even from where they'd stalled without being savaged.

As I watched the skirmishes going on all across the terrain below the hill, bracing myself without any idea what action I'd need to take, it became increasingly, nauseatingly clear that we weren't winning quickly. We might not be winning at all. Beings whirled around each other, more essence plumed into the air, but the leviathan's horde of minions had managed to surround and divide us. It was too vast for my allies to overcome in a few decisive strikes, no matter how much my magic had ramped up their abilities.

My magic.

The answer came to me like a punch square in the chest, unmistakable and painful. There were two ways the leviathan's minions could be stopped: through killing, which wasn't working out at the moment, and through shattering the hold on them with someone else's sorcery.

And the only sorcerer anywhere nearby was me.

For a second, my legs locked and my breath caught in my lungs. There were *so* many of them—thousands, swarming all across the landscape around me. Undoubtedly there were more in the shadows where I couldn't see them. How the hell could I reach all of them?

I didn't need to snap every single one of them out of their magical compulsions, I reminded myself. Just enough of them that the beings on my side could get the upper hand. If I didn't try, if I didn't do it fast, I'd never get the chance at all.

I closed my eyes, still seeing the carnage below playing out in the back of my mind, and yanked all the fizzing electric energy inside me into my voice.

The magic blazed through me, its searing crackle drowning out everything beyond my body. A yell so loud it scraped my throat raw burst from my mouth. Words I didn't recognize blared from my lips through the dusk. But I knew exactly what I was saying. *Don't fight for the leviathan. Shake off his control. Go free.*

Here and there, all across the battlefield, the breaking of the leviathan's spell reverberated into me with little pops like cans shot by a BB gun. They rattled through my awareness so swiftly I couldn't count them, but there had to be dozens.

It was working. The leviathan mustn't have shored up his hold on his minions in a while as he'd stockpiled his energy for his larger goal. I was shattering his magic with my own.

My heart lurched with the power resounding through my body. My chest clenched up. But I shouted again and again, hurling the energy in me as far as I could, even as my legs gave and I sank to my knees.

My head was spinning. I coughed and bent forward, my fingers digging into the grass. There was no exhilaration in my sorcery now. My entire torso was on fire. A shiver passed through me as I struggled to catch my breath.

A loud, creaky thump jolted through my awareness with enough force that I managed to raise my head. My eyes widened.

The area along the road was clear again other than the scattered, smoking bodies of fallen shadowkind. A bunch of the beings who were still moving had just heaved the first truck back onto its wheels.

Its windshield was spiderwebbed with cracks, but either the driver had survived the crash without much injury or one of the other human workers had hurried forward to take his place. The engine sputtered and settled into a low rumble. Then the truck pulled forward with a slight hitch. The others growled to life behind it.

They were coming again. I'd managed to free enough of the leviathan's minions to turn the tide like I'd hoped.

I swiveled my head, staring blearily across the darkened landscape while the turmoil inside my body radiated through every cell. The fighting had mostly moved to the rocky terrain right along the coast, near where the leviathan's eerily immense form was still poised with his head immersed in the rift. Flares of fire glinted here and there as Sorsha, Omen, Lance, and whatever other beings could bring flames to bear let loose their heat.

Had we really done it? I couldn't quite summon much sense of triumph through my dizziness, but my lips managed to form a small smile.

I sat back on my butt. I could tell that my legs still wouldn't hold me up, if they ever would again. The throbbing in my chest hadn't let up at all—my breaths were strained, as if I were trying to suck in air through the tiniest crack in my throat. But none of that mattered if we saw this moment through to the end.

The trucks roared onto the hill behind me. Shouts rang through the spaces between them as the workers hustled to drag out their cargo. I turned my head to see them setting up the half a dozen bulky contraptions, which looked like something half cannon, half crossbow, along the crest of the hill on either side of me.

One of Rollick's people paused, looking at me, but I waved him off with a feeble gesture. "We've got to shoot that monster," I croaked, tilting toward the leviathan. "As soon as you can, as much ammo as you can."

He nodded and dashed back to the truck. I wondered vaguely what story Rollick had given these people to explain the crazy task he'd assigned them with now. They clearly understood the urgency. I guessed after everything they must have seen tonight—and in L.A. for several days before—their acceptance wasn't totally surprising.

They loaded the weapons with blades like sharpened shards of a vast metal frisbee. Like the blades that had been loaded in the walls of the factory where we'd killed the behemoth. Maybe they'd even repurposed the exact same ones, just altered a little so they'd fly through the air properly when launched.

Those killing edges had brought down the behemoth. These ones *had* to work on the leviathan too.

If they didn't, we were simply doomed.

The last blade had just clanged into place when one of the workers let out a yell that sounded more like a warning than a call to action. I jerked my attention in the direction he was staring.

The leviathan was moving again. His serpentine body shook off the beings that'd gone back to harassing him, and his head was pulling free from the rift.

Panic shot through me. Did that mean he was finished? That the Highest were on their way?

I gritted my teeth against a fresh wallop of pain and forced more words from my throat. "Shoot him! Now! Keep reloading until you've hit him with everything."

Before I'd even finished speaking, the workers were springing into action. All across the line of weapons, Rollick's people yanked the firing levers.

The blades released with a series of twangs. They whirled through the air, catching the faint beams of moonlight that penetrated the thinning clouds, and slammed into the leviathan's body one after the other, each a little higher than the last.

The monster's body flinched harder with each impact. He pulled his head completely free of the rift to let out an earth-shaking snarl full of pain and fury. The clouds of essence that poured up from the wounds were so thick I could see them even against the dusk.

The beings around him fell back except for Sorsha with her flaming wings. She whipped herself toward the blades, kicking them deeper into the leviathan's flesh. The metals in our projectiles would prevent most of the other shadowkind from getting close enough to attack. But now that we were launching them, the blades were enough.

Rollick's people scrambled to reload the weapons. They

fired again, marking a path up the serpent's undulating body almost all the way to its jaw.

The leviathan twisted and shuddered, dodging a couple of the blades, including one that would have struck it in the skull. We could only hit it from the one side, and I didn't know how deeply the metals were digging in even with Sorsha's assistance.

But it was faltering. With the next barrage, it only avoided one. Its body sagged, slowly crumpling over toward the sea. Smoke gushed upward from its huge carcass like it was the burning wreckage of a vast ship.

The men at the weapons stepped back. They still had a few blades left, but they couldn't aim properly while the monster was slumped over in the water instead of stretched upright. It didn't seem to matter anyway. The leviathan was barely even thrashing now, just twitching here and there without finding the strength to get up. Those wounds couldn't heal while the metal was embedded in him.

We'd done it.

I almost gave in to the relief of that thought and slumped over myself. The soft grass called out to me. But as I tipped forward, leaning my weight onto my arms, a quaver of energy surged across the hillside, dissonant enough to set my teeth on edge and make every hair on my body stand on end.

I yanked my gaze upward. A gasp snagged in my throat.

Something was coming through the rift. Something huge and bulbous, like the head of a whale with an eye that must have been larger than my entire body. That eye blazed blood red, rolling beneath its heavy lid.

It was *wrong*. That was the only way I could describe it.

Shivers wracked my body just looking at it. The air around it vibrated; an off-key pealing sound split the air.

The ocean hollowed out beneath the leviathan's still spasming body. The water twisted and churned. Rocks along the shoreline cracked open or outright disintegrated, pebbles blasting across the ground. My skin felt as if it were about to crawl right off my body.

That—that thing had to be one of the Highest. The leviathan had called them through after all... and he wasn't gone yet. He wasn't totally dead, which meant his magic was holding on, and the immense being whose very presence was unraveling the fabric of my world was pushing even farther out.

I thought I saw lips pulled into a grimace on that gigantic head. The blazing eye kept flicking this way and that. Along with the bone-deep wrongness, my strongest impression was that it didn't want to be here at all—but it couldn't pull itself back.

Would it be able to retreat now that it'd started passing through even *if* the leviathan finally died, or would the momentum be too much? How much damage was it going to do even before we could answer that question?

The grass beneath my fingers was crinkling, suddenly parched dry. A cloud overhead burst apart with a boom of thunder and a shower of lightning bolts. The beast in the rift groaned, and a crack opened up right through the shoreline into the ocean floor.

Terror and pain screamed together all through my body. I could barely feel my limbs. But my eyes fell on the leviathan's smoking body, and one tiny thought penetrated my stupor like a needle threading the last inspiration I might ever get through my mind.

The leviathan had the power to call that horrifying thing through... and his power was now up for the taking.

I shoved myself down the side of the hill. My limbs flailed like they were made of jelly; every choked breath burned in my chest. I dug my fingers into the grass and heaved out with my knees, propelling myself forward with every bit of strength I had in me.

Dark wings flapped overhead. Crag grasped my shoulders. "Where are you going, Softness?" he asked in a low, pained rumble that I barely heard through the rising thrum of wrongness.

"Get me to the leviathan," I rasped out. "Please."

I didn't think he wanted to follow that order, and I hadn't put any sorcery into it, but the gargoyle granted my final request. With a growl, he lifted me into the air and carried me over the shattering rocks to the monster's crumpled body.

I flung myself out of Crag's arms down on the nearest wound. As I opened my mouth, the fiend's essence rushed up my throat, nearly suffocating me. Stiffening my body, I gulped and gulped, no matter how the noxious smoke seared at my insides, no matter how tightly the vise around my heart clamped.

The leviathan's essence prickled through every nerve in my body. My pulse stuttered and faltered. It was too much, like I was trying to drink down the entire ocean, more than any one body was meant to hold.

But I needed it. I needed to hang on just long enough to—to—

There was no room left in my head even for thoughts now. Just drink, drink, drink.

When I couldn't stand to suck in one more puff of essence, I flipped over onto my back and stared up at the rift. My mind was whirling like the whipped-up clouds overhead. The huge, unnatural presence above me felt as if it were about to tumble down onto me and squash me flat.

I opened my mouth and let out the sorcery I'd swallowed, all of it, on top of the talent I'd already possessed, pleading to whatever other powers might exist to let it be enough.

"*Go home!*" I screamed in the language of the magic. "*Go back through the rift. Get away from here!*"

Agony cut through the center of my chest. My heart seemed to split in two. My vision hazed with growing blotches of black. But I felt my magic smash the leviathan's last lingering spell with a cracking sensation that rebounded into my body.

The Highest being groaned again, but there might have been relief in it this time. As my pulse dwindled to nothing and the pain spread through every inch of my frame, it jerked back into the rift. The last thing I saw before my vision blanked completely was its bulbous head slipping out of sight.

The catastrophe was done... and so was I. I had the sense of a tear tricking down my cheek, but a strange contentment swept over me before my awareness blinked out.

CHAPTER TWENTY-EIGHT

Quinn

Something was beeping. In kind of an annoying way too. If there was an afterlife, surely I'd earned a spot someplace that didn't come with irritatingly repetitive noises?

And if there wasn't an afterlife, why the hell was I hearing anything at all?

My eyelids fluttered. My body twitched on the firm padding it was lying on, and a thin fabric surface shifted with it. An ache woke up in my chest, but weirdly distant and fuzzy, as if the parts of my body were scattered around me instead of all attached in one piece.

I registered groggily that I'd felt this way before. The bright lights, planes of white around me—

A deeper sense of recognition jolted my eyes all the way open. I blinked, staring at the hospital room I'd somehow ended up in. The ache sharpened and eased, intensifying and retreating with every thump of my heart.

Of my heart?

As I stared down at myself, at the hospital gown cloaking me, a nurse hustled into the room. "You look like you're doing well," she said in a soothing voice. "Everything's on track. Your immune system has responded well so far. It's a long process fully adjusting, but of course you're an old hat at this—you know how it goes."

She flashed me a smile, but I was too distracted by taking in the fresh stitches marking my chest to return it. Fresh stitches sealing a fresh incision, right over the area where my last surgery scar had been.

How could— It didn't make sense. Was I dreaming? I blinked hard as if that might wake me up if I was, but all that happened was my head spun a little before my thoughts settled down again.

The nurse said something else that I missed completely. Then she bustled out of the room. The second the door clicked shut behind her, four monstrous men wavered into being out of the shadows, surrounding the bed.

I gaped at all of them, but I had enough of my wits to quickly check them over for any new damage. I thought Crag had a few more scars marking his face and arms than he'd sported before, and Lance had a new one cutting across the golden skin at the crook of his shoulder, but otherwise they weren't noticeably worse for the battle we'd somehow all survived. They smiled down at me in their own ways.

"What—" I croaked, and swallowed hard. "How—"

Rollick chuckled softly and brushed his fingertips over my hair as if he were afraid to touch me too firmly right now. "I have enough resources at my disposal to get giant crossbow-cannons manufactured with a few days' notice. Did you really think I couldn't find you a new heart?"

"But I—" My gaze shot directly to him, focusing on his face. "Where did it come from?"

He held up his hands. "I took a perfectly legitimate route. I wouldn't go against your sense of morality, even if it doesn't totally align with my own. I simply saw to it that you were bumped to the front of the list."

A strange emotion swelled inside me, so bittersweet it brought tears to my eyes. "That's cheating," I mumbled. "I stole someone else's spot, and—"

"Stop right there," Torrent said in his best no-nonsense tone, folding his arms over his chest. "If things had been the way they were supposed to be, you'd have had months if not years of warning to work your way up the list in priority. There's nothing *fair* about anything you've been through in the past couple of months."

"And I bet none of the other people on that list just defended the entire world from destruction," Lance pointed out with a broader grin.

Crag let out a rumble of agreement. "You can't save billions of lives and tell us we're not allowed to save yours," he informed me gruffly.

I sank back into the hospital bed. Maybe they kind of had a point. Maybe I didn't need to feel guilty. Maybe... maybe I actually deserved a second chance at this whole transplanted heart thing, without a legacy of toxic magic attached to it.

I glanced at Rollick again. "I hope you made sure this one doesn't come with a supernatural bonus."

He outright laughed. "No more sorcery for you. Such a shame when for a few minutes there, I'd imagine you were by far the most powerful sorcerer the universe has ever known."

I made a face and closed my eyes. "Not a title I had any interest in claiming."

Rollick hummed to himself. "There are a couple of people here I think you might want to see. Your parents are in the waiting room. I can have the doctor let them in if you're ready for other visitors."

My spirits leapt, and my eyes popped open again. "They're out of the bunker? Of course they're out of the bunker. Everything really is okay?"

Lance beamed at me. "No more storms, no more waves. No more tricksy ancient beings enslaving the rest of us."

Torrent's smile turned crooked. "The Highest were so offended by the assault on their autonomy that they collapsed that particular rift completely. So, as far as I know, there isn't even a portal left that's large enough to fit them if someone decided to give it another shot."

"Good," I said, a renewed wave of relief washing through me. I paused, studying each of them in turn. The familiar faces that didn't look at all monstrous to me now stirred up a pang of affection not even the aches of the transplant could overwhelm. "What happens after this?"

Rollick shrugged. "We assumed you'd go back to your regular life, your college courses and the rest. Unless you had some other plans."

"No. That's good. I just mean—what about you? What about *us*?"

I didn't need their protection anymore. They didn't

need the special powers that had emanated from my chest. Neither of those facts made a difference to me, but these men didn't think or feel like regular humans did. I couldn't take anything for granted.

But Crag was leaning down to press a gentle kiss to my temple. "We'll be with you as long and as much as you want us there, Softness."

"Nowhere I'd rather be, baby girl," Lance declared.

Even Torrent's expression brightened. "If we can make it work when we're being chased by murderous fiends, I think we can handle a peaceful regular life just fine."

"Unless you've had your fill of us," Rollick said in a teasing tone.

"No," I said with total determination. "Not at all." Not ever, I suspected. And now... now I might have decades more with them.

I didn't want to have to totally hide that fact. I paused. "I would like to see my parents. But... I'd like you all to be here while I talk to them too. Where they can see you. They should know that you're sticking around."

The demon nodded. He vanished for a moment, and my stomach twisted at the thought of how Mom and Dad might react. They'd been stunned and horrified by the realization that monsters existed at all. How were they going to accept four of those monsters as a permanent presence in my life?

Well, they'd just... have to, one way or another. I wasn't hiding who I was or what mattered from them again. It wasn't my job to act as a human shield, to protect people from *myself*. If I deserved anything, it was to set that one worry aside after all the protecting I'd already accomplished.

Rollick reappeared in the same spot as before. The other men flickered out of view when the doctor opened the door to motion my parents in. As soon as Mom and Dad were inside and the door had closed, they solidified into physical form again.

Mom let out a soft yelp that she smothered with a hand to her lips. Dad flinched. But then they relaxed, presumably recognizing the men as the companions I'd introduced them to back at the bunker. Their gazes jerked back to me, and they hustled over.

"Sweetheart, I'm so glad you're okay," Mom said in a voice taut with emotion, leaning over to hug me gingerly. "The doctors say all your results look fantastic so far."

"You've always been a fighter, kiddo," Dad said, sounding pretty choked up himself, and squeezed my hand.

"I've still got a lot left to do," I said. Fatigue rolled over me, reminding me that no matter how long I'd been lying in this bed, my body had just been through more than one kind of marathon. My eyelids drifted down, but I held on to alertness long enough to add, "There won't be any more monsters around. Not like the ones that were hurting people. But these guys—they're staying with me. We're going to keep looking out for each other."

My parents lifted their gazes to the monstrous men. I couldn't say they looked overjoyed at the thought. Mom's attention lingered on Lance's claws and Torrent's supporting tentacles, and Dad's brow knit as he considered Crag's stony jaw. But Mom simply rubbed my shoulder.

Dad tightened his grip on my hand reassuringly. "They've done a good job of that so far."

Mom inclined her head. "And it's good to know you

have someone else to turn to when you need it. You should have someone other than us. No matter what kind of people—or... whatever—they are." She shot my men a smile to show she didn't mean her comment as an insult.

Rollick gave them one of his charming grins. "We're people enough in all the ways that count. And Quinn definitely has us."

"Good." Mom sounded like she meant it.

The relief I'd felt before sank right through to my bones. My eyes drifted all the way shut. Rollick teased his fingers over my hair again, and I started to drift off, content with the certainty that everyone in the room was perfectly happy to see me get my rest.

It was really over. I really *could* rest, for the first time in weeks. No more sorcerer heart. No more magic pulsing through my veins. No more murderous, psychotic fiends out to kill me.

I was a one-hundred-percent-normal human being again. But that didn't mean I wasn't changed. I knew about so many amazing things out there in our world that most mortals had never imagined could be true. And *that* magic would stay with me no matter how short or long the rest of my life might be.

CHAPTER TWENTY-NINE

Five years later

Quinn

I got out of the car on the opposite side of the street from the building and hesitated before turning to face it. I'd come out to see the construction while it was in progress several times, of course, but not since all the outer walls, one of the final steps, had been put in place. Now it was finally going to look whole. Real.

I swiveled on the sidewalk quickly, wanting to take it in all at once. Gazing up at the looming skyscraper, my breath caught in my throat.

It was somehow even more than I'd imagined when I'd first started sketching the building out years ago, not long after I'd returned to my classes. More than any of the concept drawings or blueprints or even my visits during the earlier stages of construction had prepared me for.

I'd never told anyone this, but in my mind, from the very beginning, I'd thought of it as *The Monster*. To everyone I worked with, that name would have called up negative associations. But in the building before me, I saw everything the concept had come to mean to me.

It was broad as well as tall, huge and imposing and a little twisted with ripples breaking through the upward jut of the otherwise straight edges. But the outer walls with their reflective panes were tilted at just the right angle to reflect the southern sunlight without bouncing it into a passerby's eyes. The massive structure *glowed*, like something magical that'd sprung up on this city block.

It was my ode to the types of monstrousness and magic I'd learned to appreciate. And somehow it was standing here in front of me, the first major solo design I'd ever had accepted and constructed. I'd accomplished that dream.

How many more were still ahead of me?

As a smile crossed my lips to match the swell of awe and joy inside me, a figure drew to a stop on the sidewalk a few feet away. I glanced over to see a girl who looked to be in her early teens, a wave of hair so pale it was nearly translucent curving against her cheek as she gazed up at my building from beneath the shade of her sweatshirt's hood. Her bright brown eyes had widened. Her sinewy frame was weirdly tensed, as if she were grappling between stepping closer to the structure and yanking herself away from it.

"Wow," she said in a soft voice, her fingers tightening

around the strap of her backpack. And then she shivered in a way that instantly set me on the alert.

"Are you all right?" I asked. She'd sounded appreciative when she'd spoken, so I couldn't tell whether the shiver had been provoked by the building or something else—maybe whatever had made her so tense in general.

Her eyes darted to me with a flicker of anxiety. "Yes," she blurted out. "Sorry. I just—I've got something to do."

She spun on her heel and hustled off before I could say anything else.

I watched her go, my smile dwindling. But then a gaggle of tourists halted farther down the street to exclaim over the building, and the rush of happiness came back. I glanced the way the girl had gone, but she didn't reappear.

I hadn't spent all that much time here in San Francisco. Maybe it was weird for strangers to talk to each other here, and that was why she'd hurried off. In any case, there wasn't much I could do about it.

A tickle of someone else's joy seeped into my chest. My smile returned, and I crossed the street to walk around the side of the building.

Even though my sorcerer powers had vanished when I'd lost the heart that'd granted me them in the first place, a thread of my connection to my monstrous men had remained, possibly from the traces of their essence that must have wound into my other vital organs. I could only sense the faintest hints of their strongest emotions, but sometimes that was enough to recognize their presence.

I was just coming up on the maintenance door partway down the side alley, which *should* have been locked, when it swung open to reveal Rollick's handsome face and his usual sly smirk. "Are you going to come in and check out your opus from the inside or what? The rest of your entourage is getting impatient."

I laughed and slipped inside, finding myself in a shadowy hall where the three other men who couldn't simply stroll down the street without being stared or even screamed at were waiting.

Lance tugged me to him with a pleased hum. "Is it everything you wanted it to be?"

"It's perfect," I said, returning his embrace.

"Wait until you see the view." The dragon shifter shot Crag a pointed look, and the gargoyle held out his hand to me. I stepped toward him and let him scoop me up into his arms.

"I'm doing well enough that I could manage the stairs, even this many," I had to inform him, though I didn't exactly mind being cradled by his stony strength. After the usual precarious first year, my doctors had gradually eased off monitoring my new heart. It thumped away in my chest now as if it'd always been a part of me. And hopefully, given that it hadn't come with any supernatural strings attached, it'd keep pumping for many years more.

Crag let out a gruff sound. "This is much faster. The elevators aren't running yet. No power."

"And we're not letting you play around with the electricity, Ms. Fix-It," Torrent teased in his dryly even voice from behind us.

"Fine." I patted Crag's well-muscled shoulder. "You can be my winged elevator."

He gave a rumble of a chuckle and stepped to the edge of the elevator shaft. I spotted the car down below on one of the basement levels, leaving the space above us totally empty other than the cables. With a push of his clawed feet and a flap of his wings, the gargoyle leapt up into the air.

My other men disappeared into the darkness, but I knew they were traveling with us. Crag couldn't move quite as fast as he normally might have when he was working with such a narrow space, but we soared past a few floors with every sweep of his wings. The exhilaration rushed through me, leaving me grinning.

At the top floor, Crag set me down by a ladder to a maintenance hatch that reminded me with a hitch of my pulse of my last urban exploring adventure before my life had become full of monsters. I clambered up the rungs without hesitation, shoved the hatch wide, and pulled myself up onto the rooftop of the first ever building I could take full credit for designing.

The sprawl of the city spread out before us, glinting with lights of different colors as evening started to creep over the streets. We were high enough up that I couldn't hear the thrum of the traffic passing by below. When I turned, I could make out the glinting ocean waters beyond the buildings along the coast.

"Who needs walls when you can be up here," I said with a laugh, and inhaled deeply with a gust of wind that tossed my hair back over my shoulders.

Rollick, who'd emerged from the shadows alongside the others to join me, arched his eyebrows. "Rethinking our current living arrangements, sweet mortal?"

I thought of the apartment back in Jacksonville we all shared now—as much as my shadowkind men needed a physical living space. Rollick had insisted on contributing enough funds that I could afford a corner penthouse, which had almost as amazing a view as this, the ocean in one direction and the city streets along the beach in the other.

Since none of the men needed to sleep, we could manage with a two-bedroom, the second bedroom set up in case they wanted to relax with a little privacy. Or entertain themselves while keeping out of my hair when I was working from home. Mostly, though, we'd fallen into a rhythm of living alongside each other that had quickly felt completely natural.

I could have had the place to myself whenever I wanted —I knew all I had to do was ask—but there was something comforting about knowing that just about anytime I called out, at least one of them would be in hearing distance.

"I'm always happy coming home to Jacksonville," I told the demon with a playful swat. "Which means you're also not convincing me to move to Miami anytime soon."

He grabbed my hand and pressed a kiss to my knuckles. "Then it's a good thing there are handy rifts I can jump through between the two, isn't it?"

My other three men had been content to putter around Jacksonville and the area nearby with occasional daytrips abroad, enjoying their favorite aspects of the mortal realm without straying for long from my side. Torrent had started anonymously donating small sculptures he made out of found natural objects to a local gallery that'd been excited by them, but that was the grandest of their ambitions.

Rollick, on the other hand, hadn't waited much time before getting started on rebuilding his legacy as he'd always said he would. His new hotel stood on the most popular stretch of Miami Beach, flocked to by human and shadowkind guests alike.

From what he'd said, the shadowkind needed a refuge like that even more now. The Highest hadn't stirred from the depths of the shadow realm again, and no other monsters had rampaged across the mortal realm since the leviathan's death, but the near-catastrophe had left a lot of the mortal-side beings shaken. Humankind seemed to have brushed off the craziness of those few weeks with our usual dogged resistance to anything beyond our understanding, but the shadowkind wanted to know they had like-minded companions they could turn to if anyone tried to steal their freedom or the land they considered a home again.

Lance let out a soft growl at the sight of Rollick's affectionate gesture and grabbed my other hand. He leaned his head close to mine and nipped my earlobe before murmuring, "I heard there's something humans like to do to make a place really their own. 'Christening' it, I think they call it?"

My cheeks flushed. "And you figured we'd do that up here, huh?"

An unusually mischievous glint had lit up in Torrent's sea-green eyes. He extended one of his tentacles to tease around my calf. "What better spot to celebrate our daredevil lover's great achievement?"

A thrill shivered through me, affection and excitement twined together. The men I loved knew me so well, both what was important to me and what got me off. And I couldn't say the proposal didn't have a significant appeal.

I nudged Lance with my elbow. "What are we waiting for, then?"

He let out an eager little snarl and pounced, snatching me up and flipping us over with his usual acrobatic grace. The next thing I knew, I was sprawled on top of his lean frame while he stretched out on a flat section of roof, and he was pulling my mouth down to his.

The sudden movement had left my pulse racing, and the flick of Lance's tongue between my lips only keyed me up more. I kissed him back hard, reveling in the wonder of the moment—that I'd accomplished this much, that I had these men with me. That I was here, alive and well, at all.

Seconds later, the rest of my men had gathered close around me and Lance. Crag lowered his head to kiss the side of my neck. Rollick slid his hand up under my shirt, tracing the line of my spine with a giddying caress. Torrent stroked my thigh with his hand while his tentacles glided over my legs where my skirt left them bare.

When one tentacle rose to the apex of my legs, squeezing my clit with a deft sucker, I whimpered against Lance's mouth. He took the opportunity to adjust the angle of our heads and kiss me even more deeply, as if he were trying to devour me whole. Then he released my mouth to nibble along the line of my jaw, pushing me up over him high enough that he could grab the bottom of my shirt.

He yanked the thin cotton garment over my head, and then Rollick claimed my mouth for himself. The demon's kiss was as searing as ever, with no hesitation about participating in this joint effort now that we had years of collaboration behind us. He trailed his hand back down my spine and snapped open my bra in the same movement.

As the straps slid down my arms, Lance dipped his head

to catch the peak of one breast between his lips. Crag closed his rocky hand over the other, the warm but rough texture of his palm brushing over the nipple to perfect effect. I rocked helplessly against Torrent's pulsing tentacle, already feeling way too close to the edge. But then, these men could always take me there so quickly.

Lance tapped the tips of his claws against my side and, when I gasped, scraped them delicately over the skin. At my shiver, he sucked harder on my breast. Torrent picked the exact same moment to tuck the tip of his tentacle right inside my panties, the suckers plucking directly at my flesh, and I came with a rush of bliss that propelled a cry from my throat.

Rollick drank the sound down, and then Crag was tugging my head toward him, his strength tempered by the gentleness he always offered me. "We'll take you even higher than that, Softness," he said gruffly, and melded his mouth with mine.

Torrent was busy sliding the panties right off me. He nudged my hips a little higher and turned toward Lance, with a grin I could hear in his voice. "I can think of other places our woman would appreciate those claws."

I quivered with anticipation as Lance lowered his hand. He grazed the vicious talons ever so carefully over my folds and clit. Needing to hold so perfectly still only amplified the thrill of the sensation. I gasped, aching for more.

Torrent didn't leave me hanging. The second Lance withdrew his claws, the other man plunged his tentacle into me with just enough force to send my thoughts spinning with the surge of delight. I moaned and clutched at Lance beneath me, then pressed my lips harder against Crag's.

Rollick flicked his own shorter claws over my untended breast, adding to the symphony of pleasure that was swelling through me all over again. My mouth tore from Crag's with a guttural groan, and Lance beamed up at me.

"What do you want now, baby girl?"

"You," I mumbled. "Inside me. Give me the dragon cock."

He chuckled. "I'll never deny you that."

He was so good at his vanishing act now that my body barely shifted from where it'd been braced above him before he'd returned to physical form, now sans clothes. His monstrous cock with its thicker head rubbed against my clit, and Torrent withdrew his tentacle to make room. The wind licked over my back, chilling me for just an instant before Torrent leaned close enough for his warmth to envelop me. "Will you take me too, Quinn?"

Lance thrust up into me at the same moment, so my first answer was nothing more than a gasp. "Please," I said, breathless and shaking.

My gargoyle and my demon were still kneeling on either side of me, now fully naked in their monstrous forms. I gazed down at Rollick's two cocks and lowered my head to take the upper one into my mouth. It slid past my lips as Torrent prepared my back entrance with strokes of his tentacle, and the heady sensation of being triply filled careened through my nerves.

When I tested my teeth against Rollick's shaft, he hissed a breath and clutched my hair. I sucked him down as far as I could, swirled my tongue around him as I eased back, and released him only to draw his second cock into my mouth. He swore at the pursing of my lips around his rigid length.

I might have teased him more if Torrent's cock hadn't filled me then, gliding into my ass to match Lance's rhythm from beneath. Instead, my groan reverberated over Rollick's cock.

I brought my mouth back to his upper shaft and gripped the lower one with my hand, knowing from experience how to best ensure he unraveled. Crag kissed my shoulder and resumed his fondling of my breasts, not one to be left out. I pumped the demon's pair of dicks with the same blissful force my other two men were applying to me, bringing tongue, lips, teeth, and fingers to bear.

"I'm never going to get tired of seeing that hot mortal mouth around my cocks," Rollick rasped. His head tipped back, and he stiffened for just a second with a twitch of both shafts before he came, his smoky, salty release spilling down my chin and over my hand.

Before I could wipe my mouth, he leaned in and lapped his own cum off of me. I shuddered at the unexpectedly hot gesture, adding to the fire of passion searing through me with every rock of my lovers' bodies beneath and behind me. Then I turned to my gargoyle, wanting to bring him with us too.

Crag showed no qualms about kissing me while the taste of his fellow shadowkind must have lingered in my mouth. When I reached for his stunning gargoyle cock, he groaned. His hips pumped into my grasp instinctively.

I couldn't fit my mouth around more than the head of his shaft, but that was enough to make him shudder with delight. Then everything blurred into one string of motion, my body swaying between all of my men, the bliss blazing through me higher and hotter. And here we were up on top of a towering building, one that I'd helped bring to life, a dizzying distance from the regular world below.

The thought of that height and a fresh gust of wind over me somehow spurred my pleasure on even more. I whimpered around Crag's cock and pumped him faster, and just as he jerked with the first spurt of his release, Lance and Torrent hit the most sensitive spots inside me in perfect unison.

I came again, shivering and clenching around them, my mind blanking with the flare of total ecstasy. Torrent's breath broke and Lance let out a choked snarl beneath me as they followed me over the edge.

For a few minutes after that, I wasn't aware of much other than the bliss still racing through my nerves and the heat of my lovers' bodies around me. As I came back to myself, I found I was lying on my back, propped up between the four men to keep my skin off the surface of the roof, gazing up at the seemingly endless indigo of the evening sky. I grinned up at it, flooded with hope.

"This is just the beginning," I declared—to the sky, to my men, to the world stretching out all around me. "There's so much more I want to do, and there's no power in existence that can hold me back."

Lance hummed happily. "Especially not while you have us by your side. And we're not going anywhere."

Torrent tucked a tentacle around my waist, adding to the joint embrace. "I can't wait to see what you'll pull off next."

I closed my eyes, drifting on pure joy. "Neither can I."

ABOUT THE AUTHOR

Eva Chase lives in Canada with her family. She loves stories both swoony and supernatural, and strong women and the men who appreciate them. Along with the Heart of a Monster series, she is the author of the Gang of Ghouls series, the Bound to the Fae series, the Flirting with Monsters series, the Cursed Studies trilogy, the Royals of Villain Academy series, the Moriarty's Men series, the Looking Glass Curse trilogy, the Their Dark Valkyrie series, the Witch's Consorts series, the Dragon Shifter's Mates series, the Demons of Fame series, and the Legends Reborn trilogy.

Connect with Eva online:
www.evachase.com
eva@evachase.com

www.ingramcontent.com/pod-product-compliance
Lightning Source LLC
Chambersburg PA
CBHW051142190726
48290CB00006B/1954